RICK PARTLOW
DROP TROOPER BOOK SIXTEEN
KILL CHAIN

www.aethonbooks.com

KILL CHAIN
©2024 RICK PARTLOW

This book is protected under the copyright laws of the United States of America. No part of this publication may be reproduced, stored in a retrieval system, or transmitted, in any form or by any means, without the prior permission in writing of the publisher, nor be otherwise circulated in any form of binding or cover other than that in which it is published and without a similar condition including this condition being imposed on the subsequent purchaser. Any reproduction or unauthorized use of the material or artwork contained herein is prohibited without the express written permission of the authors.

Aethon Books supports the right to free expression and the value of copyright. The purpose of copyright is to encourage writers and artists to produce the creative works that enrich our culture.

The scanning, uploading, and distribution of this book without permission is a theft of the author's intellectual property. If you would like to use material from the book (other than for review purposes), please contact editor@aethonbooks.com. Thank you for your support of the author's rights.

Aethon Books
www.aethonbooks.com

Print and eBook design and formatting and design by Josh Hayes.

Published by Aethon Books LLC.

Aethon Books is not responsible for websites (or their content) that are not owned by the publisher.

This book is a work of fiction. Names, characters, places, and incidents are the product of the author's imagination or are used fictitiously. Any resemblance to actual events, locales, or persons, living or dead is coincidental.

All rights reserved.

ALSO IN THE SERIES

CONTACT FRONT
KINETIC STRIKE
DANGER CLOSE
DIRECT FIRE
HOME FRONT
FIRE BASE
SHOCK ACTION
RELEASE POINT
KILL BOX
DROP ZONE
TANGO DOWN
BLUE FORCE
WEAPONS FREE
COLLATERAL EFFECTS
DOWN RANGE
KILL CHAIN

[1]

One by one, bits of the universe detached from the mass of white in front of us and streaked backward into the identical lobe of glowing energy behind us. I wasn't sure how long I'd sat there in the command chair and watched the fabric of reality put on the private show for me. It could have been hours.

There was nothing else to do on this ship. Nothing remained of the virtual reality systems we'd had on the *Orion*, either for entertainment or training. This millennia-old Predecessor ship came equipped with the warp drive that could take us home, but it lacked the amenities of the Fleet vessel it had replaced. No gym, no galley, no individual living quarters. Just crates of prepackaged emergency rations and row upon row of stasis chambers.

Everyone else slept soundly in their transparent coffin, hibernating through the long, cold winter, waiting for the first gasp of spring. Even Captain Nance had given way to the tug of incessant boredom and taken his turn at the big sleep. But one of us had to be up, just in case. In case of what, I still wasn't sure. This ship had been built tens of thousands of years ago by the Predecessors, a species descended from theropod dinosaurs that had barely survived the mass extinction sixty-six million years ago, and even for them it had been an experimental design never tested. If things went bad, there wasn't a damned thing any of us would be able to do about it.

Particularly not me. I was a Marine Drop Trooper, not some sort of scientist, and even when I'd been the beneficiary of a nanovirus that had rewired my brain and given me access to a supercomputer the size of a universe, it had been more a matter of being told something was right rather than figuring it out myself. Now that I'd been cut off from all the useful parts of the vast neural network by the hive mind that called itself the Unity, I didn't even have *that* advantage.

I still commanded this mission though... what was left of it. And rank having its privileges, I'd scheduled myself to be awake for the last leg of the trip, the one that would take us back into the Cluster. Back home. Vicky had wanted to be awake for it too, but I needed some time alone to think. And beyond that, I'd decided that if we were disappointed yet again, if this didn't work, I wanted to be the one to find out first.

We'd been searching for a way home ever since the unplanned journey through a one-way tunnel into the fabric of spacetime... how many years ago had it been now? It was hard to remember, since so much of it had been spent in those stasis pods.

Nine years, ten months, and fourteen days. And that's if there are no time dilation effects from this ship's spacetime inflation drive, which is an unanswerable question as of yet.

I frowned at the intrusion on my private thoughts, though there was no one around to see it.

"I told you, Jim," I murmured a reply to the voice inside my head, "that I wanted to be alone."

You know that's not really possible anymore, Cam, the AI

tsk'ed. *To quote your Bible, I am with you always, even unto the end of the age.*

"Are you trying to depress me? Because it's working."

You don't have to speak aloud, you know, Jim assured me. *I can hear you just as well when you merely think the reply.*

"I know. I'd just like the chance to talk to you out loud without people thinking I'm crazy."

Or maybe without *me* thinking I was crazy. It was easy to believe that sometimes, even without the AI whispering sweet nothings into my brain from the implant computer wrapped around my brain stem. The computer had built itself out of the nanite assemblers injected into my brain by the larger version of the AI I'd named Jim, in a vain attempt to rewire me before my exposure to the other beings who lived inside that universal mind drove me insane.

The Unity had saved me from that fate, although not out of altruism on its part. I'd used the power of the connection to the network to wipe out an engineered species the Unity had created and seeded this galaxy with, and that had been enough to attract the hive mind's attention. The thing had cut me off from the power of the network... except for an awareness of *it,* just enough knowledge to keep me aware of its constant pursuit.

Another reason I'd wanted to be alone when we dropped out of the warp drive. I hadn't sensed the Unity's presence since we'd activated the drive and I'd gone into stasis, though I wasn't sure if it was the drive or the hibernation that had done it. If it *was* the drive, then there was the very real possibility I could get hit with the awareness again when it cut off, and I wanted time to deal with it before I wound up scaring the others to death.

Is that the real reason? Jim asked, far too attuned to my moods for my comfort. *Or is it that you think the experience will leave you cowering and helpless and you don't even want Victoria Sandoval to see you that way?*

"Why don't you make yourself useful," I grumbled at the AI, "and figure out how long we have left?"

You could do that yourself, Jim chided. *Three minutes and thirty-five seconds, approximately.*

Three minutes. I'd know in three minutes. So many disappointments, so many times the rug had been pulled out from beneath us, and in three minutes we'd be back in the Cluster, back in the Commonwealth. I wondered how the Fleet would deal with us. They'd surely written us off as KIA years ago, and getting anyone to believe our story would be a miracle. I mean, the ship and the aliens—Jay and Bob and Dr. Spinner—would give some evidence, along with the helmet camera records from the surviving Vigilante suits. But none of that would explain the network, or the powers it gave to the Predecessors, or how it had destroyed them.

Whom the gods would destroy, they first make mad.

"Was that you, Jim, or just my memory?"

Both, technically. If you don't remember it, then neither do I.

A flashing yellow light in the main display warned that we were less than a minute away from the drive deactivating. No braking involved, because the ship wasn't technically moving at all. Instead, she expanded the fabric of spacetime behind her and contracted that in front of her, sort of like a cosmic boat propellor. All we had to do in order to stop was cut off power to the field, no bruising deceleration necessary. What I wouldn't have given to have a ship like this from the beginning. So many of my friends would still have been alive.

The contorted vision of the universe expanded into the sort of star field I was used to... and, more importantly, the ones I *knew*.

"Jim," I hissed, half a question, half a prayer, "tell me..."

According to the files you had me download from the Orion, *we are, indeed, back in the collection of star systems you call the*

Cluster, at the system catalogued as C63452-9, colloquially known as Waypoint at the edge of the group of stars constituting the Commonwealth.

I sank back in my chair, disbelief warring with relief, sapping all my strength, and I couldn't bring myself to move or even speak for what might have been minutes. We'd done it.

We were home.

"Jim," I said finally, "wake them up."

"Where are we?" Vicky asked, rubbing at her eyes as she sat up in the stasis chamber. Blinking, she looked around at the other transparent coffins popping open around us and the blank confusion on her face changed to annoyance. "Why didn't you wake me up for your shift?"

I didn't answer immediately, just staring at her. Hers was the first human voice I'd heard in three months, and even the plaintive tone sounded beautiful to me. Grinning like an idiot, I leaned in and kissed her, not caring about the stale taste of months in stasis, just happier than hell to see her.

"We're back," I told her, on the verge of tears. "We're back in the Commonwealth. We finally did it!"

Her eyes lit up and she laughed, throwing her arms around my neck.

"What did you say?" Chase asked, leaping out of his chamber and tripping on the side of it, sprawling face first but ignoring the embarrassment and pain and scrambling back to his feet. "Sir? What did you say?"

"We're back," I told him, laughing, not holding it against the young communications officer that he'd been one of the crewmembers who'd been willing to allow me to sacrifice my life to get them back here. I'd been ready to do it, but he didn't have to be so ready to let me. "We reached the Commonwealth."

"Put some damned clothes on, Chase," Captain Rafael Nance grumbled, pushing himself out of his chamber and grabbing the uniform tucked beneath it. I didn't mind Vicky emerging from stasis in her underwear and I hadn't noticed Chase because I'd been too distracted by his pratfall, but Nance was over twice my age and didn't wear it well, and I was grateful he took his own advice. He nodded to me as he pulled on his pants. "We're in the Waypoint system, right?"

"We are," I confirmed, handing Vicky her clothes. "We're at station keeping right now, but once we get the crews to their stations, we can head to the colony world. I think it's called Plateau."

He grunted, stroking his beard.

"Been there once before. It's high and dry, like southern Utah except where it's more like Antarctica." I nodded, despite never having been to either of those places. "Settlements are all down in a canyon over a kilometer deep, down where the big river runs through the northern continent. You can't even see 'em from orbit. And unless we catch a ship on a cargo run, they won't see *us* either."

"Why so grumpy, Cap?" Commander Yanayev asked, stretching her arms toward the overhead to loosen the kinks from stasis, though there was no danger she'd reach it, not in a ship designed for Predecessors who were all over two meters tall. "You'd think we hadn't just gotten home against all odds after years of trying."

The *Orion*'s helm officer was as casual as if we'd just pulled into a refueling stop on the way to routine cargo run, but then she never did seem to lose her cool. Well, hardly ever.

"Cap'n Nance is just mad because the Fleet's going to make him shave off his beard," Wojtera cracked, fastening the straps of his boots. He didn't even try to keep the broad smile off his face and seemed ready to burst into song at any second. "Me, I can't wait to get back to the R&R center on Eden and hook up with some willing females. The opportunities for companionship have been a little sparse since we left Yfingam."

"You mean since that Vergai chick dumped you," Yanayev said *sotto vocce*.

"Bellina didn't want to leave her family," Wojtera said peevishly, following Nance as he headed up to the control room. "And who can blame her? She would have been leaving behind everything she knew to go with us to a whole civilization of complete strangers."

"Well, it worked for us!" Jay said, hurrying to catch up to us as we trailed behind Nance.

Bob nodded silently, and he would. The two of them were from the same world as Dr. Spinner, though he didn't appear nearly as enthusiastic about being along for the ride. Maybe that was because he'd had his mind taken over by Lilandreth the Resscharr and spent months as a vegetable after I killed her. One of the last things I'd been able to do with the power of the network before I'd lost it was repair his damaged brain.

Jay and Bob came from one power bloc on their world, Spinner from another, but I couldn't tell the difference between any of the bronze-skinned humanoids except that Jay was taller and skinnier, Bob was shorter and stockier, and both of them were younger than Spinner. Jay and Bob had come along with us in the hopes of a better life than the isolation and unimportance that was all they had to expect from their lives back home, while Spinner had come along out of a sense of scientific curiosity. Maybe that curiosity had an expiration date.

"You guys help Doc Hallonen make sure everyone is thawed out and ready for duty," I told them, motioning at the hatch for the next compartment. "Tell Lt. Springfield to get a squad armored and ready just in case. And get my armor ready."

I didn't wait to see if they did it since it had mostly been busy work to get them all out of my hair. Which needed cutting badly after three months. Grasping Vicky's hand tightly as if she might slip away like a dream if I let go, I watched as the bridge crew took up their spots at the stations Jim had instructed the ship's systems to fabricate for us. The Predecessors had relied heavily on their gravity-control technology to keep them from flying around the bridge in battle and didn't have to sit down for comfort since their knees bent backward. Lacking both the anatomy and the trust in technology they had, I preferred acceleration couches with safety harnesses.

Though there was something to be said for that gravity-control technology... and the warp drive this thing had. By the time we made it to the bridge, the ship was already moving, the stars shifting in slow motion compared to the speed we'd managed on the way here, yet a thousand times faster than we would have been able to manage on the *Orion*. Fast enough that the planet—Plateau, Nance had called it—grew from a rust-red spot to the size of a basketball in mere minutes.

Not completely red, of course, not like Mars, though the world showed the threat of meeting that dead world's fate eventually. There were no oceans, just long inland seas that cut the continents into slices, but I also noted a lack of green along their shores.

"Why isn't there any plant growth on the shores of the seas?" I asked... of Nance, I supposed, since he was the only one who'd spoken of a familiarity with the place.

"They're all more dead salt lakes than seas," Nance said, making a face. "Salinity is over thirty-five percent on all of them. Nothing grows, not even algae. The only fresh water is underground—or deep in the canyons. That's where the life is."

And those were definitely visible from space, again resembling the deep chasms of Mars, at least a few hundred kilometers long and God only knew how deep.

"Y'see that one?" Nance went on, pointing at a scar across the upper end of the northernmost continent. Well, the *section* of continent, since the entire planet was essentially one big continent. "That's the Rift. Shadewater is near the center. Chase, you figure out the comms on this boat yet?"

"Think so, sir," the younger man said, fingers dancing through a haptic hologram, face screwed up in concentration. "Not getting any transmissions."

"You wouldn't from up here. Try bouncing a signal off one of their satellites." Nance speared me with a glare. "You know, we haven't named this girl yet. It's bad luck, sailing on a ship you haven't named."

I blinked, then shook my head.

"I thought you'd name her," I confessed. "You're the captain."

Nance snorted derision.

"I fly her, but you're in command and you know it." He shrugged. "At least until the Fleet gets ahold of us and throws us all in a loony bin after we tell them what happened to us. May as well give her a name in the meantime."

I shared a look with Vicky and she smiled, though there was a sad tinge to it.

"What about Top?" she suggested.

"I like that," I agreed. "She's the CSS *Ellen Campbell* as far as I'm concerned."

Nance tilted his head to the side thoughtfully, like he was considering whether or not he approved of the name, but Chase interrupted the conversation and his ruminating.

"I sent a hailing signal," he reported. "Bounced it off one of the comm-sats. But I'm not getting any reply except the automated confirmation of the signal from the satellite."

Nance scowled.

"Goddammit, why can't anything ever be simple?"

"We're an unknown vessel," Yanayev chimed in. "With a signature no one's ever seen before, claiming to be people who were probably declared dead years ago. They might not *want* to respond to us."

"She has a point," Captain Emily Nagarro agreed. Clad in the black uniform of Fleet Intelligence, she didn't have an official station on the bridge, but as the senior intelligence officer on board she did have a standing invitation. "They might think we're pirates or Tahni or God knows what else. We'll probably have to talk to them in person."

"We don't have any landers," Nance sighed. "No Intercepts, no drop-ships. The only way to land is to set this thing..." he frowned and raised a hand in apology, "... to set the *Ellen* down, and I can't honestly say there's enough open ground down there to accommodate her girth."

"There's one other thing that can land without the *Ellen* touching down," Vicky countered, eyeing me. I nodded.

"Get us as low as you can, Captain," I told Nance. "Chase, get ahold of the armorers. Tell them to get my Vigilante ready."

One more drop. Maybe the last.

[2]

I'd lost count of how many drops I'd logged since that first training mission in Armor school. Hell, I'd even lost count of my *combat* drops, and one seemed to blend in with another until I barely noticed the rush of adrenaline anymore.

This jump was different. The *Ellen* wasn't a drop-ship, wasn't an Intercept cutter—she was nearly the size of the *Orion*, a starship that looked at home in orbit or traversing the black between the planets and so totally out of place deep within the atmosphere of Plateau. Maybe if she'd been screaming at full speed in a desperate strafing run, I could have accepted it at a gut-level. But instead, she hovered just above the mouth of the Rift canyon like something from a dream, and when I jumped out of her utility airlock, it felt like I was a depressed Corporate Council middle manager diving headfirst from an office building window.

It would have been suicide in one of the older Vigilantes, the ones we'd left the Commonwealth with, or certainly one of the cruder models we'd cobbled together on Yfingam for the Vergai. The maximum safe jump altitude for one of the stock suits was four hundred meters at Earth-standard gravity, and the

Ellen hovered at least a kilometer above the river valley floor. Still, I didn't hesitate and neither did Vicky, confident in the abilities of the Predecessor-tech reactor and jump jets installed by the Resscharr on Lilandreth's world. The thrusters could keep us in the air for half an hour or more and could easily land a suit from a thousand meters up.

Dropping into the Rift felt almost like passing through a doorway into a different world, the dry and lifeless sandstone giving way to the thriving green and blue of the river valley as we descended.

"I'm not picking up any EM transmissions," Vicky said about halfway down, her voice barely audible in my headphones over the roar of the jets.

"I noticed." Not so much as a spike on the meter at the corner of my helmet HUD to show an automated air traffic response, much less a message. No laser line of sight either. Not a single indication that anyone had seen us. Or that there was anyone *to* see us.

There was nothing else to say, and neither of us broke the silence until the buildings came into view. They'd been hidden by an outcropping of the cliff wall overhanging the river, giving Shadewater its name, and even in the glare of midday that shadow kept the settlement a good ten degrees cooler than the surrounding trees and brush. The river ran wild over the rocks scattered through it, frothing in desperate fury as if the rocks had invaded its territory and deserved to feel the full measure of its wrath. Some people got their jollies rafting over rapids like that, but I thought even the foolhardiest of the extreme sports types would have given this area a pass.

Certainly no rafts braved the waters today. No poles dipped into the isolated, still pools at the water's edge, no tractors plowed the flood plains of the valley, no groundcars wound the rough dirt tracks leading up and down the river to smaller towns. Not a single person rushed out of those houses and storage buildings and fabrication centers to stare at the Vigilante battlesuits coming down on jets of blue fire.

"There!" Vicky said when we were about fifty meters up, but my targeting system had already picked up the movement.

Fast and low to the ground, a shaggy tail trailing behind as it darted out of the open doorway to what might have been some kind of government building. Gray fur with orange highlights and canine features. A coyote. We'd scared it out of the building with the scream of jets and the billowing cloud of dust as we touched down. The turbines whined down to nothing and I stood there and let them, scanning the buildings.

Nothing on thermal, no motion other than the occasional bird flitting in and out from nests built under the eaves of the roofs of houses and businesses. Something flashed white in the doorway the coyote had come out from, and I zoomed in on the object with my helmet optics. Gnawed upon, splintered, and worn with time, yet still recognizable. It was a human femur.

"It's a ghost town," Vicky murmured.

"Alvarez, Sandoval," Nance said, his voice obscenely loud in my ear, almost disrespectful in this graveyard. "You wanna tell us what's happening down there?"

Not particularly.

"Haven't found anyone yet," I reported tersely. "The settlement looks abandoned. I'll get back to you if we come across anything significant." *In other words, stop bugging me.*

He's technically your subordinate, Jim reminded me. *You could just order him to stop bothering you.*

I've ordered you to stop bothering me and look how much good that's done.

But I'm not your subordinate.

Then what are *you?* I demanded.

Your best friend, Jim declared with malicious humor.

Wonderful.

"We're not going to fit through the doors in the suits," I told Vicky, yanking my 'face cables and popping the chest plastron. "I'm getting out. Stay buttoned up and cover me."

Light flooded the suit as the chest plate swung open and I squinted against the glare, letting my eyes adjust for a second before I twisted out of the suit. Reaching back inside, I pulled out the pulse carbine from its niche in a recess on the side and extended the stock.

"Be ready to bust through the wall if I scream for help," I added.

"You know I'd walk through walls for you, Cam," she said, only half kidding.

Before deciding on a direction, I stopped and took a deep breath through my nose. No smell of rot. That was a good sign, at least in the sense that it meant I wasn't going to walk into one of the buildings and stumble on a half-eaten corpse. Bad in the sense that it meant whatever had happened here had happened a long time ago.

The one-story office the coyote had run out of looked official despite its lack of signage, and I decided to start there. I stopped a few meters away and knelt beside the femur. I wasn't an expert on forensic archaeology, but the bone looked at least a year or two old, and it did *not* look as if it had been dug up from a grave. Someone had died and been left where they fell.

Male, Jim informed me. *Adult. A centimeter or two taller than you, probably.*

I didn't bother asking how he knew. It was likely in among the data he'd downloaded from the *Orion*'s systems, and even a truncated version of the AI that was able to squeeze itself into my implant computer could still analyze the length and shape of the bone and compare it to the samples in its memory.

Rising from the coyote chew toy, I brought the carbine to my shoulder and ducked inside the one-story structure. The door lay on the floor just inside, the lock blasted off with an energy weapon, I judged, but the hinges ripped apart with brute force. Maybe a battlesuit could do that, but I didn't know what else could have managed it.

It *was* a government office. Local government, because I doubted the Commonwealth would have bothered with the place. There was nothing worth having in this system other than the minerals in the asteroid belt and the atmosphere of the gas giants, but even those weren't worth the investment because of shipping times... and because of the reality that nearly every system had their own asteroid belt and at least one gas giant. They were only worth mining if the system supported the infrastructure, like 82 Eridani with two habitables, one of them being the Commonwealth military headquarters.

Places like Plateau only existed because some group of misfits had managed to cobble together the money to fund a single run out to the edges of the Commonwealth with a couple fabricators, frozen cattle embryos, and a load of genetically engineered seed. It was a rough life, even rougher than the one Vicky and I had tried on Hausos, but some people just wanted not to be bothered. I didn't begrudge them that, but it also meant they had no protection other than whatever they could kludge together with their fabricators and black-market patterns.

The theory was that they wouldn't have anything worth stealing, which wasn't exactly true. To some of the lowest, bottom-of-the-barrel elements among the raiders of the Pirate Worlds, humans were always worth stealing, particularly when they couldn't fight back.

That hadn't happened here. *Someone* had put up a fight, or else the dismembered bodies scattered across the floor of the government office had all died of natural causes and been ripped apart by scavengers. There were at least half a dozen bodies, or at least that was the best estimate I could make counting arms and legs.

Six, Jim confirmed. *And from the damage to the ones and the clothes, I would say they weren't killed by energy or projectile weapons.*

Then what? I wondered.

Unknown. The bodies have been stripped of flesh, or I might be able to discern cause of death.

I touched my earbud.

"We got bodies in here," I told Vicky. "Six of them. Bones."

"Copy. No current threats?"

"Not yet." An intact data terminal caught my eye. "Hold on, I'm going to see if I can access their records."

Picking my way through the field of bones should have been creepy, should have sent the hackles rising on my neck, but unfortunately this wasn't even in the top ten of grisly scenes of death and destruction I'd experienced in my short life. I brushed the bones aside with the toe of my boot, their rattle dry and mocking. Beneath one of the bodies was a gun. I paused and picked it up.

Stamped metal, probably mined locally and fabricated here in town. Ejecting the pistol's magazine showed me the truncated missile shapes of Gyroc rounds. Not guided, not slaved to a targeting system, no explosive or armor-piercing warheads, just the basic miniature rocket weapon available almost everywhere. It had only three rounds left in a magazine that could hold twenty, and I looked around the inside of the office for impact points.

There. Above a desk made from real wood, three craters blown in the adobe wall by the rocket projectiles. All three at least half a meter above where a human head would be. Nothing that tall could have fit in this room, but if the guy was shooting wildly, why were the impacts less than ten centimeters apart? He had to have been aiming up there.

Or something redirected the rounds in that direction, Jim suggested.

Whatever that meant. I ejected the live round from the gun's chamber, then set the gun gently and respectfully back on the floor, tossing the ammunition aside. It clinked spitefully, a mocking sound, amused by my confusion. The data terminal should, I reckoned, be powered by the solar collectors I'd spotted from the air, out past the overhang. No one had bothered to destroy or steal them, which might mean no one had bothered to disconnect them either.

The screen of the terminal was old, cheap to replace and easy to fix, and the crack along the corner wouldn't keep it from working. I tapped the surface of it with my bare fingertip and it snapped to life with an emblem that looked like a cross between a family crest and a corporate logo. I didn't care what it meant, just cared about accessing the menu. It was filled with useless shit like cargo manifests from the few supply ships they were able to attract with the paltry income they'd managed from selling exotic meats to the rich. No more than one every six months, it looked like as I scrolled through. The last one had been over two years ago.

As I scrolled through the records, I noticed that a *lot* of the last things they'd inputted had happened two years ago. The last reports on the crops harvested, livestock born, slaughtered, processed, and packaged for shipment. Fabricator output, requests for spare parts, everything ended two years ago. None of that told me more than the bones though.

Why are you screwing around with a touchscreen when you have a computer inside your head? Jim asked petulantly.

I paused and looked up as if he were standing in front of me.

"How the hell would I give you access to it?" I demanded.

Plug your 'link into the input jack, you technological infant. I can access it remotely.

"God, you're such a bitch." But I did as the AI instructed and pulled out my datalink, folding out the jack and plugging it into the side of the terminal.

The screen flickered, the menu scrolling so quickly I couldn't follow it before ending on the logo again.

"Well?" I asked, shrugging. "What did you find out?"

Read it for yourself.

The terminal flashed through the menu again, but this time when it settled into a function, it wasn't a mass of text but a video. Not one recorded by the colonists—who would they be recording a video *for*? These didn't seem like the kind of people who liked hearing themselves talk. No, this was an official announcement from the Commonwealth government broadcast wide over every InStell ComSat through the wormhole jump-gates to every connected system and from there to every military ship, cargo ship, and registered passenger carrier not just in incorporated colonies but every unofficial settlement and even to the Pirate Worlds.

It wasn't used too often, or at least it hadn't been back when Vicky and I had been on Hausos, and I figured that was because even the officious idiots who ran the Commonwealth knew that crying wolf would make everyone ignore the warnings. Which was more of an indication this was serious than the grim look on the face of the too-pretty woman who made the announcement —she was likely a computer construct anyway, despite the Patrol uniform she wore. There was a date in the corner and, unless I and our suit and personal datalinks had lost count, it was almost exactly two years ago.

"This is an official announcement by the Commonwealth Patrol Service," she said, enunciating each word as if to emphasize how important it was that everyone pay attention. "An extremely contagious virus has been spreading through the colonies via independent cargo vessels. This Transformation virus affects the human brain and nervous system, causing violent behavior and narcissistic delusions of grandeur. Infection is airborne, and those who've been influenced by the virus will do everything in their power to pass the virus on to others."

"What?" I blurted, frowning in confusion. A virus? Viral infections could be dangerous for settlers out in the Pirate Worlds, where people hadn't received the standard nanite treatments at birth that were given to all residents of the megacities and the larger colony worlds, but other than that... the notional Patrol officer interrupted my doubts, continuing her announcement.

"All Commonwealth colonies are under strict quarantine, and any unauthorized spacecraft attempting to land will be fired upon." The woman closed her eyes for a moment as if allowing the listeners to digest the news. "While we lack the ability to enforce this on unincorporated settlements, we strongly advise you to cut off contact with other systems until you receive further notice from official sources. There is currently no known test for this virus, but if you notice anyone acting strange or showing... unnatural abilities of any kind, it's recommended that you notify local authorities... and that they respond with lethal force. This may seem drastic, but if this virus spreads, it will mean the deaths of thousands, perhaps millions. Please remain vigilant for any future amendments to this alert."

The recording ended but I stared at the screen, unable to move. I'd expected a pirate attack, something explainable. This was *not* explainable.

Of course it is, Jim observed. *You simply don't want to think about the explanation.*

"Cam," Vicky called, a note of concern in her voice, "what's going on? Is everything all right?"

A chill traveled up my back, and maybe it was sweat drying in the shadow of the cliff, but maybe it wasn't. Maybe I knew exactly what Jim was talking about.

"No," I told Vicky, being honest with her and myself. "I don't believe it is."

An inhuman shriek brought my head around, but before I could turn toward the closed end of the office, something that smelled like death hit me and I went down hard.

[3]

Air flooded out of me in a whoosh, the hard edges of the pulse carbine punching into my side and driving out my breath under the weight of what felt like a tattered sandbag. Stars exploded in my vision and sharp edges tried hard to pierce through the fabric of my fatigue shirt, but I thrashed sideways and whatever had landed on my back was now on top of me.

Rancid breath filled my face as a living skull slavered at me through a mouth full of rotting and broken teeth and fingernails fifteen centimeters long clawed at my eyes. His forearms were as skinny as toothpicks, yet the muscle inside them was like corded metal, fueled by desperation and twice as strong as any man I'd ever fought before. The darkness of the office couldn't conceal the rags of his clothing hanging off him like a tent, or the open sores on his skin weeping puss.

"No!" His voice sounded like a man gargling with broken glass, like he hadn't spoken aloud in months. "No! I was the last! You can't be here! You're all dead! I was the last!"

"What the fuck are you talking about?" I grunted, not seriously expecting an answer but hoping to distract him.

"You were Changed," he hissed at me, spittle flying, fingernails coming closer to my eyes, shutting out everything else, all my focus on the jagged edges. "There's only room for one!"

The fuck?

I couldn't hold back that desperate strength, not with his weight atop me, but I could redirect it. I lurched to the right and the zombie went off balance, tumbling away. He rolled, growling and snapping like a wild animal as he tried to get back at me, and I barely had time to swing my legs around between us. The zombie lunged again, but his torso slammed into my outstretched boots with enough force to bend my knees into my chest, to knock me onto my back.

Adrenaline gave me a momentary jolt of strength to match his madness and I pistoned my legs forward, rocketing him across the room into the opposite wall with a crunch that must have been ribs breaking. Any normal man would have been out of commission after a hit like that, but this maniac bounced off like he hadn't felt it, stumbling back toward me.

The martial arts I'd practiced for the last few years with Top paid off in a kip-up that took me back to my feet, a move I never thought I'd use in a real fight. It took me into position to block the slashing downward blow he aimed at my face, and I caught the arm against my chest and used his momentum to throw him over my hip. Crashing into the desk, he suddenly looked smaller than he had before, less an undead monster and more a withered, sickly old man.

I didn't try to swing around the carbine, instead drawing my service pistol from its chest holster.

"Stop!" I yelled at him. "Don't do it!"

His head came up, broken and pointed teeth bared in a snarl, and he tensed for another spring at me. I touched the trigger and the pistol pushed back against the web of my hand, cold gas kicking the round free before the mini-rocket ignited. No time for it to get to full velocity, but this guy wasn't wearing body armor. Or much of anything. The round punched through his chest with a flash of the igniting warhead and he jerked backward, eyes rolling up into his head before he slumped to the floor.

I kept the gun trained on him, not trusting that he wouldn't make one more run at me, that whatever madness had kept him going all this time might keep him alive through the fist-sized hole in his chest, but he didn't move.

I stumbled back against the desk, feeling every bruise.

"Hey, Vicky," I rasped into my audio pickup, reholstering my gun, "remind me never, ever to get out of my suit again."

"A virus?" Nance repeated as the replay of the video ended, his expression a mirror of the one I'd made when I'd heard the message. "That doesn't make one bit of sense."

"Neither does this bullshit about shooting anyone who shows the symptoms!" Dr. Hallonen added, her pale face beet red at the suggestion. "Even if the virus turns people rabidly violent, surely they could be restrained with less-than-lethal weapons!"

The *Ellen Campbell* lacked an operations center, the compartment where we'd met for these conversations on the *Orion*, but we were making do with the ship's bridge. There wasn't anyone to keep secrets from anymore really, but not everyone could fit in the control room, which limited the immediate attendance to the bridge crew, Nagarro, Springfield, Vicky, and me. And, for this discussion, Doc Hallonen. We'd brief the others once we had a coherent response to give them. And once we decided what to do next.

Everyone muttered agreement with Hallonen... everyone except Vicky and me. She knew what I suspected and didn't like it, but we didn't want to spring that one on them with nothing except guesswork to support it.

"That's not the only thing that doesn't make sense," Lt. Springfield said softly, frowning at the footage I'd brought back of the inside of the buildings. She pointed at the bones inside the government office. "Some of the bodies were shot, but here and in a couple other places, everyone was... ripped apart. By what? Animals? I didn't see anything on the scans larger than a coyote or a bobcat." She peered over at me. "Why did they introduce bobcats and coyotes?"

I rolled my eyes. Like I would know... but then I *did* know, thanks to the implant computer.

"Rodent control," I told her absently. "Rats and mice get into the food shipments and there's no way to stop it. Commonwealth immigration control won't allow housecats because they wipe out native bird species, but coyotes and bobcats are acceptable."

"Well, the damned coyotes and bobcats didn't tear people apart," she went on. "Not unless they'd already been dead for at least a few weeks. And as nasty as that guy was who tried to claw your eyes out, he didn't do it with his bare hands. So what killed them? It was either the getting ripped apart or something that didn't leave a mark on their clothes."

I had no real answer, but I pondered the woman who'd asked the question. When all this had started, Jesse Springfield had been a junior platoon leader, not *quite* just out of Armor school but close enough. She'd been quiet, a mouse in a corner waiting for orders from Captain Solano, so soft-spoken I'd barely been aware of her existence until mounting casualties had forced her into a command position.

I barely recognized that young officer in the woman who sat across from me on one of the spare acceleration couches. Her features had sharpened, her eyes hardened, and she'd somehow evolved into as good of a company commander as Captain Solano had ever been, someone I could put in charge and depend on to keep my Marines alive.

And I didn't know a damned thing about her. The thought slapped me in the face hard enough to make me want to deny it instinctively, but it was true and it was on purpose. I'd stopped trying to get to know the other Marines after Top died. I'd stopped trying to get to know *anyone*. I trusted Springfield with my life and the lives of dozens of the Marines under my charge, and if someone had asked me if she was married I couldn't have answered without checking her personnel file.

She's not, Jim assured me.

"That warning talked about strange abilities," Nance mused, stroking his beard. "Could this whole thing about them turning violent have something to do with it?" He looked a question at Hallonen. "Maybe this virus is shutting down their pain receptors or something and they're killing people with their bare hands because they don't feel the damage they're doing to themselves?"

"And what stopped all those guns I found from killing them?" I pointed out, though the argument was half-hearted. I knew the truth—well, I had an intuition that Jim had told me was almost certainly the truth—and didn't really want to get to that point yet. "I mean, that... Changed, or whatever he was, wasn't bulletproof."

"Maybe they did, eventually," Springfield argued, hands spread demonstratively like she was in some college debate class. Or the ones I'd audited on video anyway, since my own college degree had come from remote learning on a troop carrier. I did recall that Springfield had gone to the Academy, and I didn't even need the implant computer or Jim for that. "You found a couple bodies that had been shot. They could have been the killers, surviving one bullet wound after another until they finally succumbed."

"We're trying to build a castle from a couple bricks here," Vicky judged, staring at the deck as if she was afraid to meet the eyes of the others, afraid they'd read the truth there. "Maybe we should just head back to Earth. We only stopped here to make sure the drive worked and we were in the Cluster." She shrugged. "It did and we are. Everything beyond that is just us chasing our tails. Let's go to the source and we'll find out exactly what happened."

"This could be a big problem," Hallonen cautioned, reverting to doctor mode. I'd gotten used to her being the hard-nosed Fleet medic for years now, and it was still jarring when she actually sounded worried about our health. "If we can't treat this with medical nanites, there might be no way to stop it."

"This was two years ago," I reminded her. "If it *is* treatable, then surely they've figured out a way to do it by now. And if anywhere is safe, it'd be Earth. They'd never let this thing take hold on Earth. They'd shut down all access to the solar system first." And I hoped that didn't sound as much like wishful thinking to everyone else as it did to me. "How long will it take, Captain?" I asked Nance. A question I knew the answer to already and had to shush Jim from repeating to me again. This wasn't for my benefit.

"With this drive?" He snorted, joy at the thought of the abilities of the *Ellen Campbell* apparently overriding his concern about the colony at Plateau at least for a moment. "A week. Maybe a little under."

"That fast?" Lt. Springfield asked, her eyebrows shooting up in disbelief. "From all the way out at the edge of the Cluster?"

"You have to understand, Lieutenant," Commander Yanayev explained with the patience of a tech-head helm officer talking to a Marine grunt, "that the Transition Lines don't work based on physical proximity. That's why it takes less time to get from Earth to 82 Eridani using the Transition Drive than it does to get to Proxima Centauri. It's all based on the intensity of the gravito-inertial connections in T-space. That's not how this... spacetime inflation drive works." She turned over a palm. "Of course, it's also a hell of a lot faster since, as far as I can tell, the speed is based on how much power you have to draw from, and this thing has a small black hole at the heart of its reactor."

"Then get us out of here, Captain," I told Vance, putting a commanding tone into the words to remind him that just because we were back in the Cluster didn't mean this operation had turned into a democracy. "Set course for Earth, as fast as this damned thing will go."

"Aye, aye, Captain Alvarez," he acknowledged, throwing me a salute I assumed was ironic, since he'd bothered to remind me of the disparity in our actual military ranks.

He was a Fleet captain, an O-6, the equivalent to a full bird colonel in the Marines, while I was still an O-3, a Marine captain. Yeah, he'd agreed along with everyone else that I should take charge once Colonel Hachette fell in combat, mostly because no one else was crazy enough to want the job—surely not *him*, even though he was the ranking officer—but that didn't mean he was going to let me forget it.

Everyone turned back to their stations, a sigh running through the collective as if everyone realized simultaneously they weren't going to get any answers for at least a week and would have to deal with it. I indulged in a heavy sigh myself, not from the delayed satisfaction but out of relief that the conversation was over.

"We should PMCS our suits," I told Vicky, an excuse to get the hell off the bridge before anyone else asked me a question. She nodded, understanding in her expression, and we headed out.

I should have known it wouldn't be that easy. Nagarro stood in the corridor, arms folded, waiting for us, an ebon statue of some ancient warrior goddess guarding the road to the afterlife.

"You know what's going on, don't you?" she accused. Well, the woman *was* in Fleet Intelligence, which was supposed to mean she was smart, though I couldn't swear to that after dealing with intelligence types for way too long. "I could tell from the minute you both got back that you both know something."

"We don't *know* anything," Vicky insisted, leaning into the words like she was pushing back against Nagarro's pressure. "You've seen as much as we have. And we don't plan on guessing and getting everyone worked up over nothing."

Nagarro glanced back at the bridge, and her stance changed as she took a step closer.

"I understand that, but I'm your intelligence analyst. If there are possibilities to be planned for, I need to know what they are."

The look on her face said she was sincere, but I'd heard that one of the first things they taught Intelligence officers was how to lie convincingly. She might just be as curious as everyone else. Vicky shrugged, leaving it up to me.

"If I hear of this on the grapevine, or from anyone else, even Nance," I warned her, "then you're going to be out of a fucking job. Even if it's only until we get to Earth and someone has the brains to bust me back to a company commander, or right out of the service, you'll be cleaning the damned toilets on this ship. We clear?"

"Yes, sir," she said, nodding firmly.

I took one last look around, then motioned for her to walk with us away from the bridge, just in case.

"You know what happened to me, right?" I tapped the side

of my head. "Back on Homecoming? Before I fought Lilandreth?"

"Of course," Nagarro confirmed. "That AI changed your brain structure so you could access the... whatever you call it. The power."

"The network," I suggested. "But do you know *how* the AI rewired my brain?" She shook her head and I went on. "It used an engineered, self-replicating nanovirus." I made an equivocating gesture. "Specifically tailored for my DNA, as I understand it, since the AI assured me it wouldn't affect Vicky when she entered the lab. But if one of those AI can tailor one to me, I can't imagine it would be much trouble for them to make one that would... *infect* anyone."

Nagarro's eyes went wide and she halted mid-step, hand going to her gut like she'd been punched.

"And you said it would drive you insane, eventually," she whispered.

"Now you're getting it," I agreed. I started to go on, then rubbed at my eyes. They felt like they had sand in them, which was one of the side effects of stasis. "This is just speculation. Probably paranoia, though God knows, if they're really out to get you, then paranoia is just good sense. Either way, it's been two years. Whatever was going to happen has already happened."

She nodded.

"And the worst-case scenario?" she wondered.

I had to think about that for a second. When I reached a reasonable conclusion, I looked to Vicky. I had no one left on Earth that I gave a shit about, but she'd left her mother and brothers behind. Her uncles. I could see it on her face that she understood very well the worst-case scenario.

"The worst case," I told Nagarro, my eyes not leaving Vicky, "is that when we get home... there may not be a home to go back to."

[4]

No one spoke.

They hadn't spoken much the whole week, the days passing slowly, like we were all still frozen in stasis. The ship had grown us cots, provided bathing facilities after a little prompting from Jim, and we'd managed to sleep, eat, and pretend things were normal, but the fevered anticipation everyone had felt cruising into Plateau had faded away into a low-level dread.

It was worse now that we could see it. The *Ellen* had dipped below lightspeed somewhere inside the orbit of Jupiter, and I think we'd all known it then before we'd seen it. The quiet had told us. Once we'd slowed under the velocity of an EM signal, the comms board should have been flooded with them. Even though we weren't in any of the normal Transition zones for the system, the Fleet sentinel stations would have spotted us and a dozen cruisers would have been all over us in under a half an hour, micro-Transitioning right in our path.

That didn't happen. No hailing messages, no traffic control warnings, not so much as an advertisement for the latest in virtual reality visors. Silence.

"Maybe it's the drive," Yanayev had suggested. "It distorts

the fabric of spacetime. It could be shutting out signals. Hell, it might be keeping sensors from even noticing us."

"That would make it a hell of a defense shield," Wojtera added, his professional curiosity getting the better of him for a moment.

The notion that it was just *us* and not everyone else had lasted all the way until we'd reached Martian orbit.

"Jesus God," Nance breathed, as close to a prayer as I'd ever heard from the man.

"Station keeping," I rasped, because Nance wasn't about to order it.

Yanayev was enough of a consummate professional that she obeyed, though she didn't acknowledge the command. Mars—the Mars we'd left—had been the heart of industry in the solar system. Mineral resources came in from the Belt, sometimes as processed ore, sometimes the whole rock pushed in with fusion drives dug right into the surface of the asteroid to be smelted into shapes and sizes fitting the needs of the Fleet or the Corporate Council. Metallic hydrogen from the gas giants, and finally, exotic matter from the massive particle accelerators well within the orbit of Saturn, powered by solar collectors kilometers across.

All of it converged at the Martian shipyards to be molded into cruisers, Intercept cutters, drop-ships, Corporate freighters, and whatever else the Commonwealth needed. The shipyards were a silvery web woven by a spider the size of a moon, visible from thousands of kilometers away. Or they had been.

What was left of the installation drifted in tatters, a spiderweb in the corner of the ceiling of our living room back on Hausos that Vicky had brought down with a broom. Glittering in the distant sun with a ghost of its former grandeur, it dwarfed the burned-out husks of the partially built starships still clinging to the errant strands in a failed promise of what might have been.

Still, there was a chance that Yanayev had been right about the drive field stopping signals.

"Helm," I told her, an exercise in tradition now, because I could have carried out the order myself through my headcomp or given it silently to Jim, "shut down the drive field."

Yanayev glanced back at me sharply, but again, she carried out the order. Nothing seemed to change from our view on the bridge, but she shook her head, cursing under her breath.

"Without the drive on station keeping," she told me, "we're being pulled in by Martian gravity. We're not in a stable orbit."

"It's only for a few minutes," I assured her. "Chase, are you picking up anything?"

The comms officer peered at the display floating above his station, not speaking for a long moment, but then he shook his head.

"All I'm getting are automated navigational beacons. Not a thing from the surface, nothing from Deimos or Phobos."

"Send a broad-wave transmission," I told him. "Use the *Orion*'s ID codes."

Chase nodded, his expression bleak as he complied. I watched the curve of the red planet on the main viewer with a nostalgia for a place I'd never been. I'd never had the chance to visit Mars, and now I'd probably never have a reason.

"Tactical," I asked in rote recital, knowing the answer before I asked the question, "what are you reading on the surface?"

"Radiation," Wojtera reported, the word dragged down by a grim fatalism. "No thermal readings... nothing above the background levels. Not so much as a functional reactor. It's the same everywhere we can see from this orbit—Lowell City, Bradbury, Zubrin, Olympus..."

"I'm not getting any response," Chase added, shaking his head.

I looked around the bridge, noticing the same look on every face. Hopelessness. The same thing I felt. We were the hobbits returning home to the Shire after the ring had been destroyed, but instead of finding an industrial nightmare, we'd found burned-out ruins. Thank God Tolkien hadn't written *that* ending, or no one would have still been reading his books.

Unfortunately, it seemed like God wasn't as keen on happy endings as Tolkien.

"I remember when I sailed my first command right out of those yards," Nance said, his wistful reminiscence unexpected. He stared at the screen, a muscle twitching in his cheek as if he was about to cry. "The troop carrier *Tarawa*. She was a beauty. Lost her during the war."

"I was on Mars when we got the news that the war had ended," Chase put in hesitantly, glancing around like he thought the rest of us would make fun of him for sharing a lame story. "I was a freshman at the Academy, spending my summer in training at Phobos base. I was too young to drink, but the bartender at the O-club there served me anyway. That was the first time I ever got drunk."

I'd always thought of Chase as a kid, but until that moment I don't believe I'd ever realized how *much* of a kid he'd been when he signed on for this mission. Now… my chest tightened, Now he'd left his youth in strange systems far from home, given up a chunk of his life, and here at the end of our mission he'd come home to *this*. All of them would be facing the same thing, all the ones who'd traveled through that gateway so many years ago, not just the people here on the bridge but everyone on the ship… and *I* would be the one they'd turn to. That was more terrifying than the devastation on Mars.

The stars streaked by outside the ship, so fast it didn't seem real, as if this wasn't a real spacecraft but a simulator and we weren't moving at all. That was the problem with all this ancient alien technology, from day one. It didn't feel real. At first I'd thought it was because the tech made things too easy, but the death, the sacrifice, the terror made it clear that wasn't the case. The problem was that it took the humanity of it. Everything we'd come across out here had removed us one more step from our origins, from that little piece of land my parents had with chickens and goats. Once upon a time, I'd thought every step I took away from that past was a step forward, but lately I'd started to think that every step had been in the wrong direction.

Blackness swallowed us again, interplanetary space so far from Mars and the desolation there that we might have been in another solar system, and if we'd been on the *Orion*, we'd have spent an hour getting out of the gravitational influence of the red planet before we micro-Transitioned into minimum safe distance from the Earth-Moon system. Not with this thing. It was minutes between Mars and Earth, days between systems. If we'd had a fleet of these things, the war with the Tahni would have lasted a month.

"Any other spacecraft?" Nance asked Wojtera.

"No, sir." The Tactical officer's answer was as redundant as the question. Any of us could have told by looking at the sensor readout that there was nothing around, no sign of civilization, no trace of the defense platforms that had once guarded every approach to Earth.

Part of me expected to find the planet gone, a lifeless rock with the atmosphere stripped away and a huge chunk of it splintered and tumbling the way we'd found out there, where the infected Predecessors had opened wormholes and killed off entire populations. But it was only a few minutes before the big, blue marble showed up ahead of us, the same as it had been the last time I'd seen it.

"Oh, thank God," Chase murmured, seeing it at the same time as I did, half the sphere lit up by the Sun, half shrouded in darkness. The Moon made its way around the mother planet in a stately dance like a wind-up doll, everything proceeding as it had for billions of years.

"Still no signs of activity," Wojtera cautioned, as if trying to point out to Chase that it was too early to celebrate. He frowned, staring harder at the display. "There's... vestiges of radioactivity on the Moon. Might be from a reactor leak. Might be from a fusion blast. Not a recent one."

I didn't respond, waiting until we were closer, knowing that the readings from Earth would be masked by the atmosphere this far out. There was no back-and-forth of order and confirmation the way I'd grown used to on the *Orion*, and not just because the ship was new to us. None of them wanted this to be real any more than I did, and the entire crew seemed to be holding their breath as the Earth grew ever larger in the holographic projection at the center of the bridge.

"Low orbit, Helm," Nance said, his face abashed as if he'd just realized that he'd been neglecting his duty as captain.

The *Ellen Campbell* skidded into orbit like a baserunner sliding into third, shrugging off the laws of physics, though by now I was getting used to it, as if the abilities of the ship were a reflection of my own impatience to find out what had happened. Asia slipped below us, still bearing the scars of a nuclear war fought two centuries ago, and thank God I knew enough history to recognize the stained, blackened swathes of desert as old wounds or I might have panicked.

A glance at Chase showed that the comm officer already had his ears open, searching for signals, so I didn't bother jostling his elbow. There wouldn't have been much coming out of the ruins of old China anyway, though once the south Pacific rolled blue and wild beneath us, the entire bridge seemed to lean forward in anticipation. The Hawaiian islands had the largest ground-based sensor array in the western hemisphere, and if anyone was left, they'd have to see us.

We passed over the islands without a word from comms, without a single intercept fighter launched to meet us.

"No energy readings," Wojtera told us. "Nothing from the North Pacific fusion plant, nothing from Trans-Angeles."

"Hey," Yanayev spoke up, squinting at the sensor display. "Where the hell is McAuliffe?"

I blinked. I hadn't thought about the station, mostly because I'd never been there, but McAuliffe was the largest orbital facility in the Commonwealth, built up around the kernel of what had once been the first commercial space station.

"It's there," Wojtera said grimly, pointing to a dim sensor reflection coming over the terminator. He didn't have to say anything else. We could all see it. No reactor readings, no thermal output at all. No sign of activity around it other than a hazy cloud of debris.

Close to a hundred thousand people had called that station home.

"Wait!" Wojtera exclaimed, light coming into his eyes for the first time since we'd come out of FTL. "I'm getting something! It's not much... a reactor, but a tiny one, about the size of the power plant on an Intercept cutter." He turned and met my hopeful stare. "It's active. There's something down there, some kind of settlement, if not a city."

"Where?" I asked him.

"Just outside of Jackson, Wyoming."

"That's the middle of fucking nowhere," Chase murmured. "Why would there be anyone out there at all?"

"We have to go down there," I said. "It's the only thing we've seen so far. Maybe we can get some answers there."

"Shouldn't we check Trans-Angeles first?" Chase asked plaintively, a hint of panic in the question. "It's the largest city in the world. There's got to be somebody..."

"There isn't," Vicky declared flatly, the first words she'd spoken since we left FTL. Her face was expressionless, the cold mask she wore in combat, and I doubt anyone else could have read the pain she hid behind it. "There's no one down there. If there were, we wouldn't be able to miss it. And..." finally the façade broke for just a heartbeat, the catch in her voice giving evidence to what she really felt, "... the Underground would be uninhabitable without power. There's not enough ventilation. None of the other levels could get water without the reactors and the desalinization plants." The mask slipped back into place and the set of her jaw hardened. "If things broke down here like they did everywhere else, the entire city would have to be evacuated within a week or everyone would wind up dying of thirst or asphyxiation. The same thing would happen in any of the megacities. Someplace isolated, with a small population might be the only area we'll find survivors."

We were strapped into our seats or I would have taken her in my arms, the rest of them be damned. She'd just realized she'd probably lost her entire family, and the fact that it had likely happened a couple years ago wouldn't make it easier to deal with. But that would have to wait until later.

"Woj," I told the Tactical Officer, "feed the sensor readings to the Helm." I nodded at Yanayev. "Take us down."

"You two going to use your suits as shuttles again?" Nance wondered, cocking an eyebrow in curiosity.

I stared at him for a second, not because it was a bad question but more because he'd shown no reaction at all to the probable deaths of billions of innocent people. The isolation on board the *Orion* for several years with few stops planetside hadn't been good for Rafael Nance. Maybe he needed to see this firsthand.

"No," I decided. "This ship can land. I think it's about time you landed her."

[5]

Among the death and destruction and despair of my travels across the galaxy, there had still been beauty. I'd seen spectacular vistas, raging rivers, canyons unimaginably deep, mountains that had extended nearly out of the atmosphere. Yet even among the grandeur of those alien landscapes, the abrupt ascent of the Teton mountains from the snow-covered splendor of the valley below stood out, a natural beauty that was uniquely of Earth.

The remains of a road ran through the valley, cracked and broken, overgrown from disuse, and irrationally amid the apocalyptic revelations of the last few hours, I felt a deep sadness that the magnificence of this place had been abandoned, seen only in photos and videos by all but a few.

This was once Grand Teton National Park in the old United States of America, Jim informed me. *Visited by millions of tourists every year before your Sino-Russian War.*

It wasn't my war, I reminded him as the *Ellen Campbell* cruised just a hundred meters above the valley floor. *I'm not Chinese or Russian.*

More yours than mine. After the war and the Crisis that followed due to the disruption in your economy, most of the populations of North and South America and western Europe were relocated into the megacities and the road systems were mostly shut down. The national park system was abandoned.

I knew all that, of course, or I would have if I'd spent a moment thinking about it, because it was buried inside the computer files. It was still sad.

"How far are we from the reactor?" Chase asked, obviously not as appreciative of the view as I was.

"Just a little farther," Yanayev murmured.

"Twenty klicks," Wojtera replied more helpfully. "Southeast. But to find a landing spot that'll fit this thing, we need to circle around another ten. Past the old city."

The *Ellen* practically crawled through the valley, slower than the groundcars of centuries before, past the ruins of what had once been Jackson, Wyoming, back when there'd been such a place. I knew all about it now that I'd bothered to check the files in the headcomp. It had been a playground for the ultra-rich, a tourist magnet back when tourism had been a thing, but all that had been abandoned after the war.

Decades later, a few top-level executives from the Corporate Council had taken possession of some of the larger and more remote ranches and refurbished them, using them as vacation getaways. Where we were headed was one of them, according to the maps, a ranch owned by Corporate Council royalty dating right back to the beginning—Patrice Damiani. I'd heard of her, of course. All of us down in the Underground knew about the gods who lived in the towers. We envied the Surface Dwellers, but for the Corporate Council types who occupied the spires as far above the Surface as it was above the Underground, there was no point even in envy or avarice. That life was beyond us.

Now those towers were just as lifeless and hopeless as the Underground. Maybe Patrice Damiani had made it back to her ranch after whatever disaster had befallen the cities. Maybe she'd come out and yell at us to get off her lawn.

There were bison in what was left of the town, picking at the grass that had overtaken roads and parking lots where it wasn't covered by the fresh snow, and I felt a conviction that if we waited long enough up here, I'd see wolves move in to hunt them. Instead, we kept moving, past the town and over the bare foundations where suburban houses had once stood. Entire neighborhoods had fallen to a fire decades ago, maybe a century, because the trees had regrown around them, leaving only bare stone as a testament to the money that had allowed them to live here.

Something moved under the evergreens, a gray against the snow, too distant to make out.

Coyote, Jim informed me.

Fitting. The coyote had been the avatar of the trickster god among the indigenous peoples of this area, and surely this had been the greatest trick of all—on us, flung far afield into the outer galaxy in an effort to save our civilization, only to return to find it destroyed. On the human race as a whole, perhaps. We'd reached the stars, fought two wars for our right to control them, yet something had ripped it all away at the height of our power.

"That's the source," Woj said.

It wasn't pretentious, I'd give Patrice Damiani that much. She hadn't turned the old ranch into a castle or a Swiss chalet, she'd just set her designers and construction crews into making it the epitome of an old west ranch, as imagined from watching old movies. The main house was two stories, at least two thousand square meters on the interior not counting the guest houses, the barns, the corrals and, of course, that fusion generator buried underground and covered by what looked like an innocuous work shed.

And unlike every other building we'd seen, this one was

intact. And in use. Horses stared up at us from the corrals, whinnying in terror at the massive cylinder floating in the morning sky. People tried to calm them, half a dozen men and women dressed in work clothes that wouldn't have looked out of place back when this place had been built the first time.

"That pasture," Nance directed, pointing a few hundred meters north of the ranch house at four hectares of open fields, lush and white with the early spring snow. "Take us down there."

The order was almost a grumble, and if Nance hadn't argued with me—much—about landing the *Ellen* on the ranch, neither had he seemed happy about it.

"It's not natural," he'd declared sullenly, "for something this size to land."

Yanayev, on the other hand, positively beamed at the challenge, squeezing the Predecessor starship between the trees at either side of the field and bringing us down as gently as a down feather. I didn't even know we'd landed until she nodded at me, hands coming off the controls dramatically.

"You want to come?" I asked Vicky softly as I unstrapped from the seat.

"Try to keep me away," she said, then gestured at her uniform. "Suits?"

"No, I think we've freaked these people out enough for one day. Probably better if we demonstrate that we're human." I nodded at the spray of snow still settling back to the ground in the wake of our landing. "We'd better grab jackets though. You too, Captain Nance."

"What?" he asked, eyes going wide with confusion.

"I'd like you to come along for this."

"Why?" Nance demanded, and I wondered if he was going to go all the way through the Ws, but laughing at him didn't seem appropriate under the circumstances.

"Because this is important enough for you and Nagarro to be in on it," was the only answer I'd give him.

Of course, the real one was that he needed to be off the damned ship and breathe real air before he totally lost touch with reality, but there was no tactful way to say that in front of the crew.

"Let's go," Vicky said, "before those cowboys all run away from the aliens."

———

"Who the hell *are* you guys?" the old cowboy demanded.

A bushy, gray-streaked beard framed a rounded chin and chubby cheeks and from the Stetson on his head to his boots. The only thing that didn't fit in with the frontier image was the pulse pistol held loosely in his right hand, down by his side. It was a military-issue weapon, which had me curious. Guns were tightly controlled on Earth, though I wouldn't have been surprised to see them out here on the private reserve of the people who made the rules and didn't have to live by them. But not a pulse pistol.

The two younger men on either side of him weren't visibly armed but they *were* visibly terrified, and I was sure both of them would turn and run if I yelled *boo* at them. Me, I was armed, and even though I'd left my service pistol in its holster, I was fairly certain I could clear it and put a round through the older guy's head before he brought up that pulse weapon. That would have been a suboptimal outcome, however.

"I'm Captain Cam Alvarez of the Fleet Marine Corps," I told him again, hoping the words would penetrate his stunned surprise this time. "This is Captain Vicky Sandoval, my wife and second-in-command." Vicky nodded to the cowboy, hands resting on the pulse carbine slung over her shoulder. "Captain

Rafael Nance, Space Fleet, and Captain Emily Nagarro of Fleet Intelligence."

"I'm Jose Contreras," the cowboy told us, boots shifting in the eight centimeters of snow that covered the field. "People call me Joe. I run this place for the Damiani family. You say you're with the military," he went on, gesturing at the *Ellen* behind us with his pistol carelessly enough that Vicky's right hand wrapped around the grip of her carbine. "But what the hell is *that* thing?"

"Joe," I said, trying to phrase my reply to keep this all plausible for him, "we've been gone quite a while on an extended assignment well outside the Commonwealth. Part of our mission involved salvaging Predecessor technology." I nodded back at the ship. "That's where this came from. But like I said, we've been away a long time. We got back and found..." shrugging helplessly, I motioned around us, "... all this. The cities are abandoned, everything's destroyed. Your fusion generator was the first sign of habitation we found. We were hoping you could tell us what happened."

Joe stared past me, still regarding the ship with a mixture of awe and distrust. It loomed over us, twice as big as the ranch house yet barely putting an indent in the snow, most of its weight being supported by the gravitic field.

"You... *found* that thing?"

A stiff breeze knifed through me, and it took every bit of self-control I had not to stuff my hands into my jacket pockets. Nance didn't even bother, huddled under his field jacket like it was a tent, the holstered pistol on his belt forgotten and abandoned to comfort. Nagarro at least *tried* to look prepared, though she openly shivered. Joe and his cowboys had the good sense to be wearing gloves of course, as well as hats. My ears at least had the manners to go completely numb so I wouldn't have to feel how cold they were.

"Hey, you know, I figure you've all been living out here your whole lives so this weather is nothing to you, but we're all cold as shit. Any chance we could take this inside?" I jerked a thumb back at the *Ellen Campbell*. "I could show you around the ship, if you'd like, get out of the wind."

Joe shook his head.

"Naw, I don't think I'm ready to get inside that right yet. But we have coffee on inside the house. You can come on in and I'll tell you what I know." He grinned. "We got central heating and everything." He eyed Vicky dubiously. "I'd appreciate if you'd leave the artillery outside though."

Vicky frowned, but I made a quelling gesture.

"No problem. Captain Sandoval, you can leave the carbine in the ship." I offered Joe a tight smile. "After all, if anyone here means us harm, this ship has gravitic weapons that can blow apart an asteroid. Compared to that, what's a pulse carbine?"

Joe blanched but didn't rescind his invitation. Vicky handed her long gun off to a Marine inside the airlock at the nose of the ship and followed us inside, though I noticed she kept her hand inside her jacket where she'd concealed her shoulder-holstered duty pistol. She watched the far-off faces watching us as Joe led us to the main house, workers eyeing us from the bunkhouse. No, not just workers... children too, half hiding behind their curious parents, their eyes white and wide.

"How many people live out here?" I asked Joe, trying to estimate in my head given the size of the buildings.

"Before everything that happened, we only had about a dozen," he told me, pushing the front door open and holding it for us. Warmth shimmered through the door like a heat mirage in the desert, and I sighed in relief as I crossed the threshold. "The families of the ranch hands used to live in housing a few klicks down the road. But since... well, we have to share the same food, and the power plant here is a lot more reliable than the solar collectors they use in the older houses. So now we must have about thirty, I think."

"You can't grow your own food here, can you?" Vicky asked, glancing over her shoulder at the snow before she wiped her boots on the mat and stepped inside. "Not just the weather, but that soil didn't look like much for crops."

"You a farmer besides being a soldier, Miss Vicky?" Joe asked her, an amused chuckle rumbling in his deep chest as he pulled off his gloves and sheepskin jacket. Just the jacket would have been worth more than the average Surface Dweller in Trans-Angeles made in a month, and that was if it was made from cloned skin. A jacket made from an actual sheep would be worth more than any of them made in a year, though I thought this guy might have gotten it the old-fashioned way, given the flock of sheep we'd spotted in an adjoining field, fenced in and grazing.

"I was, for a while," Vicky sneered. "And I'm a *Marine*, not a soldier, Mr. Contreras. Before that, my husband and I used our separation bonus after the war to start a small farm and ranch on Hausos. And before that, we fought from one end of the damned war to the other."

"Well, thank you for your service," Joe said, offering an off-handed salute. "Though at this point, I don't suppose it would matter if the Tahni had been running things instead of us."

"Yeah it would, Dad," one of the hands who'd come along with him to meet us objected, and I finally noted the family resemblance between them. Both the younger men were his sons. "The Transformation Virus didn't affect the Tahni. If their military hadn't been destroyed, they would have walked right in and wiped out everyone who was left."

Joe grunted but waved the boy off.

"Go grab us some coffee, George. Bring it in here."

Here was a living room bigger than the entire enlisted

barracks for our company back on Inferno, reaching up the entire height of the two-story structure, framed by polished wood beams and decorated with the mounted heads of bison, elk, pronghorn, and black bear. I wondered how old *those* were, and if even the Corporate Council Executive Board would be bold enough to hunt the local wildlife, given the strict conservation laws on Earth.

"They're all new," Joe told me as if he'd read my mind, though he'd most likely just followed my gaze. "Ain't no hunting laws when there ain't no government. And as your wife pointed out, we need food. And yes, we *do* grow some of it here. Seed genetically engineered for this soil, but the rest... well, sit down and I'll tell you all about that."

Two couches faced each other, a polished oak coffee table between them, both of the sofas upholstered in what had to be real leather. Joe sat down on one of them and waved us into the other, which might have been crowded if the damned things weren't as long as a queen-sized bed. The kid who I assumed was Joe's younger son, maybe sixteen years old, sat at the other end of Joe's couch and watched us carefully, though what he intended to do if we tried something wasn't clear.

Joe said nothing, waiting for the older boy to bring out a tray with seven coffee mugs—real ceramic, of course, given whose ranch this was—and hand them around. No one had asked how we wanted it, so I assumed it was black and wasn't disappointed when I was right. It was also strong as hell, and only a lifetime of perfecting a poker face kept me from grimacing in distaste. Vicky took a sip with a neutral expression and Nagarro actually seemed to enjoy it, but Captain Nance spluttered his first gulp of the stuff, looking as if he would have done a spit take if it weren't for the bear-skin rug on the floor—which was, undoubtedly, real.

"Sorry," Joe said, the upturned corner of his mouth demonstrating he wasn't the least bit apologetic. "Cowboy coffee can take some getting used to."

"Joe," I said, cutting through the niceties, "what happened? I got a ship full of people who've been waiting to see their families and loved ones for years and they're all pretty keyed up, as you can imagine."

Joe's mischievous smile faded away, replaced by something bleak and forlorn.

"You have t'understand," he began, "we're a little isolated here. Even though we *can* get onto the net here, most of the time we're too busy to spend much time on it. Even the kids. So we didn't get the beginning of this. All I know is that it started in orbit..."

"It started in another system," George interrupted. At his father's peevish glare, he shook his head. "I looked up everything I could once it all started. They said that the outbreak started somewhere in the Periphery systems or the Pirate Worlds even... somewhere far away. And from there, it came through Belial."

I nodded, knowing what Belial was even if I'd never been there. A private pleasure station in the Alpha Centauri asteroid belt, it was a gray area legally, without the stricter customs regulations of a place like McAuliffe.

"But then," George went on, "whoever started it arrived at McAuliffe, and you know how the traffic from Earth to McAuliffe is." The boy's cheek twitched. "*Was*. It hit the megacities from there and spread like wildfire."

"There's some... strange videos that came outta McAuliffe there at the beginning," Joe allowed. "I think I got one of them saved on the house's local server."

The cowboy pulled out his 'link and scrolled through the menu for a couple minutes before a hologram sprung up from the center of the coffee table.

The video was two-dimensional and poor quality, not because Belial had poor quality security systems—I knew they didn't—but more because something unknown was interfering with the electronics. Static blossomed in the feed every few seconds, making it hard to discern depth or details. It was a fairly open space, one of the many zocalos on the station from the look of the sales kiosks. People were running, and from their motion I thought it was likely in one of the outer layers, somewhere the angular momentum from the cylindrical station's spin was close to Earth-normal gravity.

I couldn't see what they were running from, but whatever it was they were desperate, terrified, slamming into each other and striking out to get away from it. Then there was what I at first thought was more static, but it persisted, and gradually I recognized it for what it was. I'd been near a tornado once, long ago on the plains of Hausos, and when a twister was passing by the air seemed to fill with swirling debris, moving so fast you couldn't make out the individual bits. Something was catching bits of merchandise, clothing, building materials, and furniture and spinning it through the air at cyclonic speeds.

A tourist stumbled into the frame, a pudgy, ordinary-looking man with a bad haircut and a jowly face distorted in terror. He staggered toward a vendor kiosk, putting out a hand to steady himself as if against a heavy wind, but something was eating away at the hand, stripping the flesh from it, and he screamed, soundless in the video-only feed. White bone was visible from beneath bloody skin and muscle all the way to the wrist, and bile rose in my throat, along with the horrible thought that the man was about to be flayed alive before my eyes.

Instead, the tourist's head imploded in a spray of red that was instantly added to the vortex. The rest of his body slumped to the ground, his clothes slowly but surely reduced to tatters by the storm.

Something walked into the frame deliberately, without a stagger or a stumble or a hint of panic. It might have been a man, once, or a woman, but whatever it had been was lost in a mass of shining metal. Bare, silvery bionics had replaced arms and legs and shoulders and hips, and more metal was melded in obscene conjunction with the skin on either side of the thing's face, replacing ears with rounded amplification discs and eyes with glowing green oculars. Even the jaws were hinged metal, the teeth sharpened to points, fitting just past each other to make up a picket fence of gleaming silver. In the center of it all, a single hint of what had once been a handsome, human face was a straight, aquiline nose.

I knew what the thing was. This wasn't some poor bastard who'd been badly injured and required bionics because they were cheaper than the cloned replacements not everyone could afford. No, this was quite obviously an Evolutionist. They were a religion, of a sort, men and women who wanted to take the "next step" beyond humanity, to replace themselves with machine parts that would eventually make them immortal. Most people called them Skingangers, after the criminal element that had risen from their midst. That might not have been fair, but it was close enough to the truth to be a stereotype, and I had no trouble imagining this particular Evolutionist being involved in something illegal.

The big metal thing paused in front of one of the larger vendor kiosks, staring at it with cold, inhuman eyes for long moments. The polymer frame of the kiosk vibrated, shaking faster and more violently until it shattered and sailed away with the rest of the particulate wind. Beneath it, a little girl cowered, her arms covering her face, her dark braids fluttering in the unnatural wind.

Her hands jerked away from her face, as if something had grabbed her by the wrists and forced them down, and her head tilted upward hesitantly, wide, dark eyes staring into the green oculars of the Skinganger. No more than ten or eleven, the little girl screamed, as silently as the tourist had, and began to float upward, her body stiff as a board, unable to move a muscle of her own volition.

"Turn it off," Nance begged, his voice a low moan.

"Wait," Joe insisted.

I wanted to look away but I couldn't. The little girl stared hard at the Skinganger, and slowly the look on her face changed from terror to a hard, cold smile. The Skinganger raised off the ground a meter, arms thrown outward, jaws working helplessly as if seeking for something to rip and tear. Metal wrenched violently away from flesh in showers of sparks and fountains of blood and something unseen, something from inside the little girl, tore the massive creature into component pieces.

The girl glanced casually at the camera and cocked her head sideways. The picture went dark.

The air had been sucked out of the room, and all I could do was stare at the blankness where the video had been, the coffee mug hanging in my hand, forgotten. Finally, Nance broke the silence, speaking for all of us.

"Sweet Jesus."

[6]

"Tell me that's not real," Nagarro pled, shaking her head in violent denial. "That had to be some kind of computer animation."

Jim? I prompted.

It could be faked, of course, he replied, not sounding overly surprised at what we'd seen. *But nothing about it is inconsistent with what we know. Given the population density in a station such as Belial...*

Yeah, I got it.

"I can't swear that it's real," Joe admitted, "but it was right after that video went public that things started to change." His hands wrapped around his mug and he leaned back in his seat, eyes focusing on a memory. "Everything... fell apart quickly. Like within days. A full quarantine was put in place and we stopped getting the weekly shipments of food and supplies. Not just people and supplies that stopped moving either. The government put a complete lockdown on the net, on *all* communications. The only news coming our way was official announcements, and those stopped after a couple weeks."

"It was scary as shit," George added.

"Let's watch our mouth, George," Joe chided gently. "But yeah, I was thinkin' we might be looking at the end. I was just about right too. We didn't have no VTOLs here, just a couple hoppers, and those only have a range of a few hundred kilometers." He snorted a laugh that was more rueful than humorous. "Don't know if you've noticed, but there ain't a damn thing within a few hundred kilometers of here."

"You were trapped," Vicky declared, sympathy in her voice, her earlier hostile vigilance gone now. "No way to get to the cities even if you wanted to."

"We tried calling for help," George put in. He looked at the coffee mug in his hands and set it down on the table, apparently having lost the need for any more caffeine. "We tried over and over. Especially when Mom..." the kid rubbed at his eyes.

"My wife," Joe said, a haunted note to his voice. "Felicia. She... she was riding and got thrown, got hurt too bad for the medical gear we had with us. She needed an auto-doc and we tried to get help out here, but the one military comm station we got ahold of told us there was no one to transport her."

The younger kid—I still hadn't gotten his name—sobbed, shoulders shuddering, eyes squeezed shut, and George put a comforting hand on his brother's shoulder.

"She passed away a year and a half ago," Joe told us. "Right up in the master bedroom. Ms. Damiani would have had a regular fit if she'd known, but she and her son lit out of here when things started to go bad. Well before the communications cut off. They were the smart ones. If *I* was smart, I would have asked them to take us with them when they left the planet."

Well, that answered *that* question. I wondered if the rest of the Council bigwigs had made a run for it too.

"And that's the last you heard from the outside?" Captain Nagarro asked. She'd recaptured her composure at least, though I saw in her eyes that she still hadn't accepted the reality of it.

She was hoping he'd say no so she could tell herself that things had worked out, that everything was okay.

"No. About nine months ago, we got a visit from a private freighter that had been flagged for something called the Commonwealth Provisional Government. They dropped us off fresh supplies and the pilot told us they'd be back about once every three months, that they'd be using this place as a base to rebuild things on Earth once they had the free manpower."

"There's someone out there then," Nagarro sighed, leaning forward as if he'd justified her hope. "There *is* still a government."

"According to the woman who brought us the supplies, and her pilot." Joe shrugged. "I s'ppose they could have been lying, but at the time I was so happy to have someone bringing us resupply I wasn't in the mood to be too nosy."

"Did they say where they were based out of?" Nance asked. "We need to link up with them. If there's a functional government, that ship out there could help."

"They didn't say." Joe seemed to finally remember the coffee mug and took a long sip out of it. "Probably because it wouldn't have done us any good. Not like we had a starship we could fly out there with. All I know is they were supposed to be back here two weeks ago with the next shipment."

"Two weeks late?" Nance grunted. "That doesn't sound good."

"No, it doesn't," I agreed, then pushed myself out of the too-comfortable couch. It had been designed for high-level executives to plant their asses on and feel like they were getting a massage. To me, it felt too soft. I paced around the perimeter of the furniture, hands in the pockets of my jacket, because otherwise I wouldn't have known what to do with them. "If what happened to the Commonwealth is the same thing that happened to the Predecessors, I don't know how the hell they'd stop it. This provisional government could have already fallen to the infected."

"The Changed," George provided. "That's what they started calling them before the communications blackout."

"Fallen to the Changed then," I corrected myself. "Either way, you don't know where they were operating out of and they haven't shown up." Sighing, I turned to the others. "Inferno? Hermes?"

"If Inferno was still holding out," Vicky told me, "then they would never have abandoned Earth. You know that. They would have come back and evacuated these people... anyone who was willing to leave. And they wouldn't be flying a commercial freighter around either."

She was right about that, though I didn't want to admit it.

"Hermes, Eden, Inferno, Aphrodite," Nagarro ticked them off on her fingers as she spoke, "they all have the same problem. The cities there are heavily populated. This thing spreads like a virus, right? Viruses spread fastest in places with higher population density, which is probably why the megacities here on Earth fell so quickly."

"The Periphery then?" Vicky asked her, and I thought she was impressed with Nagarro's analysis, which was a rarity. Like me, Vicky had bad memories of intelligence screw-ups during the war. "Maybe the Pirate Worlds?"

"You all do what you want," Joe told me, "but me and mine'll stay here before we let anyone drag us to the Pirate Worlds. I reckon we'll do just fine here. If you want to do anything for us before you go chasin' off after what's left of the Commonwealth, maybe you could find out if there were any more people around who're scrapin' by and could use a better place, like one with a fusion plant and a bunch of livestock, and give them a ride back here."

"Not a bad idea," Vicky admitted. "We found this place first because of the power plant, but there are nature reserves out there, biological research stations, maybe just people living in the old cities like Tijuana."

"Hell, you fellas could stay here, if you wanted," Joe offered. "I mean, if you change your mind about leavin'. We got enough buildings around here that could be fixed up. We could feed and house at least a few hundred people."

"Thank you for the invitation, Joe," I told him, "but we're all still in the military, which means we took an oath to serve the Commonwealth, and we can't give up on that until we find out there isn't any Commonwealth government left to serve."

"Cam, you reading me?" Wojtera asked, his voice buzzing in my earbud. "We've got incoming."

Shit. I looked to the others. "You getting this?"

They jumped up from their seats, and the Contreras family followed a bit more hesitantly.

"It came out of T-space just outside Lunar orbit," Woj went on, sounding abashed. "We didn't pick it up at first because frankly, the sensors on this boat are a lot more complicated than I'm used to and I didn't even know they could detect anything at this distance through the atmosphere."

While he spoke, I jogged to the door, opening it to a wind-blown sprinkle of falling snow in my face. The sky had clouded up again while we'd been inside, and fresh powder laid itself down in just another reminder that March in Wyoming wasn't quite the same as March on the plains of Hausos—or in Tijuana.

"What's it look like?" I asked, jogging back the way we'd come, clearing the ranch house until I could see the *Ellen* again.

"Nothing too big," Woj said. "Maybe a commercial freighter. Small enough to make landfall if they want."

Commercial freighter... I thought about what Joe had said and slowed to a walk, looking upward as if I could see the thing through the snow clouds.

"Should we try to hail them, sir?" Chase asked.

"It's a risk," Vicky warned. I started, only then realizing that she and the others had caught up to me. "If it's the... Changed, then we can't know for sure that just the technology on our ship will be enough to deal with them."

"I don't think you're going to have to worry about calling them," Woj said. "They're burning for orbit and their current course is going to take them down over the Rockies. Given that you're standing on top of the only active fusion reactor on the continent, it's not a bad guess that they're heading your way."

"Do you want us to prep for takeoff, sir?" Yanayev asked. "There's still plenty of time for you guys to get back here."

That would have been the smart thing to do. If this ship was hostile, we'd be totally safe inside the *Ellen*, unless they were the Changed. Maybe even then, considering the space-warping abilities of the Predecessor vessel. But if we retreated to the ship and took off, they'd probably see us as an alien threat. We were here to gather intelligence.

"No, stay buttoned up," I told her. "We came here to talk, and we're going to talk."

And I'd just have to hope they were in the mood to listen.

We stood out there in the snow way too long. Maybe that was just a reflection of how spoiled I'd gotten by the Predecessor technology that I expected every ship to make it down from orbit in a few minutes, but this was a conventional commercial freighter, and it took the better part of an hour. My face was numb, and Nagarro and Nance had retreated back indoors with Joe's sons, though the old cowboy stayed politely out there with the two crazy Marines.

It didn't come *straight* down either, of course, not after they caught sight of the *Ellen Campbell* filling up an entire pasture. The distant whine of the jets came first, well before the black dot against the clouds, shaping a wide, cautious arc around the valley, scanning for threats most likely.

"They're hailing us, sir," Chase informed me.

"Connect me through my 'link," I told him.

"You're up, sir," he said almost immediately. "Go ahead when you're ready."

"Unidentified vessel," a woman's voice repeated, harsh, stern, like a drill instructor, "this is the Commonwealth Provisional Government transport *Diana*. This settlement is under the protection of the Commonwealth government and military, and any aggression against it will be met with force."

"Well Goddamn," Vicky murmured, raising an eyebrow. "She sounds like a Marine."

"Attention Provisional Commonwealth vessel *Diana*," I replied, "this is Captain Cameron Alvarez of the Commonwealth Fleet Marine Corps, acting commander of the Fleet Intelligence ship *Ellen Campbell*. We've been out of the Cluster for several years. We mean no harm to this settlement or anyone here. If you could land, I'd really like to talk to you face to face."

No response came, and I thought maybe she wasn't buying it, that the freighter would turn around and make a run for T-space to call for reinforcements or just give up on the place altogether if there were no reinforcements to be had. But the *Diana* didn't turn and run; she pulled tighter into her arc, descending not into the pasture but into the courtyard behind the ranch house, coming down right on top of us.

Vicky cursed and shielded her eyes from the debris kicked up by the landing jets as the two-hundred-meter cargo hauler roared its defiance of gravity, a dozen landing struts extending from the belly as she touched down. Joe's ranch hands had taken the livestock back to the barn, but in the distance, a klick away in the field beyond the *Ellen*, sheep surged away from the sound and light and heat, huddling against the far fence as they bleated their fear.

I very purposefully didn't blink or flinch or cover my eyes. Whoever had been on the other end of that comm line had sounded tough, unyielding, and I sensed it would be a bad idea to show weakness this early. Besides, the heat from the belly jets felt damned good after spending an hour in sub-freezing temperatures. Steam poured off the ship and the ground beneath it. The snow pack melted and vaporized, the curtain of superheated water vapor thick enough that I didn't even notice when the belly ramp lowered.

Not until the tall, broad-shouldered woman sauntered down it. She didn't *look* old, could have been anywhere from thirty to two hundred and thirty, but there was something about the set of her eyes, the supreme confidence of her step that made me guess she was somewhere on the spectrum closer to the latter age. She only wore a uniform in the sense that her combat boots, olive drab fatigue pants, brown tank top, and leather flight jacket were nearly uniform for independent spacers. So was the heavy pistol tied down in a gunfighter rig on her thigh. For some it might have been an affectation, an attempt to look tough. Not with her.

Her long, powerful stride brought her nearly nose to nose with me in seconds, her piercing gaze weighing me like God at the last judgement. Behind her, a man emerged from the steam, dressed in a similar fashion. A head taller than her, bald, with cheekbones that could have sliced through steel, he would normally have been intimidating in his own right, yet I barely noticed him past the woman.

"I'm Korri Fontenot," she declared, "Fleet Intelligence. You wanted to talk to me?"

[7]

"Is that a fucking mastodon?" Rafael Nance asked, pressing his nose against the window of the groundcar like a child on a tour of a zoo.

"Yes, Captain Nance," Korri Fontenot said with a droll indulgence. "Demeter was originally established as a biological research station for the reintroduction of extinct animals—the ones we had enough DNA to recreate. They call them Revenants."

Looking out the front windshield of the car, I could believe it. The northern continent of the world was part subtropical rain forest and part boreal where it climbed back up the major rivers into the mountains. Amity had been built in the center of the two, nearly in the center of the continent at the confluence of two of those rivers, or so it had appeared from the air on the way in. We'd landed around noon local time, which I preferred. Getting my first view of a world at night was unsatisfying. Or at least my first view in a long time.

"The city's about twice as large as it used to be," I said softly. Where we'd landed the *Ellen Campbell* at the edge of the spaceport would have been nothing but forest during the war, and from the port facility buildings to the first structures of the town proper was where the landing field had been.

"You've been here before?" Fontenot asked, glancing back at me over her shoulder.

"Eyes on the road, hon," the big, bald man next to her said dryly, arms crossed. His name, I'd found out back in Jackson, twenty light-years and a week away, was Jagmeet Singh, and he'd been a bounty hunter up until a few years ago, when he'd taken a job working for the new government. "Unless you want me to drive."

Fontenot snorted at the idea but still looked back in time to avoid a cargo truck she'd unintentionally been playing chicken with.

"Yeah, I was here during the invasion," I confirmed. "Unfortunately, with all the stasis and time dilation shit, I couldn't even tell you how many years ago that was."

"Yeah, get back to me when you're so old that you start losing the first thirty or forty years' worth of your memory."

I frowned across Singh at her.

"I know it's not polite..." I began, but her raucous laugh interrupted me.

"Let's just it this way, Captain Alvarez... think of the oldest person you ever met and add twenty years."

I thought about Top and decided Fontenot was probably wrong but decided not to argue about it.

"Still, you were here during the war. You should bring that up with the boss. It'll give you two something to talk about."

I bit down on the questions I wanted to ask because I figured she probably wouldn't answer them. She hadn't been too forthcoming back on Earth, and since we'd taken separate ships to the Delta Pavonis system I hadn't had the chance to press her on any of the details. I wasn't sure she trusted us yet, and she hadn't so much as told me the name of the person I was coming to meet.

If it had been important I would have kept pushing, but we were here and we'd find out everything soon enough. Another scream of jets overhead drew my eyes upward through the sun roof. Another ship coming in. There'd been dozens of them taking off or landing when we'd come in, as busy as any port on a major colony, but one thing had struck me about it. Most of them had been commercial vessels, and I hadn't seen any military ship larger than a cutter since we'd arrived in the system.

"I forgot you went to Demeter," Vicky said from the back seat. "I was in OCS for that. I heard it was bad."

"It was more than bad," I confirmed, shuddering at the memory. Fontenot had bemoaned the loss of her early memories, but there was one I would have loved to get rid of. "It was a nightmare by the time we got there. I'm glad I didn't have to sit around and watch how it got that way."

"Oh, yeah," Fontenot laughed softly. "You and the boss are gonna get along fine."

I would have expected the Chairman of the Emergency Council to have a bigger office... but then again, there wasn't really much in the way of office buildings in Amity. Every square meter of the place seemed to be packed with apartment buildings, townhouses, warehouses, fabricator shops, and factories, like someone had plopped Victorian London into the middle of the 18th century wilderness of North America. Without the smokestacks belching pollution and the child labor, I hoped.

The Emergency Council offices had been crammed into what I thought must have been the original colonial government offices, or at least the ones they'd rebuilt and remodeled after the war. When I'd last seen them, they were half-destroyed by the battle to retake the city from the Tahni. That had been a close-run thing, mostly accomplished by the local militia aided by intelligence assets. *Unspecified* intelligence assets, as usual, though the rumor was that it had involved special operators from the DSI—the Department of Security and Intelligence, the civilian intelligence agency—as well as Fleet Intelligence. Then again, we always heard rumors about that kind of thing and no one who knew would ever talk about it, not even Top or the Skipper.

However the capital had been retaken, it had been the end product of a year of guerilla warfare. I'd met a few of those guerillas afterward, burying civilians who the Tahni had let starve to death as retribution for the sabotage and the assassinations. They'd been hard people, as patched and threadbare as their clothes, unwilling to let their Gauss rifles get more than an arm's length away even with every Tahni on the planet confirmed dead or captured. I couldn't have imagined any of them settling back into the idyllic, pastoral lifestyle they'd lived before the Tahni came, but I wasn't at all surprised to find out that this world was the heart of the surviving Commonwealth.

The people walking past us in the hallways and up the stairs to the third floor had the same sort of hard look, and I wondered if what had happened here the last two years had been close to what they'd experienced in the war. A few of them ignored us, probably used to seeing new faces in and out of this city every day, but others stared openly, probably having heard where we'd come from or what we were driving. No one said a word to us though until we reached the top floor.

It was less hectic up there than down below, and I thought maybe the design of the outer offices with their gauntlet of aides and secretaries and functionaries was designed for that, to keep the detritus out and reserve access to the inner circle for those who had problems only they could solve. The desk we approached just outside of a door marked *Chairman* was surely the Cerberus guarding the gates of the otherworld, although the frumpy-looking woman sitting behind it wasn't a three-headed hellhound.

"Hey there, Korri," the woman said cheerfully. "You and Jagmeet have a nice flight?"

"Oh, it would have been great if the man didn't snore like a diesel engine, Claire," Fontenot laughed, nudging Singh with an elbow.

"Oh yeah, right!" Singh protested, spreading his hands. "That's the fucking pot calling the kettle black right there! I don't think you snored that much when you were half metal!"

My face must have reflected my confusion, because Fontenot sighed and explained.

"I used to have some replacement parts left over from the first war with the Tahni, but I had them taken care of a few years back. Thank God, because I probably couldn't have the work done now." She turned back to Claire. "The boss is expecting us."

"Go on in then," Claire said with a wave. "You know him... if he doesn't know you're here, those other two will."

I was about to ask Fontenot who these other two were, but she didn't give me the chance, pushing past the desk and giving a perfunctory knock on the door before throwing it open. I shared a look with Vicky, Nance, and Nagarro, wondering what the hell we were getting ourselves into. The office was small, plainly furnished, almost spartan. A desk—real wood, but out here that was just a matter of the materials available rather than conspicuous consumption—and a half a dozen chairs clustered around it. A few physical pictures hung on the walls, family photos I supposed, old-fashioned still frames. The only concession to modern technology in the office was a holographic map of the Commonwealth, decorated with colors and shapes that probably meant something to the people running this place but nothing to me.

Three people occupied the office as promised, one behind the desk, two across from him. The woman drew my eye first, not because of her striking looks, though she did have those— short, dark hair, smoldering eyes, and the sort of perpetual skeptical tilt of her head that reminded me of Vicky. No, what attracted my attention was the impression she gave of barely restrained violence, that beneath her Fleet Intelligence blacks lurked a hunting leopard, ready to pounce without warning.

The man sitting beside her wore the same uniform, but on him I thought it looked out of place. Not just the Intell black fatigues, but any uniform at all. His hair was a wave of slicked-back brown, out of regulation just enough to let anyone military know, some little measure of rebellion against the hand he'd been dealt, and I had the gut-level intuition that he was a man who wouldn't have minded never wearing a uniform again. He was too handsome for it, for one thing, and I figured he must have come from a well-to-do family who could afford to have his genes tinkered with in utero to be the best him he could be. Either that or he'd just hit the genetic lottery.

There was something else off about him, though it took me a moment to figure it out. He was... *outsized*, I suppose was the word. Muscular beyond what our Marines were, and we were infamous for spending our off time lifting weights. This guy was jacked, like a professional athlete with cloned muscle implants. Dangerous, like the female, though perhaps in a different way.

But the last man, the one behind the desk... well, if the other two could have been intimidating on their own, when they were in the same room as this guy it was clear who was in charge. He stood as we entered, offering a hand. He wasn't much taller than me, built powerful and rangy, neither did he share the sculpted features of the Intelligence officer, his face much more normal, but there was something indefinable about him. His handshake was firm without trying to crush my fingers, but I could tell he had the strength for it he wanted to.

"Captain Alvarez," he said, nodding a greeting, "I'm Randall Munroe."

"Cam Alvarez," I said, then motioned at the others. "My wife and XO, Victoria Sandoval, Captain Nance of Space Fleet, and Captain Nagarro of Fleet Intelligence."

"I'm Colonel Kara McIntire," the short-haired woman said, unfolding from her chair with the grace of a dancer or a martial artist, "director of Fleet Intelligence." She cocked an eyebrow toward Nagarro. "Which, I suppose makes me your boss, Captain."

"Yes, ma'am," Nagarro said with a curt nod. "If I may... what happened to General Murdock?"

McIntire and the too-handsome guy exchanged a glance and the man sighed.

"I'm afraid he passed on even before... all this," she said, gesturing expansively. "I understand you've been gone quite a while, and I'm afraid a *lot* has happened in the interim." She shook herself like she'd just remembered where she was, then offered a hand to the man in black beside her, pulling him forward. "This is Major Deke Conner, my second-in-command."

"Pleasure to meet you," Conner said, his voice as smooth as his looks.

"Please, have a seat," Munroe invited us, motioning to the rough-hewn wood chairs across from his desk. "I think we have a lot to talk about. I've only had a sketch of a report from Major Fontenot..."

"If you don't mind, sir, ma'am," Fontenot said, "me and Jagmeet have some paperwork to file and well..." she motioned at the rest of us seated. "You don't have enough chairs in this rathole of an office."

Munroe struck me as the serious type and I braced myself, expecting him to chew the woman out, but instead he chuckled as if this was a recurring joke between them and motioned assent.

"I'll read you into it at dinner, Korri," McIntire promised as the door closed behind the two of them. It all seemed very casual, not quite what I'd expected, but I got the impression the familiarity was from the fact that they'd all known each other and worked together for years.

When Munroe turned to me, his eyes took on a cold, calculating glint that I was certain had been the very last thing many men had seen.

"Talk to me, Captain Alvarez," he invited.

"This is gonna take a while," I sighed, then motioned between Vicky and myself. "The two of us used our separation bonuses after the war to homestead on Hausos, a former Tahni possession…"

"I know you," Munroe interrupted like I hadn't been speaking. I blinked and stared back, uncomprehending. He aimed a very Marine-NCO-style knife-hand at me. "We've met."

"Have we?" I asked, shaking my head. I tried to run everyone I'd ever come across through my memory using the headcomp, but Jim basically told me that there was insufficient data and I couldn't count on pulling up memories I'd had before he'd implanted the computer.

"The shuttle down to Inferno off the transport from Earth," he told me. "When we were both reporting for Boot Camp."

Then it hit me like a sledgehammer between the eyes, a memory as vivid as if it had happened yesterday…

. . .

"I've been out in space for two weeks," the guy next to me in the shuttle complained, "and I haven't seen anything but the inside of a ship."

He was about my age, I thought, maybe a year or two younger, but with one of those lean faces you thought might be older at first. He had his hair buzzed short like he'd already been getting ready for Boot Camp before he even boarded the ship to Inferno. His accent was familiar to me. I'd heard it sometimes in the Zocalo, from the rich kids who came down there to slum. I didn't know what the hell a rich kid would be doing in the Marines, but that wasn't my business.

"You'd rather have been riding outside in a suit?" the girl on the other side of him wondered, chuckling so softly I almost couldn't hear it over the distant bang of the maneuvering thrusters taking us out of the docking bay of the transport.

As the shuttle emerged from the metallic womb of the ship, the light of the system's primary star whited out the image in the passenger cabin's overhead viewscreens for a second until it adjusted the contrast. The ruddy brown and algae green of Inferno came into focus as the merciless glare of 82 Eridani faded in the background, and I sighed in anticipation of the misery. They'd warned me it would be hot. The Underground was never hot.

"There's your view, buddy," I said, nudging the guy who'd complained. "Get used to it. We'll be spending a lot of time there."

"Eden's just an orbit over," he mused, eyes fixed on the scorched desert and steaming jungles below us. "Temperate, comfortable, a paradise."

"You been there?" I wondered.

"Me?" He shook his head. "Naw, I've never been off Earth. Just audited it a lot, virtual reality and stuff. That's why I joined. To get away... from Earth, I mean."

"Yeah," I murmured. "I guess most of us joined to get away from something."

"Secure for boost in thirty seconds," the shuttle's crew chief warned us over the intercom. "Things are gonna be uncomfortable for a few minutes."

I made a face, remembering the shuttle I'd taken from the Trans-Angeles spaceport to McAuliffe Station.

"I'm Randall Munroe," the lean-faced kid told me, sticking out a hand.

I stared at it, cocking an eyebrow. Shaking hands was a rich people thing. He seemed to remember that suddenly and reddened, offering me a forearm. I bumped it with mine.

"Cam Alvarez," I returned.

"Maybe I'll see you around down there," he said, grinning.

Rich people sure were talkative. He sounded lonely though, and he also sounded like a guy who wasn't used to being lonely.

"Yeah." It wasn't likely, but no use bringing him down any more. "Good luck."

"Holy shit," I murmured, rocking back in my chair at the impact of the memory. "How the hell did you remember that?"

"Let's just say," he told me with a shrug, "that my mother had enough money and enough pull to make sure I had a near-perfect everything before I peeked my little head out of the womb."

"She didn't care about your looks then?" Vicky asked him bluntly, then rolled her eyes when I stared at her, horrified. "Not that you're ugly, but look at *him*." She pointed at Deke Conner. "*He* definitely had prenatal gene therapy to get those looks, but you look kind of... normal."

This time, all three of them laughed, and I decided without any other evidence that I liked this guy.

"I kind of ruined their work," Munroe admitted, "when I decided to ditch the whole Corporate Council Executive lifestyle and join the Marines."

"Why?" I blurted. "I mean, I know why I joined—I didn't have any choice. It was go to war or go to jail. But why would you choose to give up life in the towers for a chance to get yourself killed?"

"I was a patriot." He shrugged. "Blame my grandfather—he was a United States Marine. Whispered in my ear since birth that it was an honorable calling. My mother made it easy by being such a manipulative, controlling bitch."

"And who was that?" Vicky wondered.

"Patrice Damiani."

I shaped a silent whistle.

"Your mom," I said slowly, "is Patrice Damiani? The number two in the entire Corporate Council?"

"Was." His voice went wistful. "She died during the last battle of the Psi War."

Nance had been looking back and forth between us like he was watching a tennis match but now he spoke up.

"What the hell is a *Psi War*?"

"I think I can guess," I said grimly.

Munroe exchanged a look with McIntire and she spread her hands.

"It's not like it's a secret to anyone. Anyone *here*."

"Well, it's not exactly how I envisioned this," Munroe said, "but you brought a damned Predecessor ship here, so you're obviously significant enough to break protocol for. I'll brief you before you brief me." He offered a lopsided grin. "But as you say... this is going to take a while."

[8]

"I wish Korri were back in here," Munroe began, "because the first part mostly involves her." He sighed and rubbed at his eyes. "Then again, it's probably better that she isn't. It all started with her granddaughter stealing a Predecessor artifact from a Corporate Council lab out on the Periphery. It contained a sentient AI that melded itself with her brain."

I wouldn't know anything about that.

"The AI rewired her to accept it, and that gave her... abilities. Telekinesis of a sort, through channeling thought into Transition Space and converting it to kinetic energy."

"I'm familiar with the concept," I told him. Vicky glared at me, but to hell with it. We were either going to report what happened or not, and there was no point in lying to them. Munroe's expression showed that he noted the comment but didn't let it stop him for the moment.

"The Corporate Council had fallen apart a few years before." He snorted humorlessly. "That's another story for another time, though not one that's pertinent to the current situation. But elements left over from their corruption, rogue former DSI agents and Corporate Security Force mercenaries, came after her, wanting the abilities she'd gained for their own purposes. She went to her grandmother, and Korri and her friends tried to help her by following the advice from the AI."

"That's always a mistake," Vicky murmured.

I heard that, Jim said.

Shut up, I'm trying to listen.

"The AI was able to use the abilities it gave to Jackie to take their ship out of the Cluster," McIntire took up the tale. "It led them to a world they called Homecoming."

I looked up sharply but decided not to interrupt her this time.

"Things went... wrong." McIntire sighed. "Another long story, and in no way Korri's fault, but the end result was, the Transformation Virus was brought back to the Commonwealth."

"No," Deke growled, eyes darkening at a vision the rest of us couldn't see. "The end result was that *billions* of people died. Every major city on Earth is an open grave that we're never even going to begin to be able to clean up. We'll wind up having to fusion bomb the damned places and start over. If we ever even get a big enough population to make it worthwhile."

"When did you get so bitter?" McIntire asked, reaching over to grab the man's hand and squeeze it. Ah. I hadn't realized that about the two of them.

Deke shrugged, didn't look like he wanted to answer.

"It just hits me sometimes when I don't expect it," he admitted.

"Tell me about it," Munroe agreed. "The virus didn't affect everyone. Maybe one in a hundred thousand, maybe even more than that. We never had the time or opportunity to run any tests. Just a few people in each colony, just a few dozen or a couple hundred on Earth... maybe. Again, we don't know for sure. They were basically gods... or demons, if you prefer. They couldn't be shot, couldn't be *touched*, and they surrounded themselves with an army of thralls under their spell. Soldiers who weren't afraid of death or pain, who'd keep fighting until they died. And they weren't just fighting *us*. Because y'see, the worst part about the Changed wasn't that they all became psychopathic narcissists with delusions of grandeur, it was that, more than they wanted to kill us, they wanted to kill each other. The war between the Changed was what wound up destroying most of the colonies and most of the megacities. What was left of the military wound up retreating here because we were the one colony that hadn't been infected."

"It all sounds about as horrible as I imagined it would be," I told Munroe, "but that doesn't answer the main question I have. How in the hell did you *beat* them?"

"*We* didn't," Deke corrected me. "Cal did." I frowned at him, wondering if I'd missed something, but McIntire filled us in.

"Caleb Mitchell," she said, and the hair stood up on the back of my neck. I'd heard the name before. "He was the only one infected by the Transformation Virus who didn't let it take him over."

"How the hell is that possible?" I blurted. "How could he fight the ghosts?"

All three of them stared at me like I'd just admitted to being an axe-murderer, and I cursed at the slip. Too late now.

"I was infected," I admitted. "I was able to hold out for a few weeks, but by the end I knew they had me. And then they didn't."

"Cal fought off the ghosts the same way he fought off anyone else who ever fucked with him," Deke said with the conviction of the old priest in our parish in Tijuana speaking about the power of the Holy Spirit. "By being the baddest, toughest, most strong-willed son of a bitch who ever lived."

"According to him," Munroe said, with not quite the wholehearted belief of Deke Conner, "the... network, he called it, the fabric of Transition Space, was like a huge quantum computer, and the AIs the Predecessors had sent into it to try to use it against the Skrela had overwritten it with their own... patterns."

"Yeah, I got that part," I confirmed. "I got way too familiar with their *patterns.*"

"Cal overwrote them," Deke said, grinning. "With himself. He erased those damned things like a fucking exorcist."

"Shit," I murmured. "Then he's every bit the badass Chang said he was."

"Chang," McIntire repeated, rising from her chair, fists clenching. "*Robert* Chang? Where the hell did you hear that name?"

The others didn't try to answer, not even Vicky. They just looked at me.

"We met him," I said, "on Homecoming. We went there trying to find the Northwest Passage to finally get back to the Cluster, but he showed up in a Resscharr ship and told us he'd just closed it off."

"Yeah, that fucker closed it off and left us high and dry," Deke muttered, arms crossed.

"You were with him on Homecoming," McIntire snapped, then pointed out the window in the general direction of the spaceport. "Is he on your ship?"

"No, he wanted to be left behind," I told her. "Jim..." I shut my mouth, opened it, and tried again. "The AI we found on a world called Waterline, where we found the ship, thought he could help Chang. Make him less insane, closer to what he was back before he started duplicating himself." I winced at a sudden realization. "And you were the friends he told me he felt so guilty about screwing over."

"I believe Caleb Mitchell did more than just get rid of the

ghosts," Munroe said, eyeing me closely. "My son was among the infected as well. This was after the network was cleansed, but it was still troubling. But then Captain Mitchell took most of the Changed with him along with his family and headed out of the Cluster. That was just a few weeks ago, but my son Cesar, along with every Changed who stayed behind just... lost their abilities. Lost their connection to the network."

"Oh, shit," I sighed. "That was the one hope I had coming here once we found what had happened to Earth. That some of you still might have the power."

"Hope for what?" McIntire asked me.

"I think it's time," I said, "that I told you about the Unity."

"This is good, right?" Vicky asked, one hand on my arm as we stepped back out into the summer sunlight.

I hadn't noticed how warm it was here back when we were in the groundcar. Something else I'd grown to hate about the constant travel was never settling into one season or another. Funny, since Tijuana only had two seasons, dry and wet, while the Trans-Angeles Underground had lacked even a sky, much less weather. But our time on Hausos had spoiled me, given me a taste of seeing the same patch of ground, living through winter and spring and summer and fall. The last several years consisted of stepping off the lander into a different terrain and different climate every few days, and the only place we'd stayed for more than a brief visit was Yfingam.

I had a feeling I'd be calling Demeter home for the foreseeable future though.

"Which part?" I asked, standing on the street corner, waiting for the groundcar to take us back to the *Ellen*. I assumed the promised cargo trucks would meet us there to unload both our personnel and gear and bring all of it into Amity. "The part where they're going to let us stay here while they decide what to do with us, the part where they obviously don't trust any of us, or the part where none of them bought the idea that the Unity is an existential threat, much less that it's on its way here?"

I didn't have to keep my voice down, because the two of us were alone at the curb. Nagarro had been asked to stay for a private debrief with her new commander, and Captain Nance... well, he'd decided that since he had no personal belongings on the *Ellen* and wasn't going to be allowed to fly her for the moment, there was no reason to ride back out.

"You're the commander," he'd reminded me, waving as he headed into the commercial part of Amity. "You can break the news to the others. I'm going to go get a beer."

Bastard. I wanted a beer too.

"No," Vicky said, kicking me in the ankle just hard enough to make me look up from staring at the pavement. "The part where you don't have to worry about the ghosts anymore. Everything's back to normal and there's no danger you'll turn into a violent psychopath. Plus, now there's no way for the Unity to track you down."

"I wouldn't be so sure of that," I told her. "The Unity weren't affected by the ghosts, and I doubt they'll be affected by whatever this Mitchell guy did that cut off the network from humans."

I'd exaggerated a little, I decided, when I'd thought of Amity as Victorian London. It was more like an early twentieth century New England manufacturing town, though again minus the smog. London even up until the time we'd left the Cluster had an air of age to it, the weight of history pressing down on every cobblestone... unless the ViR travelogues I'd accessed on the public net in the Underground hadn't been accurate.

Amity had no such feel to it. It had been around less than fifty years before it had been nearly destroyed in the war, and now most of it was even younger than that. No buildfoam or plasticrete here though, no temporary dome housing that had wound up being used for decades because no one wanted to bother to build anything more permanent. No, these buildings were constructed from local brick and wood or old-fashioned concrete and cement. The green fields and distant forests only contributed to the image, and not even the freighter making an overflight of the city at three thousand meters could change that.

"Maybe we should just consider ourselves lucky," Vicky said, and there was a bleak note to her voice, a sagging frown on her face that reminded me of what we'd found on Earth and what it had meant to her. "A lot of people would fall down on their knees and thank God to be where we are now."

I slipped an arm around her, pulled her toward me.

"I'm sorry. We've been gone so long... I guess it's easy for me to forget you still had family back in Trans-Angeles."

"It's not your fault," she said, accepting the hug, though from the tightness in her shoulders not entirely comforted by it. "I haven't even sent Mom a message in years, even before we left the Cluster. Not since Hausos."

"We were pretty involved in the operation," I reminded her, but she was already shaking her head before I could finish the sentence.

"It doesn't matter. She..." Vicky's shoulders shook, a minute vibration, but enough to tell me she was fighting back tears. "She stopped answering. By the time we left, she'd stopped answering my messages. I think she gave up on me."

"Things happen," I assured her. "Your brothers might have kept her busy." I grinned. "They were always getting into trouble. Or maybe she decided to get married again. She would never have forgotten you."

She sucked in a deep breath and visibly composed herself, shoving her feelings into a box to deal with later when we were alone. Sometimes I wondered if she was going to overload that segment of herself and explode with uncontrollable rage, and I hoped for everyone's sake that I would be the only one there when it happened, because at least she might not kill *me*.

The car pulled up, a civilian driving it. Or least a young woman in civilian work clothes. From what I'd gathered, most of the people here worked for the provisional government in one way or another.

"You guys going out to the spaceport?" she asked through the open window.

"That's us," I confirmed, pulling open the back door and letting Vicky get in ahead of me. "Just take us to the big alien ship out there."

"Copy that, sir," she said, and I suddenly revised my estimate of her age. She'd served somewhere.

"Marine?" I asked her as we pulled away from the curb. By way of answer, she pulled the brown hair away from her temple and cocked her head to the side to show me the 'face jack implanted in her temple.

"Drop Trooper," she told me, pride in her voice. "3rd of the 198th. I got out after the war and settled here because it had looked like a nice place when we landed here to retake it from the Tahni."

"Everybody landed here but me," Vicky lamented.

"You missed an easy one," I said, grinning, hoping to take her mind off her family. "No KIA, only one casualty in my platoon, and that was from a building falling on her. The local militia did all the heavy lifting."

"Yeah, we have Mr. Munroe to thank for that," the driver said.

"What do you mean?" I asked her. She laughed, glancing back at me.

"You mean, you don't know who he is?" She laughed, then took a careful look around to gauge traffic and pulled a wild U-turn with the screech of tires. A handful of pedestrians jumped out of the way, some wide-eyed and horrified, the rest cursing and making obscene gestures. "This, you should see for yourself."

We'd been heading out of town, but her maneuver took us to what looked like it had been the center of the city back before it had been extended to deal with the influx of refugees. Traffic got heavier through the industrial districts, a steady stream of cargo trucks coming in from the spaceport, loaded down with raw materials brought in from the system's asteroid belt or the lunar mines. Demeter had larger industrial facilities in orbit, taking shipments from the belt and the mines in the atmosphere of the system's gas giants, probably manufacturing fuel for the planet's fusion plants or maybe for the ships in their makeshift fleet.

I thought she was taking us to one of the fabrication centers, though God knew for what, but instead we pressed on to a public park at the center of the old city. Given that the world was a wilderness populated by mastodons and saber-tooth cats, the park seemed incongruously tame by comparison, well-manicured lawns and stately oaks lining the place.

Our driver pulled up just in front of a huge plaque and a statue half-hidden behind it, mounted at the center of a ringed sidewalk, the focal point of what a sign told us was Liberation Park.

"Go take a look," she urged, waving at it.

Vicky rolled her eyes, apparently considering this all a waste of time, but now I was curious to venture back into the afternoon summer heat and the sun beating off the pavement to investigate. The plaque and the statue were both of bronze, polished and maintained with loving reverence in the years since the war, the statue showing two men and a woman in civilian clothes, carrying Gauss rifles, expressions of anger and resolve on their faces. The plaque...

The plaque was adorned with the face of one man, and even at short acquaintance, I knew it was Randall Munroe.

"In memory," Vicky read the inscription off, awe in her voice, "of the civilian militias who risked everything in order to free this world from the Tahni occupation. Their sacrifice will never be forgotten so long as humans walk this world." Beside the words was a list, inscribed in script so tiny, I could barely read it. The honored dead. "Jesus, there's a lot of them," Vicky breathed.

But it was the other half of the plaque that attracted my eye.

"Dedicated," I took up the recitation, "to Corporal Randall Munroe of Marine Force Recon. Stranded on Demeter after the failed initial attempt to free this world, Corporal Munroe took charge of the civilian resistance and for a year kept them alive as they attrited the enemy and sabotaged their ability to fight. This led to the rescue of countless civilian prisoners and the final liberation of the planet."

"Holy shit," Vicky said, shaking her head. "That rich prick is a war hero."

The driver had followed us to the memorial and she laughed, loud and raucous, at the comment.

"Munroe wouldn't be offended," she said, "but you'd better watch talk like that when you're out and about. The people here love him and don't put up with anyone badmouthing their hero." She walked back to the car, casting one last addition over her shoulder. "Especially his wife."

[9]

Lifeless eyes stared back at me, frozen in shock, as if they'd had a fleeting glimpse of the afterlife in that last second before death and it hadn't been what they expected.

"How did he die?" I asked softly. Doc Hallonen and I were alone in the barracks room, but speaking in a normal voice felt like it would be disrespectful with the body of the engineering tech at our feet.

He'd gone out dressed in a tank top and workout shorts. I figured if I was going to commit suicide, I'd get dressed up first. But we'd only been on Demeter for a few days, and I suppose no one had the time yet to have a dress uniform fabricated. I hadn't either. Fabricator time was hard to come by here, with so many people crammed into a city never built for this kind of population or the sort of industry the center of a new civilization required. I'd gone shopping at one of the local outlets instead, picking up premade civilian clothes for the moment until I could get some more uniforms made.

I hadn't worn civilian clothes in years, not since we'd left the Cluster, and I felt like I was wearing a costume in the jeans and t-shirt. Hallonen looked more natural in them, mostly because I was used to seeing her in medical scrubs rather than a uniform, and to me she could never look like anything except a doctor.

"No blood," she said with a cold, clinical detachment I could never have mastered. "No weapon around. I'd say poison. Not sure what or where he got it, but it was fast-acting. His roommate told me he wasn't gone more than an hour, and Technician Gow here is already cold." She looked at me, gestured with the medical kit held loosely in her hand. "I checked him when I got the word, but it was way too late even if we got him to an auto-doc. He's been brain-dead for over forty minutes."

"Do we have anyone coming to pick up the body?" I wondered, squatting beside the man, unwilling to take a knee because I didn't especially want to touch anything in the room.

It was unadorned, impersonal. A few of the crew had bought holographic photo and video displays for the temporary barracks to stream pics of their families, but most didn't particularly want to be reminded. And none of us had been able to bring much out of the *Orion* after she'd been brought down by the Unity. We were refugees, like most of the people in Amity

"That's your job," Halonen informed me. "You'll have to square things with the local cops, military police, whatever. I'll be around if they need my exam results."

Gow was younger than me, maybe in his late twenties. Subjectively. All our objective ages were totally fucked up by the time in stasis, and everyone had pretty much given up on keeping track of them. But the tech was too young to have fought in the war, that much was clear.

"Did he have anyone?"

"If you mean family," Hallonen said, arms folded as she regarded the dead man, "then no." She tilted her head sideways in a shrug. "At least, probably not. They all lived on Hermes, and you heard what they told us about Hermes. Nothing left there except some of the farms way out in the boondocks. Few enough that the provisional government already has a census and a list of the survivors, and Gow's family wasn't among them."

She moved across the body from me, kneeling down, seemingly unafraid to put her knee in whatever bodily fluids might have evacuated from Gow after his death.

"If you mean did he have any significant other among the crew, then again, no. According to Technician Second Class Melhoff, his roommate, he had a girlfriend among the Marines... Corporal Fairfield."

"We lost her back on Waterline," I said, pressing the heels of my hands into my eyes. "Jesus, this is the second suicide since we got here."

"I think it's setting in," Halonen mused. "The reality, I mean. It's hitting the people who had husbands or wives and children the hardest, of course, but I think maybe they haven't really given up hope yet, not deep down inside. They still believe things are going to get back to normal." She sniffed a quiet laugh. "Nance, of course, isn't having any trouble at all. He figures he's the captain of the Commonwealth's only warp ship, so he's doing great."

"What about you?" I nodded to her. "You have kids."

"A boy and a girl," she agreed, her expression bleak. "But they're older than you. Families of their own, and I haven't seen any of them since I got assigned to the *Orion*."

"Where did they live?"

"John was on Aphrodite, last I heard. At a geological sampling lab halfway between Kennedy City and the coast." Hallonen chewed on her lip for a moment. "He might be okay. They don't have a census of the survivors there yet, so there's a chance. My daughter, Pris... she was in Capital City. An aid to the European Cultural Minister." She shook her head.

"There's..." The surgeon's clinical detachment slipped and she swallowed hard. "There's no way she could have..."

I hesitated but put my hand on her shoulder.

"I'm sorry. I wish there was something I could do."

"There *is* something you can do," she said, her gruff mask returning as she stood. "These people have too much Goddamned time to think. Go be a commander and give them something better to do with their time. Give them a purpose."

"It's okay," Vicky said, her arm wrapped around the shoulder of a young Fleet tech as I walked through the door. I assumed he was Melhoff, the roommate. "There was nothing you could have done about it. He probably made this decision long before we arrived here."

Fleet crewmembers packed the break room at the corner of the two barracks wings in the converted warehouse, some of them sobbing, some just sitting there with half-forgotten paper coffee cups in their hands and numb shock on their faces. Some were in their utility fatigues, some the same sort of workout gear as Gow, others in locally bought civvies. No uniformity, no purpose. Lost.

"This sucks." I turned, found Yanayev at my shoulder, her eyes red, hair sticking out as if she'd been awoken from a sound sleep. And she might have been. It was early in the evening here, but most of us hadn't totally adjusted yet to the local day-night cycles. "I ran into Chuck Gow a few times in the mess. He was a nice kid."

"I don't remember him," I admitted, speaking softly not just because I didn't want to disturb the crew while they were grieving but because I was ashamed at the confession. I was in command. I should have known *something* about everyone. "I just never got to engineering back on the *Orion*."

Yanayev said nothing, just moved past me and sat down between a pair of junior officers, speaking softly to them. Comforting, like Vicky was. Maybe I should have been trying to do the same, but I didn't know what to say. It had been too long since anyone had tried to comfort me.

I sat down beside Vicky and tried to listen to what she was telling Melhoff, hoping I might be able to steal them to use with the others, but before I had the chance Lt. Springfield appeared in the door. *She* had managed to find a fresh set of utilities somewhere, though they didn't have her name or rank on them yet. I suppose that technically made her out of uniform, but then again, I wasn't entirely sure about the regs in the provisional government's military.

"Sir, ma'am," she said, looking at Vicky and me. "Mr. Munroe is downstairs. He wants to speak to both of you at your earliest convenience."

I sighed, leaning my head back against the wall. I didn't honestly want to talk to the man right now. Vicky gave Melhoff a pat on the shoulder and stood, looking back at me. I nodded and followed her and Springfield out of the room and down to the stairwell. The Fleet enlisted and NCOs occupied the third floor, Marines the second, all officers on the ground level, except for Vicky and me and Captain Nance. The three of us had been granted lodging in one of a series of townhouses at the center of the city that apparently had been devoted to housing the command structure of the new military.

Waiting at the foot of the stairs on the first floor was Randall Munroe. The man didn't wear a uniform, didn't use a rank, but everything about him screamed that he should have, that he was most at home with a gun in his hand. But there was none at his hip, and if he had a weapon concealed under his light, cloth jacket, it was well hidden.

"I'm very sorry to hear about your crewman," he told us. And maybe he was, though I had a hard time reading any emotion through those gray eyes. "I... have some experience with difficult transitions."

"I bet you do," I agreed. "I read up on the civilian resistance on Demeter during the war. How the hell did you not get the Medal for that?"

"Because of my mother," he answered without hesitation. "She wasn't happy about me running away, changing my identity, and joining the Marines. It was pretty much all I could do to keep her from dragging me back to Trans-Angeles." He made a dismissive gesture as if waving aside the entire thing, as if his story was inconsequential. "I didn't just come here to offer my condolences," he admitted. "I've been discussing your situation with Kara and Deke, trying to figure out how to best put you and your ship to use. I apologize for not getting back to you sooner." A pained expression passed across his face. "Perhaps if you'd been able to give the crew something constructive to think about the last few days, they wouldn't have had time to sink into depression."

That sounded almost like a criticism of my leadership, and I frowned but didn't comment on it. Maybe I deserved it.

"What are you wanting us to do?" I asked him.

"You have to be aware the military has been reorganized. We only have one operational cruiser, the *Teutoberg Forest* under Admiral Khan, and he's constantly patrolling the rest of the systems in the provisional Commonwealth." Munroe shrugged. "Not that we've discovered any other major threat since we allied with the Pirate Worlds, but we're weak, and there's always the chance someone might take advantage of that."

"The Unity didn't need you to be weak," I assured him. "They could have wiped out the Commonwealth before this whole Psi War business."

"Yes, well, that's a potential threat, but not one we could stop right now anyway, is it?"

I reluctantly shook my head. That part was inarguable.

"The lighters and other armed civilian ships are all we have besides the *Teutoberg Forest*, and our ground forces are pretty much all light infantry. Not even Force Recon. We had to pull in the Savage/Slaughter Private Military Company out on Highland to use their mercenary infantry. The head of the company, Keller Savage, is officially a general now."

"Who made him a general?" Vicky asked sharply.

"Well, not to put too fine a point on it," Munroe told her with a thin, taut smile, "but I did. And I propose to promote the both of you to the rank of colonel as well."

I knew what Vicky was getting at and it bugged me too, enough to say something when perhaps I should have kept my mouth shut.

"Mr. Munroe..." I began, but he interrupted me with a raised hand.

"Just *Munroe*, if you don't mind. I was a sergeant... I worked for a living."

And that was another reason why I liked this guy. Which was exactly what made him dangerous.

"Munroe," I said, "you seem like a good man. But you're a hero to the people on this world. I worry that might blind you to the scope of the systems you're trying to bring together. Not everyone is going to see you as a hero... some are just going to think you're a dictator. Do you have any plans to hold an actual election at some point?"

He grinned. Not a calculated smile that the politician I could see in him would have approved of, but an honest smile. I think had it not been for the circumstances, he might have laughed.

"I really need to tell you the story of how I got this job. Trust me, it wasn't because I wanted it. We've already had elections for local representatives to the Demeter emergency government, but the problem with elections on an interstellar level is the fact that the populations are small and scattered. In total, there are close to a billion of them, but they're spread out over fifty systems, more maybe, and most of them are preoccupied with survival at the moment. Then we have the Pirate Worlds..." he shrugged. "The *former* Pirate Worlds, I should say. We're in an economic alliance with them at the moment and we have a mutual defense agreement, but they don't have any interest in being a part of our new government and definitely wouldn't be up for a census. But they're the only organized force out there besides us, and they have a lot more warships than we do at the moment."

"You're worried about them?" Vicky asked.

"I'm paid to worry. But yeah, I spent years as a Corporate Council merc and I had to deal with the cartels. Their power is dispersed but it's not dead, and as bad as the Transformation Virus was, I don't know if it's enough to change a century of the way they've always done things. And we can't discount the possibility that some bright boy out there might be thinking that all those disorganized systems would be easy pickings. So, our first priority is to find out which systems can be fortified, which can be saved, and which need to be evacuated back to the closest worlds we can hold. Which is where you guys come in."

"You need our Drop Troopers," I said. "I haven't seen a single Vigilante since I got here."

"There are none," he confirmed. "Every single Drop Trooper we had was killed in the final battle with the Changed. You have the only ones we know about in the entire Commonwealth. It's possible there are caches of suits out there somewhere, but our priority so far hasn't been searching for them."

"And that's another thing you'd like us to do?" Vicky asked. "Search for weapons and equipment?"

"Among other things. But what I'm really concerned with is a threat that our intelligence assets have been hearing rumblings about out on the Periphery."

"A bigger threat than the Unity?" I asked him pointedly.

"I believe you," he said. "There's no way you're making this shit up, not with that ship, not with the aliens you brought with you." And the memory of Munroe and the others being introduced to Jay, Bob, and Spinner nearly made me chuckle. "But the bottom line is, that's a threat that might be here tomorrow, or next month, or next year. And from what you've said, I don't know that there's a Goddamned thing we can do about it. This... this is something we can deal with now. *You* can deal with it. If you agree to it. I can't draft you..." Munroe shrugged. "Well, maybe I could, but I'm not going to. You've been through enough, and I don't intend to disrespect that. The ship, we're going to use. Nance and his bridge crew have already volunteered to stay on, and we can crew the ship with Savage-Slaughter infantry, but as a Marine, I'd much rather have Drop Troopers on her." He offered me a hand. "What do you say?"

Vicky caught my eye and nodded, which would have been good enough even if I hadn't already decided for myself. I took his hand.

"All right, Munroe. I promised myself when I went to OCS that I'd never let get promoted out of the field. But as long as you guys won't kick me out of a Vigilante, you've got yourself a deal."

[10]

"I want to apologize ahead of time," Kara McIntire said, which is just the sort of thing I expected from an intelligence officer and yet didn't want to hear, "about the sketchy nature of our intelligence, but I think once you hear the subject of this report, you'll understand why."

We were in her office, which was actually larger and better-decorated than Munroe's, despite the fact that he was her boss. I wouldn't have expected someone as harsh and lethal as McIntire to be an art connoisseur, but paintings hung at the cardinal points of her office, a simple yet elegantly pastoral look to them. I couldn't swear to it, but I'd have been willing to bet they were painted here on Demeter from local landscapes.

After Munroe had solicited our help the night of Gow's suicide, I'd assumed we'd be called in for a briefing the next day, but no one from the government had contacted us for three days, and at first I'd thought they were dragging their feet in bureaucratic inefficiency. Then new uniforms had been delivered to the crew at the barracks and to Nance and us at the townhouse, and within an hour Kara McIntire had buzzed me on my 'link and set up a briefing.

Not so inefficient after all.

Walking from the townhouse to the government offices, the first thing that hit me was the people—or, rather, the strangers. Open spaces didn't bother me anymore, but I'd spent a good part of the last several years seeing the same faces every day, and having so many new ones around everywhere I looked gave me repeated jolts of fight-or-flight. I was sure Vicky noticed, but she said nothing, just grabbed my hand and held it as we walked.

No one stared at us this time, but there were a hell of a lot of salutes, which made me uncomfortable. We hadn't done any saluting on the *Orion*, mostly due to the fact that we were rarely outdoors in a non-tactical situation, and I was out of practice returning them, not to mention that it seemed like a huge waste of time. But I suppose they were making an effort to maintain proper decorum in order to reinforce that this *was* a real government with a real military and not just a bunch of half-assed refugees with a makeshift militia.

McIntire had also seemed a bit more pleasant to deal with when she'd greeted us at her office door, this time without Deke Conner in the office. The thing I'd noted after the quick scan of the artwork was the lack of family photos or videos. I wondered if that was a recent thing, something everyone did to put aside the pain of losing them, or if she hadn't been close to her family even before the Psi War. I would have bet on the latter. McIntire didn't strike me as someone with a lot of family ties.

The last thing I noticed was that there was no holographic display, no star map in her office. I would have expected one for a briefing like this. Maybe the lack of one had something to do with the preemptive apology.

I settled into my chair, leaned on my knees, and waited. McIntire sighed, and if I was willing to hazard a guess despite my short acquaintance with the woman, I would have said she was embarrassed.

"Our intelligence sources are scattered and unreliable," she told us. "Most of them are in the Pirate Worlds, and they'll say anything for the right barter." She snorted. "Which is the only sort of trade there is right now until we establish a new monetary system. But this source... well, I trust her a bit more than most, since I worked with her in the DSI during the war."

I tried to keep the distaste off my face but Vicky couldn't quite manage to conceal hers, and McIntire grinned ruefully.

"Yes, I know, you're both probably not fond of the DSI, but trust me, neither am I. That's a story for another time, but she and I went through the shit and she didn't ask for anything in return for this information, which makes me more likely to trust her."

"What's the intel, ma'am?" I prompted, reserving judgment on its quality until I got details.

"I don't know how well you remember the early days of the war," McIntire said, "but things were... up in the air for a couple years."

"I think we both remember it pretty fucking well," Vicky growled, a flare behind her eyes. I felt the same way, but I said nothing.

"Then you know. The outcome was in doubt, and if the Tahni had won, that would have meant the end of humanity as an interstellar power. We were desperate, which was the source of weapons and tactics like the missile cutters in the Attack Command, the drop-ships, and various other, more top secret and esoteric ideas." The corner of her mouth quirked upward. "Ask Major Conner about something called Omega Group if you want to see the veins pop out in his forehead. But that was the Fleet, the Marines, Fleet Intelligence, people who had to answer to the Commonwealth Senate. You can only imagine what an agency like the DSI was up to during that period."

"I'm afraid to," I told her. "But I have a feeling you're going to tell us."

She nodded.

"I suppose I don't have to tell you why autonomous weapons systems were banned by the Commonwealth a couple hundred years ago."

A prickle went up my neck at the words. It wasn't something I'd thought about a great deal before we'd encountered the different alien societies outside the Cluster, but the AI, the Skrela, and the Ghosts had all driven the point home.

"It was because of what happened during the Crisis," Vicky said slowly, as if trying to figure out where this was going. "The refugees."

"It's a complicated story how it came to it politically, but what happened was fairly simple. The European nations didn't have enough young people to field armies anymore, so they guarded their eastern borders with armed, autonomous drones. After the nuclear exchange between the Russians and the Chinese, tens of millions of refugees were driven out of the eastern European regions by radioactivity, fallout, fires... and starvation. There were huge hordes of them on every road out of the affected zones, all trying to get to perceived safety in the western nations. But those nations could barely feed their own after the war, and they shut down the borders." She shrugged. "There were warnings... signs, loudspeakers from the air on drones, fences. None of it was enough to turn back people whose children were starving. The automated weapons platforms mowed them down by the tens of thousands."

I nodded, not caring to imagine the tragedy. I'd seen enough I'd never be able to get out of my head without adding to it on purpose. Even back in the isolated hovels of Tijuana, abandoned by the postwar civilization, we knew about the refugee massacres, and the strictures against autonomous weapons were nearly as deeply ingrained as the Ten Commandments or the Sermon on the Mount.

"Right up until the Changed brought down the last megacity on Earth," McIntire went on, "arming AI drones was one of the few crimes with an automatic death penalty. No exile to a colony, no punitive hibernation, just a march to the incinerator chamber of a fusion reactor and a bath in plasma. We only had to use that penalty twice in the history of the Commonwealth, you know? And not once after the first war with the Tahni."

"Because people learned their lesson?" I asked hopefully. She barked a laugh.

"Hardly. Because the DSI started tracking down everyone who tried to build automated weapons systems and hiding them away in secret labs, making sure that if any useful technology were developed, it would be used by us."

"Oh, fuck," Vicky muttered.

"Exactly, Colonel Sandoval. You must understand, even when the Corporate Council under their Executive Director Andre Damiani tried to subvert the election, discredit the military, and take over the Commonwealth government—that happened while you were gone, by the way—he didn't attempt to use this technology, simply because there was too great a risk that someone would turn him in. And not even his position would have kept him out of the incinerator. But somewhere out there, those labs, those factories, those test ranges still toiled, right up until the Psi War when they were abandoned and the scientists and workers evacuated back to somewhere they perceived as safer."

"But the lab is still out there," I guessed. "And you know where it is?"

"Not exactly," she admitted. "One of the ways it was kept from being discovered was that the entire setup was constantly on the move. People heard rumors—it's easier to measure the soul than it is to stop rumors. But no one could ever report anything even if they were so inclined, because they could never say *this is where the lab is*. And without that information, it's nothing but a wild rumor that could end your career if you get caught passing it around."

"But..." I prompted.

"But this source... let's call her by her old code-name, Scorpion... told me someone has found it. Normally, I'd just send out one of my operatives undercover to investigate, but the systems are weeks away and not under our control. And if this place *is* found... it has to be destroyed. Completely. A cutter or a cargo bird couldn't carry enough ordnance to do that."

"But the *Ellen* can do it," Vicky finished for her.

"Bingo, Colonel Sandoval. And for the cherry on top, you can do it with enough Drop Troopers on board to handle anything you might run across, *and* you can get to the rendezvous with our source in a few days, rather than the months it would take from here."

"Months, huh?" I repeated, eyebrows shooting up. "Just where the hell is this place?"

"Well," McIntire said, smiling just like Top used to when some ignorant private asked her if he'd finished his work detail, "that's the other benefit. You both know the territory. The source is on your old stomping grounds. You're both going back to Hausos."

———

"Twenty people," I said, looking at the roster on my 'link screen. "That's all we're going with for the Fleet complement on this mission?"

"It's all we need," Rafael Nance said dismissively, as if I'd complained about the weather.

His eyes were on the *Ellen Campbell*, on the platoon of Vigilantes marching up the cargo ramp into her. Vicky and I had already stowed our suits, but the fastest way for Springfield and her platoon of enhanced battlesuits to get on board was to walk. Vicky had stayed in the hold to oversee the process while I'd ventured back out into the morning sun to talk to Captain Nance.

"Don't need an engineering crew," he ticked off on his fingers, "because we have no fucking clue how to repair or modify or maintain the drives or the reactor on this boat. Don't need maintenance or repair techs for the hull, life support, or weapons because we have no fucking clue how to maintain or repair *those* either. Don't need flight ops because we're only taking the one cutter with us, because this thing can—obviously—land on a planet. All we need is the bridge crew and, just between you and me..." he glanced around as if worried someone might overhear and leaned closer to me, "... we could probably get away without *that* too. One person could fly and fight this boat, I reckon."

"Why bring twenty, then?" I wondered.

"Four crews of five," Nance explained. "Three active to work eight-hour shifts, one spare so every shift can get a day off."

"Damn," I murmured. "I know we'd be better off if we had a fleet of these things, but it kind of feels like it would be better if we didn't. That'd be the end of an era."

"You're telling *me*," Nance agreed, nodding fervently. "If we didn't have the Unity to worry about, I might have insisted we blow this boat up once it had got us here."

"Is the crew already aboard?" I asked him.

"Just the XO. Everyone else'll report when we're an hour

from launch." Nance laughed. "It's not as if they need to get her warmed up or anything."

I nodded, didn't give voice to the impatience roiling inside my gut. We'd been prepping for days already and still weren't supposed to leave until nightfall, and I couldn't help but feel we were wasting time. The Unity *was* coming, sooner than later, and no matter what Munroe said about us not being able to do anything against them, we still should have been doing the best we could to get ready.

What that would mean, I wasn't sure. They had one cruiser and the *Ellen*, and that was about it for anything that could touch the Unity ships I'd seen. I couldn't figure it out and I was desperately hoping someone here could, but that would mean planning. That would mean not pushing off the preparation until they had no choice. But we were the new kids on the block, and we had to give them reason to trust us.

"I see they finally gave you a rank consummate with your opinion of yourself," Nance remarked, smirking at the birds on my shoulder epaulets. I returned the expression and mimed dusting the eagles off.

"You mean they finally formalized my status," I reminded him. "The one *you* gave me, if I recall right. You could always have been in charge of this fiasco... Rafe."

His eyes flared at the casual use of his first name, a liberty I hadn't taken the whole time I was the commander of the mission, but then he relaxed and shook his head.

"Oh, hell, now you're gonna be impossible to live with." But his laugh was good natured, and he clapped me on the arm. Then he frowned again, staring back at the road into town. "Who the hell is this?" Nance asked, nodding toward a groundcar pulling up near the ship.

The rear door opened even before it completely stopped

and a tall, rangy man in black emerged, a large duffle over his shoulder. Even with the sunglasses, I recognized him.

"Major Conner," I called to him, "didn't expect to see you here."

Deke Conner's stride was long and powerful, almost a lope, like he was walking in low gravity, and I wondered if he was native to a higher-G world.

"Yeah, well, this is an intelligence mission, Alvarez," he said, face twisted in a sneer. "And unless I missed a section in your CV, neither you nor your lovely wife is an intelligence officer."

"What about Captain Nagarro?" I asked sharply, not caring much for his tone or his attitude. "She's been with us this whole time. I think she's qualified to..."

"To *analyze* intelligence, sure," he agreed. "But we're not talking about analysis, we're talking about field work." He waved it aside. "Either way, it isn't up for discussion. Captain Nagarro has been reassigned to a desk job in Amity—with not a single argument from her, by the way. And I'm going with you." He jerked a thumb at the *Ellen*. "Does this thing have cabins, or do we all just lay out sleeping bags around a fucking campfire?"

"There are crew quarters," I confirmed, "though they're not much to write home about. Racks but no mattresses, so you might want to run back home and grab a pillow."

"Everything I need," he told me, slapping a palm against the huge duffel, "is right in here." He slung it again and continued his long-legged stride toward the boarding ramp. "See you on the ship."

"Don't want to say goodbye to Colonel McIntire?" I asked, half-mocking because he was being an asshole, half serious because I was sure I'd detected something between them before and it would be nice to think that after all these years of marriage, my emotional sensors had at least been calibrated that much.

Deke didn't even stop walking, just threw a smartass grin over his shoulder.

"We've been together long enough," he told me, "that I don't have to."

"Well, he's a real winning personality," Nance muttered once the Intelligence officer was on board the ship and out of earshot. "Gonna be a fun trip. By the way, where are your buds, Jay and Bob? And that weirdo alien scientist?"

"Dr. Spinner," I supplied.

"Yeah, him. They not interested in coming along?"

I sighed, remembering the hurt look on the faces of the two of them when I'd broken the news.

"Afraid not. Now that this is officially a military expedition, they aren't authorized to go on this mission. Munroe said he'd try to find something for Jay and Bob... and Spinner is already with the engineers, seeing if there's anything from the technology on his world that we're lacking here. He's fitting right in, but the other two seem kind of lost."

"The grass is always greener," Nance said with a shrug. "I think they're all gonna regret not staying home." He laughed sharply. "Particularly if they can't find girls who're into the exotic."

Shaking that image out of my head, I checked the time on my 'link.

"We've only got a few hours left," I said. "I'm going to check on Vicky, then pick up a couple things from town before we ship out. Anything I can get you?"

Nance frowned, forehead wrinkling in thought.

"You know, it's been so damned long since I had anything we couldn't fabricate on the ship, I honestly can't think of anything I'd want."

"Well, I can," I assured him. "There's not that many of us on board, and we won't be gone that long. The engineering crews installed a freezer and this place has shitloads of livestock. I'm bringing along some steaks."

The Unity might be coming to end us all, but by God, until they did, I was going to enjoy myself.

[11]

"Man, I could get used to this," Deke Conner sighed, watching Hausos grow larger on the main screen. "When I think of all the months I've wasted in Transition Space, stuck in a cramped, little cutter…"

I didn't reply, too mesmerized by the sight of the world that had been my home for too short a time. Hausos gleamed blue and green and precious little white, a warmer world than Demeter, with smaller ice caps and shallower oceans and rolling hills lush with grass like the steppes of Asia Minor.

"She's still beautiful," Vicky whispered from beside me.

We weren't bothering to strap in, not when there were no threats in sight, and she leaned against my shoulder, what might have been regret in her voice.

"You wish we hadn't left?" I asked her softly. She shook her head.

"No. Every bad thing that happened would still have happened, and a lot of the good things that happened because we were out there wouldn't have." She patted my arm and smiled. "And we wouldn't have ever met Dunstan. I'm just glad he and Hazel and their baby are safe and away from all this."

"That kid'll be how old now?" I asked, brow furling as I tried to do the math. "Eight?"

"God knows," she admitted. "I hope they have three or four of the little rug rats by now."

"What's it look like down there, Woj?" I asked.

"No spacecraft in orbit," he said. "But there're at least two small fusion reactors down there."

"There was only one when we were there," Vicky observed. "At the center of the settlement. I wonder when the second one was installed?"

I looked over Woj's shoulder at the placement of the second reactor.

"That one's Gamma Junction," I said, pointing at the easternmost of the two. "But the other power plant... there was nothing within a thousand klicks of that area the last time we were here."

"According to Kara," Deke said, "her source is in that Gamma Junction place." He cocked an eyebrow at me. "You used to live here. What do you think the reaction of those people would be to this ship landing right outside their city?"

"Not good," I told him. "Even before everything that happened. I don't know how much they've heard of what happened back in the Commonwealth, but they have to know contact with the government has been cut off. Seeing an alien ship the size of a warehouse landing like gravity doesn't exist isn't going to make anyone feel comfortable. We should use your cutter."

"The *Dutchman*," he corrected me, then shrugged. "The *Dutchman II*, to be exact. The first one sort of got blown up a long time ago. She started out life as a surplus missile cutter, but this new one was an Intercept." Deke grinned. "Got all kinds of interesting little tricks. Not like this boat, but we won't be helpless. So, who's going? Besides me?"

"Both of us," Vicky said while my mouth was still open to answer. When I scowled at her, her jaw set stubbornly. "There are still people down there we know... I hope. And most of them liked me better than you."

"No uniforms," I decided. "If we're going low-key, then we go in civilian clothes."

"Thank God I brought some along," Vicky said.

"What about you, Conner?" I asked, and maybe there was a challenge in the question. "You prepared?"

"Everything I need is in my duffle," he said, a tight smile the only acknowledgement of the barb. "Is this the sort of place I can open carry a gun, or should I conceal it?"

"Hausos?" I thought back to the place I knew, the farmers striding through Gamma Junction with shotguns resting on their shoulders. "Oh yeah. Before, you probably could. Now... definitely."

"Sounds like my kind of place."

———

The *Dutchman II* was tiny by comparison with the ships I'd been calling home these last few years, but the cockpit felt cozy rather than small, the embrace of the cushioned acceleration couch and the push of the plasma drive against my back familiar and comforting. This was flying, this was *human*. On the *Ellen*, for all that we'd cleaned out the stasis chambers and brought in some furniture, I could never shake the alien nature of the ship.

The thicker layers of the lower atmosphere buffeted at the delta-shaped craft and the rumbling of the plasma drive faded out, replaced by the whine of her fusion-powered jets. I checked the communications panel, wondering if there was any sort of traffic control out here, but the entire board was locked down.

For you, maybe, Jim told me. *There's been no attempt to communicate with this ship, no scans so far.*

You've been quiet lately. Did I do something to piss you off?

Constantly. But mostly, I've had nothing useful to say. And unlike you humans, I don't talk when I have nothing useful to say.

I had a thought, remembering that Jim had access to all the files from the *Orion*'s database, including the personnel files from the Commonwealth military prior to our departure from the Cluster.

What do you have on Major Conner?

There was a Deacon Edward Conner who was admitted to the Commonwealth Military Academy near the beginning of the war, but he was reported missing during the Battle For Mars after a Tahni attack on a cadet training vessel. No other records exist for anyone of that name.

Huh. That jibed with what Kara McIntire had intimated, and I put the rest together quickly, used to the Fleet Intelligence way of doing things by now.

"So, Deke," I said, speaking before I allowed my good sense to talk me out of it, "you were in Omega Group during the war?"

His dark eyes flashed toward me with the promise of violence, just for a half a second before he was able to bring himself back under control, his expression going neutral.

"I don't know what you're talking about," he said casually, attention focused on the controls as we dipped lower into the atmosphere on the planet's night side. "I was in Fleet Intelligence."

"You were a cadet at the Academy reported missing during the Battle for Mars," I laid out my reasoning as if it were fact. "After that, you fall right out of the military personnel files. That means something so top secret the Fleet didn't even know you worked for them anymore. A covert ops team, I figure. Omega Group. And the way you talked about him, I'm pretty sure this Caleb Mitchell was on it with you."

Deke laughed harshly.

"Kara put you up to this, didn't she?" Sighing, he settled back into his seat and sighed in resignation. "Doesn't really matter much anymore, but old habits die hard. Yeah, we were all on the team, everyone who survived the *Thatcher*. Ten of us, though only seven survived the war. Now, there's only three, assuming Caleb is still alive out there somewhere."

A memory tugged at the corners of my mind, and I ran the file of those cadets through my head again.

"Matt M'Voba," I said softly and this time, Deke didn't even attempt to conceal his shock.

"How the hell do you know about Matt?"

"I met him," I explained. "During the invasion of Tahn-Skyyiah, just outside the Imperial Palace. He went in with some Force Recon types, and my company stayed outside and got fucking slaughtered."

And if I sounded bitter, it was only because I was. Vicky's eyes flickered toward the deck. I thought she'd been about to tell me to stop taunting the Intelligence officer, but now her jaw clamped shut. She'd very nearly been killed in that final battle. Search and Rescue had gotten her into an auto-doc minutes, possibly seconds before it was too late, before the blood supply to her brain had been cut off too long to revive her.

Deke nodded, fell silent for a moment.

"Yeah, I heard about the casualties you guys took. Didn't know it was you."

"I was a first lieutenant. The Skipper..." I had to start again. "Our company commander had been killed on the last drop before the invasion. That was my first time leading a company into combat, and I lost..."

I couldn't say it, couldn't put it into words.

"We lost two during the first try at Demeter," Deke said softly. "Daniela and Valeria. Then Brian in the Imperial Palace. Matt and Cowboy in that whole business with Andre Damiani and the Corporate Council. Holly in the Psi War after Trans-Angeles fell. Reggie later on, after... now it's just me, Caleb, and Kel."

Kel. They'd mentioned Kel Savage as a general, the guy who'd provided the ground forces for the provisional government from his mercenary company. I didn't believe in coincidences.

"Sorry," I told him, both for dredging up bad memories and messing with him about his record.

"Me too," he agreed. "I know you guys had it bad out there, Alvarez, but trust me... it was no picnic back here either. Sometimes, I think it was inevitable, you know? Like we'd come too far, too fast. Went from riding horses to launching rockets in just a few decades, gone from nearly destroying ourselves in a nuclear war to spreading out to hundreds of planets. I mean, it took the Predecessors millions of years to get to what they had when the Skrela took them down."

"They took themselves down," I told him, then shook my head. "I got to know the Resscharr way too well when we were out there. Trust me, they're not anyone you want to be using as a role model."

"Shit, dude, there was a whole Goddamned religion worshipping them up until everything fell apart. Psychopath losers who didn't even know what the Predecessors looked like but still had themselves physically augmented because they thought the Ancients would approve. Proselytizing on every streetcorner in the bigger colonies, stockpiling weapons for the revolution when their gods returned, fighting gang wars against the Evolutionist cyborgs." He shook his head. "Like I said, it hasn't been that great back here, even before the Psi War."

He nodded at the front screens and pushed the steering yoke forward, a welcome rollercoaster dip accompanying a change in the tone of the atmospheric jets.

"There's the landing field," he told us.

He was right about that, and the patch of cracked and overgrown pavement just north of Gamma Junction's last row of buildings hadn't changed since we left. If anything, it was more run down now, more of it reclaimed by the grass and brush. No other ships took up space on the stretch of gray pavement, just a couple VTOL transports and a few hoppers, and not a soul wandered the space between them. It was well past midnight local time, and on a world like Hausos, they rolled up the streets when the sun went down.

"Hang on," Deke told us. "I'll have us down in a second."

Whatever else Deke Conner was, he was certainly a hell of a pilot. Forward thrust cut, and before my stomach had the chance to fall away with the loss of momentum and the triumph of downward gravity, the belly jets kicked us in the ass. The entire ship rang like a bell at the sudden upward thrust and I thought my spine shortened a couple centimeters, but the maneuver had the advantage of reducing our thermal signature and putting us on the ground as quickly as possible. I'd barely had time to gasp in a breath before the landing gear touched down, throwing me against the safety harness with a bouncing lurch.

"You think anyone noticed us landing?" I wondered as I yanked the quick-release for my restraints, and I didn't mean the question as snarky as it sounded.

"I'm hoping not," he admitted, hopping up from his seat. "Place like this, they might not bother with a night guard or anyone watching the field. We have a few hours until dawn. If we can get in and out before then, this whole thing becomes a lot simpler."

He paused to tie down his drop leg holster, fastening the buckle around his thigh he'd left undone while he'd sat in the pilot's seat. The weapon was large and looked heavy, though I didn't recognize it except that it was neither a Gyroc launcher nor a pulse pistol, and it certainly wasn't one of the service pistols Vicky and I carried.

"What the hell is that big hogleg?" I asked him on the way to the belly ramp, curiosity getting the better of me.

"Gauss pistol." He drew the gun, popped out the magazine, spun it by the trigger guard, and handed it to me butt-first. "Guess they didn't have these in wide issue when you got out."

The thing had *looked* heavy, and by God it *was* heavy, probably just shy of three kilos. I'd spent most of my free time on the *Orion* working out in the ship's gym, mostly because I didn't want the Force Recon guys to show up us Drop Troopers, but I couldn't imagine trying to use this thing in combat. I reversed it and handed it back to him, shaking my head.

"You must be stronger than you look."

He laughed and spun it again effortlessly before reloading and reholstering it.

"Yeah, I get that a lot."

Chill air rushed in through the open belly ramp and I cursed, taking a second to zip up my jacket. The damned weather again. Middle of summer and hot as hell in Amity, late fall and close to freezing here in Gamma Junction. No snow yet, but the sky was socked in with clouds, not a star visible through the haze.

"Wish we could rent a car," Deke murmured, sticking his hands in his pockets. "But I suppose it's the old shoe-leather express for us."

He set off, and I looked between him and the belly ramp for a moment.

"Don't you want to button up?" I asked, but before the words were all the way out of my mouth, servomotors whirred and clanked and the ramp lifted upward on its own.

What the hell? The thought was for my own benefit rather than a direct question to Jim, but the AI answered it anyway.

You're not the only one with a headcomp and an implant neurolink. Major Conner is more than he seems.

I didn't need Jim to tell me *that*. Just what the hell was Omega Group?

I considered just coming out and asking him about it again, but he'd already pulled twenty meters ahead of us walking at what seemed like a normal pace, and I refused to run to catch up to him.

"He's gonna lose us," Vicky said, a little out of breath beside me from fast-walking.

"I think he's *trying* to," I agreed. "We'll see how well he can find his way around town without our help."

Particularly at night. Gamma Junction wasn't one of those planned settlements I'd seen where every street was laid out like a grid map, every neighborhood meticulously organized and each district strictly separated. It had been built by a bunch of stubborn vets tired of living every day according to military regs, who wanted their businesses or houses wherever they pleased. There were street lights, of course, because this wasn't some Vergai village, but there was also a fog rolling in.

Deke had been right about one thing—it would have been nice to have a car. And as if whatever implant neurolink Deke had was able to call him a cab in this place where no such service existed, a car appeared. Headlights first, bobbing up and down on the rutted road as it approached from the town, and finally the gentle rumble of an internal combustion, alcohol-fueled engine, not as efficient as an electric vehicle but a hell of a lot easier to fabricate with local materials. The engine stuttered and coughed as the vehicle came to a halt, pulling up right in Deke's path, the only thing so far that could make him slow his pace.

Deke's hand went to his sidearm but he didn't draw it, waiting as a long figure exited the vehicle, huddled inside a heavy jacket, the hood pulled up.

"Are you Scorpion?" Deke asked.

"Yeah, that's me," a female voice answered. A very *familiar* female voice. "You work for Kara?"

"I work *with* Colonel McIntire," Deke said a bit peevishly.

Ignoring the whining, I walked past him, frowning as I tried to place that voice. The intelligence source, Kara McIntire's old friend, Scorpion, pulled back her hood and revealed a familiar face to go along with that familiar voice.

"Hi there, Cam, Vicky," Grace Kim said, grinning broadly. "I didn't expect to ever see you two back here again."

"That," I told her, "makes two of us."

[12]

"What the hell, Grace?" Vicky asked, shaking her head in disbelief. "You told us you were Force Recon."

I almost laughed. Vicky sounded more offended at the idea that our old neighbor from Hausos might have lied about being a Marine than she was shocked that the woman had been DSI.

The Kim house, I noted from my perch at the kitchen table, hadn't changed much since the last time I'd seen it, and neither had Grace or Harold Kim. She'd never looked old and didn't now, her face free of the lines of stress or worry I was sure she'd earned through the years. Harold seemed to have collected all those for himself. The man had the same anti-aging treatments as nearly everyone who'd served in the military or who'd been born on Earth or one of the central colonies, but the lines beside his eyes and around his mouth were deep chasms that drew his expression into a perpetual frown.

That frown was even deeper than usual now, maybe because his wife had reopened an unwelcome door into her past, or maybe because it was close to two in the morning and Grace had invited three people over for tea. It was *good* tea, though I was more of a coffee-drinker and I took a sip, watching the discomfort in Grace's eyes at the accusation. And the discomfort in Deke's eyes, which I thought was both from the fact that I was sitting with my back against the wall, forcing him into a spot where the kitchen door was behind him, and from the idea that Vicky and I had monopolized the conversation with Grace so far.

"I *was* Force Recon," Grace insisted, hiding behind her teacup defensively. "Up until Demeter. The first time. I was badly wounded, evacuated by some special operations types."

"*My* type of special operations types," Deke interjected, "in point of fact."

"Afterward," Grace went on, though she eyed Deke sidelong, "I was approached by the DSI. They were recruiting for something they called the Cadre. It involved physical augmentation, and I was already pretty broken up and ready to get some payback."

"That's where you met Colonel McIntire," I guessed.

"Well, she was Lt. McIntire at the time, but yes."

"Where are the kids?" I asked her, the thought striking me as I set down the cup and looked around. "We didn't wake them up, did we?"

Harold and Grace looked at me as if I'd grown a third head.

"John is staying at a friend's house," Harold told us. "And Missy is... married now."

I rocked back in my chair, and Vicky's mouth dropped open.

"What?" she blurted. "She couldn't have been more than five when we left!"

"That's been fifteen years, honey," Grace told her gently. She shrugged. "I know, twenty is young to get married, but out here it's hard enough to find someone you can spend the rest of your life with, no one wants to wait."

Fifteen years. *Fifteen* years. Fifteen *years*.

I guess I should have known it had been that long. We'd

spent years in stasis, and we'd been warned that there might be time dilation effects from the warp drive going that distance. But the idea that we'd been gone long enough for that little girl to grow up and get married...

"Now that old home week is out of the way," Deke interrupted, "can we get down to business? If you're Scorpion, we're here about the intelligence you have. If it's anything but bullshit."

"It was important enough for me to pay that bum freighter pilot a hundred kilos of prime beef to get him to send the message through the Instell ComSats at the next wormhole jumpgate he came to," she snapped, scowling at Deke. "You think we can afford that out here? You know how valuable that is for us?"

"Fine, fine," he said, raising his hands in surrender. "So, tell us. What do you know about the... AI drones or whatever they are?"

"It was called," she told him, "Project Rho, I suppose because that sounded sufficiently generic and nondescript that no one would think twice about it. I only knew about it because Kara heard the rumors and told me instead of her superiors. She was too smart for that. I hadn't thought about it in years until the Confluence showed up."

"The Confluence?" I repeated.

"They're..." Grace looked at her husband and he shrugged. "They're hard to explain."

"They showed up about a year ago," Harold put in. "When things were... well, really damned bad. We hadn't had any supply shipments for months, the Corporate Council station had been abandoned years ago, after they were disbanded, and no one had taken their place. We were only able to buy raw materials from the occasional independent shipping firm that bothered to stop by to take our orders. Then those ended too.

Everything started breaking down and people were on the verge of starving. That was when the first of their ships came."

"We thought they were pirates at first," Grace said. "Or worse, given what happened with Captain Eld and that Tahni asshole Zan-Thint. We gathered up our weapons and set up defensive positions, but when they landed they..." she shook her head. "They brought us processed ore, fuel for the reactor..."

"Thank God," Harold added, "because we were close to running out, and wouldn't *that* have been a fucking disaster."

"And eventually, they brought *people*. Refugees from the war who needed a safe place to stay. They set them up with their own reactor in their own settlement farther west. They call it Sophia, for some reason."

"Who the hell are they?" Deke wondered. "Are they from the Pirate Worlds?"

"They're something new," Grace told me. "No one knows where they're based, and that's how they want it. They're... a weird group. A lot of them are Tahni, which is why we didn't trust them at first. Maybe a third. The others are Evolutionists—Skingangers—and a bunch of former Predecessor Cultists, plus people they picked up along the way who were refugees or bandits before."

"What the hell would Evolutionists and Predecessor Cultists be doing hanging around together?" Deke demanded. "They started a Goddamned war with each other in the middle of half a dozen colonies! They can't be in the same fucking city without killing each other!"

"That's how we heard it too," Harold said. "But there they were." He frowned. "I'm sorry, where are my manners? Would you all like more tea?"

"No, I think we're good," Deke told him. "The Confluence, whatever they are... what do they have to do with Project Rho?"

"They're nice people," Grace said, then shrugged. "Mostly.

They're trying. But they *are* still just people, and while the Tahni and Evolutionists are pretty close-mouthed, the former Cultists have recently rediscovered just how much they like to get drunk, and when they drink, they talk. And these fellas... they talked about what happened when a group of raiders stumbled across one of the worlds they were helping and tried to attack them and the colonists."

She shaped the story with her hands, as if trying to make sense of it.

"They said they hadn't been aware of anyone escorting them, but once the attack started, a dozen ships popped out of T-space and... well, this is the part that caught my attention. They said that the ships were boosting at twenty gravities, constant. Hard enough to kill a human being." Grace shrugged. "Now, that by itself means nothing. All it would take was a few unethical coders willing to install your basic AI in a few cutters. But the thing they said that impressed them the most was how the cutters all acted together, like a swarm. Like nothing these guys had ever seen, and some of them were former Attack Command pilots from the war."

"It's still not impossible that someone else did it," Deke said, but the protest was half-hearted.

"Yeah, and who would have the time, resources, or money to pull that together?" Grace shot back. "Particularly since everything fell apart? Do you even know a force that could muster over a dozen military cutters with proton cannons?"

"Okay, okay, granted." He spread his hands. "But if no one knows where their base is, how do we find them?"

Grace's eyes narrowed, and she fell silent for a moment.

"They're coming back here, aren't they?" Vicky asked her.

"You can't cause trouble here," Harold said, face clouding over with anger. "You have to understand, we *need* their help to survive. You people claim to be the new Commonwealth government, but how long is it going to be before you can do anything for us here in Trans-Tahni space? And what the hell do we do if the Tahni decide they want these worlds back?"

"Our kids live here," Grace insisted. "Our grandkids soon, I hope. You can't start a fight here. You have to promise me, Vicky."

I don't know why I felt insulted that she asked Vicky instead of me, as if I wouldn't have cared as much about her kids, but I did.

"You have my word, Grace," Vicky assured her, ignoring the dirty look from Deke. He clamped his jaws shut like he was biting back an objection, but at least he had the good sense not to argue. "We just want to talk to them."

Grace and Harold exchanged a look and he nodded, though I thought it was with reluctance.

"They're bringing in a supply shipment here to Gamma Junction in three days."

"You can stay here, if you need to," Harold added, and if there'd been reluctance before, this invitation was practically pulling teeth. "We don't exactly have a hotel in town anymore. Not much call for it."

"We'll stay on our ship," Deke volunteered for us.

"And what do you want us to tell people about who you are and why you're here?" Grace asked. "That ship being here is going to cause a stir, you know."

"Tell them the truth," I said, earning another dirty look from Deke. "Tell them we're here from the Provisional Commonwealth Emergency Council to assess the situation out here and see what we can do to help."

"Seriously?" Deke said, goggling at me.

"The best lies are closest to the truth." I shrugged. "Besides, what else could we be? There're people here who know Vicky and me, and they won't buy that we're the crew on a tramp freighter. This gives us an excuse to ask questions."

"And what if these Confluence people decide they don't like the new government nosing around?"

"Hey," I told him, grinning, "we're just three people in a little cutter. Totally harmless, right?"

Deke sighed.

"Yeah... and I guess if we're going to keep looking harmless, we'd better go make a call and get our friends upstairs to find a good place to hide."

I might have made a mistake.

I didn't realize it until the next morning, when a loud banging on the compartment hatch brought me awake with my gun in my hand. It took me a full second before I realized where I was, that the tiny, uncomfortable bunk was on board Deke Conner's ship. Though I didn't realize I'd grabbed my pistol until Vicky's hand closed around mine, pushing the weapon down.

"What is it?" I snapped, touching the control for the overhead lights. Our clothes hung from hooks set into the bulkhead, and I took a moment to shove my service pistol into its holster before I stood.

"We got a welcoming committee," Deke's voice came through the hatch, muted and distant. "And since *I* wasn't the one who decided to tell everyone the truth, *I* won't be the one who goes outside to talk to them. Capiche?"

I yawned, checked the time via my headcomp, and yawned wider. We'd managed about five hours of sleep, which would have been a lavish, nearly decadent amount back in the war, but

I'd gotten spoiled with straight eights during our stint on the *Orion*.

"Yeah, give us a second," I told him.

"Us?" Vicky repeated, eyeing me sleepily. "I wasn't the one who decided to tell the truth either."

I tossed her clothes at her, and she stuck out her tongue but started pulling them on anyway. Wishing I had time for a shower, I grabbed a fresher strip from the drawer beside the bed and let it melt in my mouth to kill the bacteria and clean my teeth while I dressed. Peaceful diplomatic mission or not, I buckled on my gun. The last time I'd been on this world, I'd wound up in a fight for my life, and those who didn't learn from history were doomed to repeat it.

Deke waited in the utility bay, arms folded, glaring at us as if this was his mission and we'd intruded on it. I didn't bother looking at the rear-facing camera feed before I imitated Deke's earlier showing-off and had Jim open the belly ramp remotely. Watching the look of disbelief on his face was nearly worth the missed sleep.

"I'm not much of a talker before I've had my coffee," Vicky mumbled beside me.

"Don't I know it," I agreed. She still glared at me as we stepped down and into the group of townsfolk gathered in the shadow of the *Flying Dutchman II*.

Most of them I couldn't put a name to after all this time, but I recognized the faces, and if they wouldn't have remembered Vicky and me on their own, the Kims would have made sure to tell them. Grace and Harold stood off to the side, inconspicuous, as if they too were merely concerned citizens who had only found out about all this at the same time as everyone else.

"Good morning," I said, pitching my voice to carry across the gathering of over a hundred people.

It was a smallish crowd, probably because the farmers

hadn't gotten in from their homesteads and a lot of others would just be too busy running their businesses and trying to stay alive, but that wouldn't last. If these people didn't like what we had to say, the others would come and then we'd be forced to either take off and try again in Sophia or button up and hope no one broke out the heavy artillery.

"Vicky? Cam? Is that really you?"

The man who spoke was a fireplug, shorter than Vicky but broad across the chest in a way that had only been accentuated by two decades of farm work since the war. We hadn't been close friends back when, but in a place this small, everyone knew everyone else, and my main problem was trying to remember his name.

"It's really us, Bob," Vicky told him, rescuing me when Jim couldn't.

I only have access to what was in your official records, meatbag, Jim shot back.

If you're going to get pissed off at my unspoken thoughts, I warned him, *you should probably stop spying on them.*

"Grace and Harold told us you represent some new government?" Bob said, apparently having appointed himself the spokesman for the community. I wasn't sure if the position was official or if he'd just taken it on himself, but it made addressing the crowd easier, and I stepped down the ramp, face to face—well, honestly, more like nose to forehead—with the sawed-off Marine vet.

"We've been commissioned into the Marine Corps by the Commonwealth Provisional government," I confirmed. "They sent us out to the colonies in Trans-Tahni space to assess your condition and see if you need help." *That* caused a rumble of cross-chatter, and I raised a hand to settle it down. "Look," I said, talking over Bob's head at the audience, "things are *just* starting to get organized. The new capital is in Amity on the planet Demeter, and they're still bringing in refugees who couldn't survive on their own worlds, still trying to set up some kind of system of trade. But they want to find out who's in desperate need of help, which is why we're here."

Well, it was why I *wished* we were here. I hated lying to them, but I would have hated getting into a fight with them more... or dragging them into *our* fight.

"Where were you six months ago?" someone yelled from the back. I couldn't tell who, except that the voice was female. A chorus of grumbles joined her, and I put on my best quarterdeck bellow, as Top always put it, to drown them out.

"Six months ago, there was a concerted attack on Demeter by elements from the Pirate Worlds, and there were barely enough people left after the Psi War to beat it back." Or so I'd been told by Munroe, since I'd been in stasis between star systems at the time. "I know things have been tight here, but they've been pretty bad everywhere, and the important thing is, the new government wants to help now that it can."

"We're here," Vicky put in, her voice carrying even farther than mine, the pitch higher, "to find out what you need, what we can do. To find out if you're interested in being part of the new government. So please, you can talk to us here or we can arrange something in town, maybe a meeting?"

"We appreciate you coming here," Bob broke in, and his words, like ours, were intended for the audience at large, not simply the person he stood facing, "but we don't need help from any half-assed new government. All it'll mean is they'll give us crumbs now and later on, once they get a real, organized military, they'll come back here and collect taxes from us, recruit our kids for cannon fodder, and mine our resources without giving us a damn thing in return, just like the Corporate Council used to do."

Ouch. Not bad points at all, and not ones I could easily refute, particularly since I'd had those same concerns myself.

"Do you think you guys on your own can maintain a technological society here for your kids?" Vicky asked him. "For your grandkids? You know what a razor-thin edge that kind of thing runs on out here. Look how fast the Commonwealth fell after the central government on Earth collapsed. What would you do if your fusion reactor went down and you couldn't repair it?"

"The Confluence will take care of us!"

It was that same female voice, and this time the crowd parted and she stepped forward. Older than most of the others, or at least more weathered, she had the look of one of the refugees who'd been settled on Hausos after the war rather than the vets who'd come here with their separation bonus. Her hair was long and braided, her eyes dark and glinting with rebellion as she jabbed a finger in our direction.

"The Commonwealth never did a Goddamned thing for us here! When the pirates and the Tahni took us over, you two and those Corporate mercenaries were the only ones who fought for us! I didn't see a single Commonwealth Marine on this world then! Did you?" The last was directed to the others in the crowd rather than us, and when they shook their head, she went on. "When we needed help, when things were desperate, Marakit was the one who took care of us!"

"Marakit doesn't ask anything in return except what we volunteer to give her!" someone else shouted.

"Marakit?" I asked, aiming the question at Bob.

"She's the leader of the Confluence," he told me.

"And she came here?" Vicky asked, sounding as surprised at the prospect as I was.

"Well, no," he admitted. "We've only heard about her. But they all love her. The people from the Confluence talk about her all the time."

And here, like a door opened from the heavens, was our opportunity.

"Well, maybe we should talk to the Confluence when they come," I suggested. "If this Marakit is as awesome as everyone says she is, then we shouldn't have any problem coming to some sort of arrangement with her. That shouldn't be a problem, right? Us talking to them?"

Bob looked around at the others, for the first time seeming to be at a loss for words.

"Umm... no," he said finally. "That shouldn't be a problem at all."

"Then I guess we'll see you all in a couple days."

The crowd dispersed slowly, and once even Grace and Harold were gone, Vicky turned to me with a look of utter disgust.

"Fine," she acknowledged. "You're better at this talking shit than I am. But don't let it go to your head."

[13]

The scream of landing jets split the afternoon calm as half a dozen cargo shuttles descended on columns of fire.

"Wow," Vicky murmured, watching beside me. "These Confluence people don't believe in half measures, do they? That's gotta be thousands of tons of freight."

As much as it impressed us, it seemed to impress the other residents of Gamma Junction even more. Thousands of them stood at the edge of the landing field like they'd gathered for a church service, their eyes cast upward in prayer to the gods who provided for their needs. Bob and Grace and Harold were out there among them, though I couldn't pick them out from the rest of the huddled masses. We'd stayed out of the middle of the press and also stayed away from the *Dutchman II*. I figured the Confluence crews would already be suspicious of another starship on the planet without us hanging around her.

"That's a lot of personnel along with all that tonnage," Deke judged, thumbs hooked in his gunbelt.

I frowned at him. He looked more like a gunfighter than a government agent, which was, I suppose, an asset for a spy, but wasn't going to help at all to build trust with these people. I would have ordered him to stay on the ship and let us do the talking if I had even halfway believed he might obey the command. For all that Vicky and I technically outranked Deke, that was a distinction I doubted he would make.

"Too many for us to take unless we call in the *Ellen*," I agreed. "So maybe we should play it cool."

Deke smirked aside at me.

"You think you're an expert on diplomacy now, Alvarez? Since when do Marines do anything but shoot bad guys and blow up shit?"

"Since I didn't have any choice," I told him. "There was just the one ship of us out there. We shot as many bad guys and blew up as much shit as we could, but we had an entire galaxy worth of bad guys to fight. And trust me, Major Conner, as scary as things got for you here, the rest of the galaxy is just as scary. I had to work with a lot of people I'd much rather have shot."

"To be fair," Vicky interjected, "we *did* wind up shooting some of them *after* we worked with them."

Any further discussion of the matter was cut short by the first of the shuttles touching down, their boarding ramps beginning to lower before the turbines had wound all the way down. And out came the people.

"Well, fuck me," Deke said, eyes widening. "They weren't bullshitting us."

The first crew out the door were Skingangers—Evolutionists. I hadn't seen too many of them even back when we'd been undercover in the Corporate Security Force, but enough for me to recognize the cyborgs for what they were. Gleaming metal replacement parts, obvious on purpose, meant to show they were rebelling against their humanity rather than just people who'd been badly injured and couldn't afford anything better. Bionic legs, arms, eyes, sometimes parts of the jaw replaced with sharpened, metal teeth in mandibles like a steam shovel.

One of them, at least, had something of a sense of style. He was sleekly designed, the melding of flesh and cybernetics sleeker and less obtrusive than the others, and somewhere along the line he'd had silver dreadlocks implanted into his skull, sometimes hanging free like the hair they resembled, sometimes wriggling like the snakes of the Medusa. He ordered other Skingangers around with short, sharp commands and still talked more than most of the Evolutionists I'd run into.

Tahni cargo handlers followed them out, more on some ships than others, but close to the third that Grace had described. I'd spent enough time working and living with Tahni that just the sight of them didn't send my balls crawling back into my belly, but these were qualitatively different from Zan-Thint and his followers. Not overtly military, they wore the typical Tahni civilian garb, clothes woven from multicolored strip wrapped around their bodies in an intricate pattern that I could never figure how it stayed together. Most of them were younger, too young to have fought in the war. Probably too young to have played much of a role in the Tahni insurrection Deke had told us about.

The rest... well, I hadn't been sure what to expect from the Predecessor Cultists. I'd heard about them, read about them, but these men and women weren't dressed in white robes and weren't trying to make a show of who and what they were. Dressed in almost uniform gray work fatigues, they could have passed for any other normal worker... if it hadn't been for the muscles. The Cultists all had outsized musculature thanks to the implant of cloned tissue, making them look like caricatures of humans drawn by the classic superhero comic book artists of the Twentieth Century, their universal broad shoulders and bulging biceps straining against the fabric of their utility garments. Like Deke, they were all too good-looking, but unlike him they hadn't been built that way before birth, so it seemed more unnatural... and was. They'd had surgical bodysculpts in an effort to make themselves the perfect human specimens they thought the Predecessors would want them to be.

I almost laughed at the sight of them, at their conception of what the Predecessors would have wanted. To the Predecessors, humans had been a control group, left in our natural state to contrast with their creation of the Tahni. They'd had no plan for us, had even tried to wipe us out in the Great Bottleneck tens of thousands of years ago. The fact we'd refused to die made us a nuisance to some of them, a subject of study for others. Right up until the end, some of them had worked to combine our genes with those of the Tahni to make something more perfect, and right up until the end they'd failed.

Maybe these guys had gotten burned out on the whole thing during the battles with the Skingangers, or maybe it had taken the Psi War to change their minds, but they looked like they were just doing their best to blend in now.

"Only place I ever expected to see Tahni hanging out with Cultists and Skingangers," Deke added, "is in a prison work camp."

"That one looks like he's in charge," Vicky judged, nodding toward the dreadlocked Evolutionist who was snapping orders to the others, sending them scrambling to unlimber pallet loaders from the utility bays of the freight shuttles. "Maybe we should go talk to him."

"Yeah, let's," Deke agreed, and set off at the same pace that had nearly lost us last night.

I didn't try to keep up this time, just shaking my head.

"He'll fuck this up for us," Vicky said, looking as if she wanted to take off at a jog after him but sticking with my casual stride instead.

"This is his operation," I said with a philosophical shrug.

"We're here so we can get Munroe to take the Unity seriously. If he fucks it up, it's his problem."

I wasn't being completely honest—with myself, more than her. Project Rho was a disturbing concept, and I knew it better than anyone. The problem was, autonomous weapons systems had only been kept in check by the central authority not just of the Commonwealth military and law enforcement but by the Corporate Council coopting anyone who started researching it. With the Commonwealth weak and the Council gone, it was only a matter of time until that genii was out of the bottle.

"Hey," Deke called to the dreadlocked cyborg, "you the HMFIC here?"

The Confluence crew weren't armed that I could see, but given that they were all faster and stronger than a normal human, I wasn't sure they needed to be. Deke was ten meters from Dreadlocks, and I knew if it had been me, it would have been a very near thing if I could have gotten my gun drawn before the cyborg reached me. The Confluencers watched Deke with wary eyes and defensive stances, but no one moved to block his way, deferring to Dreadlocks.

"I don't know you," the cyborg said, as if that was an answer to Deke's question.

"Well, there's an easy way to remedy that," the Intelligence officer said with a shrug. "I'm Deke Conner. I work for the Commonwealth Provisional Government."

"I thought it was the Provisional Commonwealth Government," Vicky said softly as we approached the two of them.

"I don't think they've decided yet," I told her.

"You say that as if it should mean something to me," Dreadlocks responded, standing stiff and straight like a Marine at attention on a parade ground. "There is no government out here, there are only the people and their needs—and those who would help fill them."

"I'm not looking for a fight," Deke assured him. "I just want to talk to someone who makes decisions."

"We all make decisions for ourselves," Dreadlocks said. "It's when we try to decide for others that there is violence."

Deke's expression darkened like a storm brewing on the horizon and his shoulders bunched, tensing as if it was a real, physical effort for him to keep from drawing his gun.

"I've heard that the Confluence is only here to help out the colonists on these worlds," he said, not raising his voice yet somehow so much less friendly than a moment before. "I figured that meant ore, spare parts, fuel..." the corner of his mouth twisted in a sneer. "I didn't realize that bullshit freshman-level philosophy was thrown in for dessert."

And *that*, I suppose, was just enough to rouse the ire of even the most pacifistic Skinganger. Dreadlocks advanced on Deke so fast, I didn't even see the step that took him across the distance between them, just saw the metal hand flash out, reaching for Deke's throat. And stopping. I definitely hadn't seen Deke move, but somehow his hand had intercepted Dreadlock's wrist, holding it in place a few centimeters from his throat. Dreadlocks leaned into the motion, visibly straining to break the grasp, but Deke stood motionless, eyes fixed on the cyborg with a confidence that reminded me of a blasphemous prayer Top had used to quote.

Yea, though I walk through the valley of death, I will fear no evil. For I am the baddest motherfucker in the valley.

The work around the two of them stopped as the Confluencers took a step forward, uncertain, their instinct to protect their leader but also hesitant, likely because they didn't know what to make of Deke. And neither did I.

"There's no reason to get violent, metalhead," Deke told Dreadlocks, his voice not giving away any fear or strain, his arm not shaking with the effort of holding off the cyborg. "Nobody's making any decisions for you, and you can bet your sweet, rust-covered ass that you won't be making any decisions for me. So why don't you fucking relax before someone gets hurt?"

Dreadlocks' face was unreadable, too much metal having replaced flesh, one of his eyes a glowing, green ocular. But slowly, gradually, he withdrew his hand and Deke let him. The rest of the crew relaxed, not moving back to their work just yet but falling back a step, still watchful but not ready for a fight.

"I don't give a fuck if you recognize our government," Deke told him, hands falling to his side as if he didn't need to bother to keep them up and ready, so confident was he in his ability to handle the cyborg. "I'm not asking you to." He gestured back to the two of us. "We want to talk to your boss. We want to work something out with her, and if she decides she's not interested, well…" he raised an eyebrow. "That's *her* decision to make, isn't it?"

Dreadlocks regarded him silently for a long moment, and I thought maybe the cyborg was going to win the world's tensest version of the quiet game, but he finally nodded, then looked aside at Vicky and me.

"You come with us. We leave in twelve hours. No one follows, no one knows where we go. You will be confined to quarters during the flight and no weapons will be allowed." He cocked his head to the side. "We only have room for two."

"I'm going," Deke stated, eyeing the two of us. "You two wanna play rock-paper-scissors for whoever's going with me?"

Vicky turned to Dreadlocks.

"We'd be staying in the same compartment?" The cyborg nodded, and Vicky rolled her eyes at me. "Then you're going, Alvarez."

Deke looked between the two of us and frowned.

"I don't know why, but I feel like I've just been insulted."

"You're smarter than you look, Conner."

"I don't like this at all," Nance said, shaking his head. His head and shoulders were all I could see on the tiny holographic projector in the *Dutchman*'s cockpit, and I felt stupid crowding around the comm panel with Deke and Vicky like we were taking a call from grandma at Christmas. "We should try to follow you in the *Ellen*."

"You know that's impossible, Rafe," I sighed. "Even if we wanted to chance it, you're going through realspace and we're in Transition Space. We have no idea where we're going and without some clue as to what the system looks like or even what direction it's in, you'd just be flying blind."

"So we're just supposed to sit out here and wait?" he demanded. "For God knows how long? You could be weeks in Transit!"

"No," Deke said. "There's no reason for you to stay here. You can head back to Demeter."

My eyes narrowed, and I scowled at the Intelligence officer.

"Hold on a second. What happens if we're only gone a few days? We come back here and the only transportation available is this cutter, it's gonna be a long month in T-space with us breathing each other's BO."

Deke grinned lopsidedly.

"Demeter's at a wormhole junction. All we have to do is take the *Dutchman II* back to the nearest jumpgate and make a call via an InStell ComSat. Then the *Ellen* can come pick us up. Closest system is about three days from here."

"You copy that, Captain Nance?" I asked.

"Yeah, and I don't fucking like *that* much either," Nance replied. "But you're the boss."

The last was said with a glare at Deke, and I appreciated the sentiment.

"We'll be okay," I assured him. "I don't think they're taking us with them just to toss us out an airlock. If they didn't want us along, all they had to do was refuse to give us a ride."

"Yeah, but that doesn't mean this Marakit, whoever she is, won't decide she doesn't like you poking around and have you tossed into a fusion incinerator. I mean, you're not even going to have a gun!"

Deke leaned back in the pilot's seat, his arms crossed.

"He doesn't need one," he assured us. "He's got me."

The worst part was, I didn't think he was kidding.

[14]

"This sucks," Deke said, making a face. He tossed the half-eaten pita sandwich onto the plate in surrender. "I mean, I ate some seriously bleh shit during the war, but this is what? Soy tuna? Who likes this crap?"

"I do, human," a Tahni at the next table in the ship's galley snapped, looking over at us with hard, black eyes. He was older than the rest, with a long cue of graying hair wrapped around his throat, the sign of a blooded warrior. He gestured at the other Tahni at his table. "We all do."

For an integrated crew, they sure did eat separately. Which made sense, I suppose, since the Evolutionists barely ate at all, hooking themselves up to a tube of what looked like baby food once a day that fed them directly into their stomachs. But the former Predecessor Cultists didn't seem interested in mingling with the Tahni at least for mealtime, even though they were stuck eating the same shit.

"Last I heard," Deke said, returning the Tahni's glare with an amused smile, "the Tahni only ate that fucking disgusting root you planted everywhere on the human colonies you invaded."

"You humans made sure we didn't have to worry about our religious restrictions anymore," the Tahni sneered, "when you killed our emperor."

"You're welcome," Deke told him, grabbing a squeeze-bulb of water and saluting the Tahni. "I mean, who wouldn't be grateful? After all, we kept you people from wasting your lives following a false god. And we freed you to follow your own destiny, which apparently involves eating utter shit."

I said nothing, just kept chewing the disgusting soy tuna salad sandwich because it was calories and I needed calories. I'd eaten worse, though not by much. And since mealtime was the only opportunity the two of us had to get out of the tiny compartment we were confined to, I wasn't about to turn my nose up to the food.

Besides, there was always the chance the Tahni would decide to beat the shit out of Deke Conner, which would have been more entertaining than listening to the man tell stories about growing up in Toronto.

"You speak as if you killed the Emperor by your own hand," the Tahni male said, not reacting with anger as I'd expected, but more curiosity. "Who are you, human?"

"I was there," Deke admitted. "At the palace. Didn't kill the Emperor though. That was Randall Munroe, my boss."

I looked up with a mouthful of sandwich, blinking in disbelief. Deke saw the reaction and laughed.

"Oh, you didn't hear about that, huh? Yeah, he did that too, besides the whole deal with Demeter. He doesn't talk about it, didn't want anyone to know about it at the time." Deke turned back to the Tahni. "My friend Cam here was at the palace as well, but he couldn't fit inside, not wearing one of those big battlesuits. I'm Deke, by the way. Deke Conner." He grinned broadly. "Formerly of the Tahn-Kandranda."

The term meant nothing to me, but apparently it did to the Tahni because he sat bolt-upright, staring at Deke.

"Indeed. I thought you were legend." He touched a long-fingered hand to his chest. "I am Pol-Kai, once of the High Guard." His gaze flickered toward me. "I too once piloted a battlesuit. It was a proud position, you understand. Not one that most would be awarded, reserved only for the bravest and most loyal warriors. Is that how it was for your Marines?"

It was most certainly *not*, of course. Our best and brightest went to Force Recon and most of the Drop Troopers were the scum of the Earth, but I had the sense it wouldn't be politic to share that insight with this Pol-Kai, not with a whole table of rough-looking Tahni around him and me without a gun.

"Yes, it was exactly like that," I assured him. "It was a great honor to wear the armor." Eventually. "Tell me something, honorable Pol-Kai," I asked him, choosing my words carefully. "The Tahni I met after the war, they were... angry. Bitter. Sometimes at their emperor, sometimes with us humans. Sometimes with the gods themselves. But none have ever shown any inclination to work together with humans. What made you and your comrades decide to join this Confluence?"

"Marakit did," he said immediately, without a second's hesitation. "She accepts us. She has shown by her actions that she is concerned for us as Tahni, that she is willing to sacrifice her life to save ours. None of us doubt her." He gave an elaborate motion of hands and shoulders that I knew most closely translated to a shrug. "When the troubled times came, when the supplies ceased to come from your people to our home at Kandranda-Skyyiah, only Marakit thought to return to help us. Not your Commonwealth, not our own homeworld, only her."

"Kandranda-Skyyiah," I repeated, tasting the words. "That means something like Home of Death, doesn't it?"

Pol-Kai gave an expression of surprise.

"You *have* spent time among my people, to know something of our language. Even your pronunciation wasn't completely obscene."

I had, of course, though I hoped he wouldn't ask too much about it, since it had involved killing a lot of them.

"Your people call the world Hudson Bay," he went on, "since they seized it from us and made it one of their own colonies. At least they allowed us the charity of continuing to live in the home we carved out of the frozen wilderness." Oh yeah, no bitterness there at all. "But what do *you* want of Marakit, Cam and Deke?" He enunciated the words as if they were stranger than the rest of the English he'd been speaking. "Do you hope for her aid, or simply her wisdom?"

"The reason the Commonwealth supplies stopped coming," Deke told him, and I thought he'd jumped in because he was afraid of what I'd say, "was that the government collapsed during the war with the Changed. We're building it back up again, trying to tie the scattered bits of the Cluster together so that we can all mutually aid and support each other. Our job is to find out if Marakit is interested in being a part of the new Commonwealth."

It was well-rehearsed and delivered by a man used to lying, I thought, but I wouldn't have believed it if he'd been trying to convince me. Maybe that was just me though, since I already knew he was shading the truth.

"What do you think, Pol-Kai?" I asked. "Does that sound like something she'd be interested in?"

"Marakit had no love for your Commonwealth before," Pol-Kai declared, "and I can't imagine she would change her mind simply because you've given it a new name. Like my home, humans love to give old things new names and pretend it changes the nature of the thing."

"It *is* new," I told him. "Whether it'll wind up being better or worse, I couldn't tell you. But I can say that if you aren't part of building it, you'll have no say at all in how it turns out."

Pol-Kai had no response for that, or at least he had no time to formulate one before Dreadlocks plodded through the galley hatchway, every footstep a metallic thump against the grating of the deck. Dreadlocks wasn't his real name, of course. We'd learned at some point during the last few days that he called himself Vagabond. Why I had no idea and hadn't bothered to ask, though it did lend him a certain depth of imagination I wouldn't have otherwise attributed to a Skinganger.

"Mealtime is concluded," he said, looming over our table like the worst waiter in the galaxy.

"Oh, come on," Deke argued plaintively. "We're in T-space. What the hell are we gonna see that would give anything away?" He showed teeth in a smile that was an imitation of the lipless, metallic perpetual grin of one of the Evolutionists. "Besides, I haven't finished this *delicious* tuna salad sandwich yet."

If Vagabond was amused, he didn't show it.

"You were told the rules before you agreed to come."

Deke sighed and pushed himself up from the table. I quickly stuffed what was left of my sandwich into my mouth, chewing at the periphery of the cardboard-like flatbread, and left my tray on the table. I figured if they'd wanted me to bus my own table, they would have given me more time to eat.

The hike back from the galley to our compartment took us through the engineering section, which was some indication of how small the crewed sections of the cargo ship were. No hatchways, just emergency seals ready to lower in case of an air or radiation leak. If I thought Deke liked to walk fast on purpose in order to lose us, Vagabond was twice as bad... and I was twice as determined not to run. Which gave me a good look at the crew as they worked. If they didn't eat together, the

Tahni, the Cultists, and the Evolutionists certainly worked together.

Lots of Evolutionists in the engineering section, fewer Cultists, fewer still Tahni. No surprise, since the Tahni had lost an entire generation of drive and reactor techs during the war and hadn't been allowed to rebuild their fleet since. The Tahni were the foot soldiers here, the Evolutionists the techs and pilots, the Cultists... maybe the grunt workers? They certainly weren't talkative in the mess, not even to each other.

Vagabond turned and made a come-along gesture to the two of us with as much obvious annoyance as a cyborg with a face half made of metal could show.

"If you want us to keep up," I told him, letting my glare slide aside to Deke in a not-so-subtle hint, "then stop moving faster than you know we can walk."

"Puny meatsacks," Vanguard murmured, but he slowed down.

Hey, I like this guy! Jim commented cheerfully. *You know, if you replaced your weak, fleshy bits with cybernetic parts, I could provide so much more information for you. We could be a real team.*

Sorry to disappoint you, but I'd rather be inside the hardware than have the hardware inside me.

"Hey, Vagabond," Deke said, "how the hell do you Skingangers live cheek-by-jowl with the Cultists? Don't you guys hate each other?"

Vagabond stopped in his tracks and stared at Deke with one gleaming green eye and one dark biological one. His claw-like metal hands clenched, and I firmly believe that if Deke hadn't already shown he was packing some kind of augmentation himself, the cyborg would have taken a swing at him.

"We do not allow the use of that word," Vagabond declared. "We consider it a slur."

"Sorry," Deke said, raising a hand, palm-out as if in surrender. "Bad habit. I should have said *Evolutionist*."

Huh. I didn't even know enough about the cyborgs to be aware that *Skinganger* was offensive. Vagabond said nothing, just stood immobile as if considering whether or not he bought Deke's apology. Abruptly, he turned on his heel and walked again, his pace still fast enough to be uncomfortable.

"We never hated the Predecessor Cultists any more than we despise all Normals," he answered Deke's question, his voice carrying back to us despite how far ahead he'd gotten. "*They* hated us for who and what we are, and we fought them for our survival. That kind of conflict takes a life of its own."

I shut my mouth. It had been hanging open from the sheer length of the dissertation, more words put together at one go than Vagabond had said to us the entire time we'd been on the ship. Deke had struck a nerve.

"Marakit taught us," he went on, a gentler note to his voice, "that the powerless hating each other is exactly what the powerful want. They want to keep us helpless, keep us preoccupied hating and killing each other because then we'll be too weak to stand against them."

"Who's *they*?" I wondered. "Who exactly is powerful now?"

"Perhaps *we* are." Vagabond sounded far too pleased with that idea for my comfort.

He stopped and I thought we'd made him mad again, but then I noticed we were at our compartment.

"You gonna lock us inside again?" Deke asked, pulling open the hatch and stopping halfway through it, looking back over his shoulder at Vagabond.

"You suggest I could trust you?" Vagabond's head tilted to the side at an angle that no human spine could manage, as if trying to examine us from a different perspective. "You, who have likely killed friends of mine, have almost certainly killed friends of the Tahni among us?"

"Don't forget the Cultists," Deke reminded him, a hint of malice in his smile. "I took out a few of *them* back in the day too."

"But that's all in the past, isn't it?" I pointed out. Not that I was particularly interested in enabling Deke Conner's head games, but it would have been nice to get out of the compartment more often. "Isn't that what your boss says? That we need to do things differently now? You might have the power now, but we sure don't. If we did, we wouldn't be coming to Marakit for help."

"No." Vagabond's answer was decisive, without the slightest hint he'd even given consideration to the idea. "Marakit may decide to trust you, but that is her choice to make, not mine. I may have exceeded my authority in merely bringing you along."

I shrugged and followed Deke into the room, kicking the door shut behind me, then closing my eyes and leaning back against it in time to hear the magnetic click of the lock sliding into place. I didn't want to look at the compartment. I'd grown to hate it these last few days, not just because of the stale odor that seemed to come from every square centimeter along with the air ducts. And not just because of its uncanny resemblance to a jail cell or the cracked, puke-green plastic upholstery on the beds and chairs.

No, I didn't want to look at Deke. After all this time, I knew what his routine would be. Less than a minute after the door locked, he'd start stripping down to his skivvies then plop down on his cot, legs spread and big, nasty feet hanging off the end of the bed.

Sighing, I cracked an eyelid and winced, seeing exactly what I expected to.

"You know," I told him, "for a man with genetically engineered good looks, you have the most ratchet toenails I've seen on a human being. And that includes the zombie cannibal guy I found on Plateau."

"Well, excuse the hell out of me, Colonel, sir," he said, resting his head back against his interlaced fingers, the look on his face completely unconcerned with my opinion. "Maybe you had dedicated pedicurists on the *Orion*, but it's been a kind of rough and ready few years back here in the Cluster."

Yeah, and I wanted to ask him something about that, but I had to assume we were being monitored in here and I didn't want to give away anything sensitive. Not that I had a clue what Deke might consider sensitive. I pulled one of the chairs as far away from Deke's bed as it would go in the little compartment and sat down in it. I wanted to take off my boots, but there was a faint residue on every surface and I didn't especially want to feel it against my bare feet.

"How long have you and Colonel McIntire been together?" I asked Deke, trying to find a question he wouldn't object to for security reasons.

"Oh, hell, I think it's been six years now," he said, eyes closed, as if it would be too much trouble to give an exact number. "I mean, we kinda got involved while I was still a private citizen, and then things got interesting and I was... let's say, *recruited* back into the military. That was even before the whole Transformation Virus came along. We had to deal with the Corporate Council trying to mount a coup, then the whole mess with the Northwest Passage and the Skrela waiting there for us, then the Tahni trying to revolt against military rule..."

"Yeah, I keep hearing how hard it was here," I interrupted. "Out there, we lost more than half our company of Drop Troopers, three quarters of our officers. Lost our ship. Lost fifteen *years* of our lives. So, I can't say honestly whether I would have liked to be here more than there."

"I wish we had a bottle," Deke said, eyes still closed. "So we could drink to each other's troubles." Finally, one of his eyes opened a slit. "What about you? How long have you and Vicky been married?"

"Since the war ended." I shook my head. "We had it all figured out. We were going to settle on a nice, peaceful colony world, have our own farm and start a family. I should have known that was too much to ask."

"From what I hear, you've seen more in those fifteen years you *lost* than most people will ever dream of in their lives."

"Yeah, there is that," I admitted. He wasn't wrong.

"Then I suppose the question is, was it worth it? The people you lost... would they have traded it for staying here?"

By God, that *was* the question, wasn't it? It hit me between the eyes in that scummy, cramped little compartment on a scummy, beat-up freighter in the middle of nowhere. I'd been thinking about *my* loss, how much *I* missed the ones who'd died. But would Top have wanted to go any other way? Shit, the only reason she'd have wanted to come back was so she wouldn't miss out on the fight with the Unity. But Top would never have been the type to settle down, not even if they'd made her a general. And God knows she would never have accepted *that*.

"How'd you get to be so fucking smart, Conner?" I asked.

"The usual way," he said with a shrug. "Pain. Lots of pain. It's always the best teacher."

I definitely couldn't argue with that.

A blaring klaxon roused me from a sound sleep, a familiar sound and a welcome one.

"Transition," Deke said somewhere in the darkness. I felt

around for the light switch on the bulkhead beside my bunk, then winced as the overhead lamp glared at me.

Conner was on his feet, already dressing, and God knew how because I couldn't have seen a damned thing a second before—the compartment didn't have so much as a chemical ghostlight, not a single ray of illumination.

"We got about thirty seconds until the gravity cuts out," he warned, like I'd never been on a damned starship before.

Lucky for me I'd slept in my clothes, mostly because I didn't trust the provenance of the bedding, so all I had to do was pull on my boots. I'd barely strapped the second one on when reality twisted and turned and took me with it into another universe. And because we still hadn't figured out the mysteries of the universe the way the Predecessors had hundreds of thousands of years ago, once we dropped out of Transition Space, the ship's gravity faded to nothing.

The boots were made for it, though I hadn't needed them since we left the *Orion* behind, and a tap of one heel against the other activated the electromagnets built into them. Metal clicked on metal, anchoring me to the deck, but there was nothing they could do for my stomach. Not that I wasn't used to free fall, but that didn't mean I had to like it.

But it wouldn't last long. The next siren warned us in plenty of time to prepare for what came next, the rumble of the fusion drives resonating through the superstructure of the freighter, the press of acceleration substituting for gravity nicely, settling my vertebrae and my stomach back into their rightful places. I sighed with relief and deactivated the magnets.

"One gravity," Deke judged, and I nodded. "Don't know how long that'll last, but enjoy it while you can."

"I wonder if they'll leave us in here until we reach orbit around..." I shrugged. "... wherever the hell we are."

"Oh, I'd bet on it. After all, the more of this system we see, the easier it'd be for us to find it again." He pulled a deck of cards out of his jacket pocket and tossed them on his bunk. "Interested in a game?"

"You had those this whole time?" I asked, goggling at him. "We've been sitting in this damned room for days, twiddling our thumbs, and you had a deck of cards the whole time? Why didn't you break them out before?"

"Oh, I didn't want to fleece you too bad before we got here," Deke explained, grinning. "I mean, after all, your back pay isn't actually worth anything now, with the economy in the shitter, so I figure all you got to bet with is what you've earned since we commissioned you. That's in chits, you understand, exchangeable for time on the fabricators, and measured in units. Every unit is about a half hour on the fabs, and I figure you have maybe a couple hundred at this point?" He pulled the cards out and shuffled them with dexterity I'd rarely seen, even among the card sharps on troop ships during the war. "That ought to last you about an hour, so I didn't want to drain your account completely. After all, you might need to get yourself some new clothes."

"Oh, *vato*," I said, shaking my head, slipping into the slang of my youth from the surge of righteous indignation, "it's *on*. I spent the better part of eight years playing poker with some of the baddest motherfuckers who ever shuffled a deck when there was not a damned thing else to do, and I left the Marines with an account stuffed full of their money."

"Well, brother," Deke said, dealing onto the bed, "the thing about Omega Group that made us so special wasn't that we could slip onto Tahni outposts and kill every single one of those assholes, then slip out and never even be recorded. And it wasn't that we basically took Canaan all by ourselves before you Marines even landed. No, the really special thing about us, about the Glory Boys, was that we were the best-trained and most highly skilled poker players in the entire human Commonwealth."

"Yeah, well that sounds like a bunch of bullshit," I told him, sitting on the edge of the bunk, picking up my hand. I meant the part about poker. The rest I could believe.

It was all I could do to keep a straight face when I saw the hand. Three kings. Maybe I'd have the fabricator crew make me a groundcar...

The hatch slammed open and Vagabond stood silhouetted by the lights in the passage.

"Come with me. It's time."

"Oh, hell," I sighed, throwing down the hand. "That figures."

Deke grinned and tossed his own on the bed beside mine. Four aces. Four fucking aces. I followed Vagabond out the door.

[15]

"Gas giant," Deke murmured, staring at the small viewscreen in the passenger compartment of the lander.

That much was obvious, but this wasn't the typical gas giant like the hundreds I'd seen in my career. Generally, they all were much of a muchness, as the Skipper used to say. Light-colored atmosphere with darker bands, usually swirling into semi-permanent storms in oranges and yellows. Not this one. This one was a light blue with deep purple clouds in spirals running off of each other like cells differentiating in a Petri dish. Beautiful, mesmerizing, unique.

Would it be enough for us to find this place again?

There are a half a dozen systems in the astrogational files with similar colors and patterns, Jim informed me. I didn't bother telling him not to answer questions I hadn't directly asked, because this time his answer was useful.

How many within the Transition time reference? We'd been in T-space less than a week, which limited the distance we'd traveled.

Three.

All with habitables? I pressed, hoping that would narrow the field even more.

Unfortunately.

Damn.

The gas giant caught my attention, but it wasn't our destination. That was one of its moons, and there was nothing unique about this world. Every habitable moon of a gas giant I'd seen had the same look. Thick ice sheets encroaching from both poles, held off in narrow stretches by thermal features, the habitable zones left as a gift by the Predecessors.

For the Tahni. That was a secret I wasn't planning on sharing with Pol-Kai. The Tahni had started both wars with Earth because of their fervent belief that the living worlds of the Cluster were their birthright, left for them by the Predecessors. As it turned out, they were dead right about that. Maybe that should have made me feel guilty that we'd encroached on the worlds that had been the inheritance of the Tahni, but it didn't. Mostly because I'd found out the Predecessors were such douchebags.

In some ways, moons like this were just evidence of how full of themselves they were, their assumption that the Cluster would be so teeming with life that even the narrow habitable bands on these little worlds would be needed. A place like this couldn't have held more than a few hundred million, and that would have been with the population crammed into every nook and cranny, half of them underground.

They weren't intended for habitation, Jim informed me.

Stop snooping on my thoughts, I snapped, scowling. But curiosity got the best of me. *Then what were they intended for?*

They were experiments. Small-scale tests before they moved on to terrestrial worlds. Losing a moon this size meant losing, as you noted, a home for a few hundred million at most. Losing a terrestrial world would mean losing a living space that could house billions. Not to mention the ecosystem to fill it. But you're correct about the Predecessors being douchebags, of course.

The ordinary moon shut out its extraordinary parent world, filling the small screen and engulfing the lander in the rust red of its atmosphere. A shudder rocked the little ship as we passed through a layer of storms, the convection from the heat of the thermal springs mixing with the colder air off the ice sheets to spawn dark, rotating swathes of thunder and hail. My fingers tightened around the armrests of my acceleration couch and my jaw ached from clenching my teeth. I tried to relax, sucking in a deep breath, earning a lopsided smile from Deke.

"Don't like flying through storms, Alvarez?"

"I don't usually mind it," I told him, "when I trust the pilot."

The pilot in this case was an Evolutionist, though not Vagabond. The cyborg in charge sat two rows ahead of us, bolt upright and unmoving, a statue being transported to a museum. The pilot wasn't much more lifelike, not even his hands moving, resting at his sides instead of on the controls, which would have worried me if it hadn't been for the interface cables plugged into jacks at his temples. I'd seen Attack Command pilots jacked in that way, but they still had to manually operate the controls.

Not this guy. On an intellectual level, I knew he had to be using some kind of remote system that allowed him to use a headcomp like mine to fly the ship, but it *felt* like he'd just taken his hands away and decided to let Jesus take the wheel. I badly wanted to run up to the cockpit, push him out of the seat, and take over the controls myself, but seeing as how he was likely three times as strong as me, I clutched at the armrests and prayed.

Finally, we dropped out of the clouds and the constant shuddering and bucking smoothed out into a normal landing and I was able to catch a brief glimpse of our LZ. Such as it was. Steam roiled up from bubbling springs, holes in the pustules of snow patching the surface of the valley, belching trails of smoke into the perpetual twilight of a sky dominated by the gas giant. No sun to warm this harsh and unforgiving hellscape, the glow of the star blocked off by the body of the planet, and I wondered if this side of the world *ever* received direct sunlight.

But there *was* life. A mass of algae coated every surface, even the fumaroles belching poisonous clouds, and where the snow was the thinnest, hardy, sharp-edged plants sprang from rock broken down into soil. I'd have been willing to bet that the atmosphere topside would eventually be lethal, but not quickly enough to keep people from digging beneath the surface. Which had to be where the base was, because there were only a handful of small buildfoam domes dotting the surface near the paved square of the landing field. Buildfoam was a white-gray by nature, but these had been stained yellow and orange from exposure to the gasses billowing from the fumaroles.

"This place is just a vacation paradise, isn't it?" Deke observed. "I can understand why you'd want to keep it a secret. Tell too many people, the tourists would crowd in and the whole ambience would be ruined."

The shuttle touched down with a feathery grace I hadn't expected, though I credited that to the lighter gravity on this moon, refusing to give the pilot's skill any consideration. The rear viewscreen flickered off along with the interior lights, plunging the interior of the passenger compartment into darkness... for me. I knew the cyborgs wouldn't care, and I'd figured out that Deke wasn't bothered by it either. Since he wasn't wearing enhanced vision glasses, my bet was that he either had a lifelike cybernetic eye or some kind of lens implant. They'd been around quite a while, but the surgery was expensive and complicated, not something the Marines were likely to pay for. Not something I was ready to pay for either, though I suppose it would have been less invasive and dangerous than having a computer installed inside my skull.

Standing beside my seat, I waited in the gloom, just happy to be on the ground, until Vagabond cranked open the airlock and the inky blackness of the shuttle lit up to the pale gray of just past dusk, enough light to make my way down the stairs. The cold struck me first, less of a surprise given the ice sheets all around us. The ambient temperature even out here among the thermal springs was above freezing, but only *just*, and the blasts of wind coming out of the north was the icy breath of an Arctic winter.

What hit me second was the *smell*. Sulphur. Rotten eggs, among other things. Strong enough I almost gagged, and I couldn't restrain the coughing fit that racked my chest before I thought to cover my mouth and nose. Deke didn't laugh at me, but neither did he show any sign of the stench bothering him. His chest didn't move. The man wasn't breathing.

"Stay behind me," Vagabond told us, "or you will be shot."

"Yeah, I get ya, brother," Deke told him. "Nice, peaceful people here, no hate for anyone." And he said every word without inhaling, showing no sign of stress despite holding his breath.

"We do not wish anyone harm," Vagabond corrected him, not turning around. "That does not mean no one wishes *us* harm."

The cyborg led us to a secure airlock built into the side of one of the domes and the question struck me of how a cyborg could operate a biometric lock, but apparently it was keyed to an implant communications link, because the outer door swung open on its own. Utter darkness loomed inside, and I bit back a curse. The entire no-lights thing pissed me off, and I wondered how the Tahni handled it since they weren't allowed bionic replacement or cybernetic augments. I found out when Pol-Kai strode comfortably after us, his deep-set, piggish eyes concealed beneath a set of goggles that would never have fit on a human head.

It was just *me* who'd come unprepared, though I doubted if they would have let me bring enhanced vision goggles along on the trip even if I'd thought of them.

"Just put your hand on my arm, Alvarez," Deke said dryly. "I won't let you fall."

If there was any way I could have gotten by without it, I would have told him to go to hell, but it was too dark for that, and I grabbed his shoulder and let him guide me forward. And downward. The first step of the staircase caught me by surprise, the second one even more so because of how deep it was, and I nearly fell forward against Deke. Not that it would have made any difference to him, because his shoulder might as well have been a brick wall. There was no way any human being could have lifted enough weights to get that solid, and he wasn't bulky enough to have cloned muscle tissue implants like the Predecessor Cultists. I don't know what the hell these Glory Boys were, but they must have dumped everything including the kitchen sink into them.

The stairs seemed to stretch down for over a hundred meters, and by the time we reached the bottom, I thought I was going to have to offer to buy Deke dinner. But a door at the bottom opened and light flooded in, bright enough that I had to squeeze my eyes shut against the glare.

"You are the gentlemen who wished to meet me?"

Splashes of color slowly faded until a slender figure coalesced in front of me, standing at the center of a wooded glen like a faerie of old. Except the forest was a holographic projection on the walls, the grass on the glen grew out of hydroponic chambers beneath the floor under overhead sunlamps... and the faerie princess was a cyborg.

Not like the others though. This woman's bionics were black and slender, built for performance in contrast to the showy, bulky silver of the Evolutionists. The face was the same black metal that ended in a sort of terminator line just before the nose; half dark metal, half pale, olive-tinged flesh. A deep red glow flared inside a cybernetic eye opposite the natural eye with its emerald-green iris set above half a pair of soft, tan-colored lips. The human side was framed with black hair cut straight level with the jawline. The scalp above the machine side was shaved to a stubble.

"You're Marakit," I presumed.

My instinct was to offer a hand, but I drew it back, knowing the Evolutionists didn't care for contact with us Normals. Her natural eyebrow turned up in an amused gesture that might have been a smile if she'd had a natural mouth to go with it, and she took my hand in her cool, nimble fingers. I didn't gulp, but it was a near thing. All she had to do was tighten her grip and she'd shatter every bone in my hand. But instead, she shook it and let go.

"Marakit Almario," she said. "Sergeant, Fleet Search and Rescue... medically retired." She gestured with a cybernetic hand and I frowned.

"I took quite a bit of damage myself in the war," I told her. "So did my wife. Marine Drop Troopers. Had to go in the tank a few times. Grew back a significant portion of my body."

The question went unasked, but she answered it anyway.

"Genetic disorder." Cybernetic shoulders imitated a very human shrug. "Not all of us were lucky enough to be born with parents who could afford to have us engineered before birth."

I laughed sharply.

"My parents were chicken farmers in Tijuana. I suppose I just got lucky."

"Sergeant," Deke interrupted, "I'm Deke Conner, this is

Cameron Alvarez. We're representatives of the Provisional Commonwealth Government. We came here to negotiate on their behalf."

For someone who hadn't been down with this whole plan, Deke had fallen into it quickly, but I wasn't sure I trusted his version of charm to work on Marakit, and I was sure it wasn't working on either Vagabond or Pol-Kai, who stood by in this virtual garden, watching us.

"Negotiate *what*, exactly?" She hadn't offered us a seat, and I wondered if it was because she was trying to sweat us or simply because she'd been a cyborg so long, she didn't even think about sitting anymore. I jumped in, not willing to trust Deke's instincts for negotiation.

"You've built up a..." I spread my hands as I searched for a word, "... *following*, I suppose, since I wouldn't quite call it an organization, in the Trans-Tahni colonies. And you obviously have your own supply chain, which means you probably have mining operations in this system's asteroid belt and the atmosphere of the gas giant. We have mining operations too, but what we don't have is a way of delivering resources to the colonies out this way."

And we'd made all this up during the flight to Hausos, thank God, which is why I'd had time to memorize it.

"And you want to contribute to their maintenance out of the goodness of your heart, I suppose?" For someone speaking out of a bionic jaw with a voice coming out of a synthesizer, she managed to put a lot of sarcasm into that question. Deke laughed sharply.

"Naw, not exactly. Look, it's been a long fucking flight and we've been stuck in a compartment about the size of a utility closet. Can we maybe go sit down somewhere—even though you don't have to—and have a drink." He shrugged. "Even though you probably don't have to do that either. And talk about this at length?"

"Oh, I still appreciate a good drink," she told him, then tapped the side of her jaw. "This is mechanical, but the taste buds are still in there. And the stomach definitely is." She looked at Vagabond and Pol-Kai, but her gaze fixed on one of the former Cultists, a tall woman with long, braided blonde hair. "Janella, go get a table set up in the hall and bring us a bottle of that vodka your people made." She grinned at Deke, a baring of sharpened metal teeth. "I can't wait to hear what these gentlemen have to say."

Vodka burned its way down my throat, through my chest and into my stomach, spreading a pleasant warmth as it went. I sighed and sat back, admiring what the Confluencers called simply *the Hall*. It had taken another kilometer of walking, both downward and forward, to reach it, and along the way we'd passed a hell of a lot more people than I'd expected. Not just the Tahni, Evolutionists, and Cultists I'd expected, but others, Normals like me. I hadn't asked where they'd come from, but I could guess. Grace and Harold had told me that some of the colonists from the Trans-Tahni worlds had joined the Confluence.

We'd only passed through a small section of this place, but even from that tiny portion it was clear there were tens of thousands of people on this world. Maybe hundreds, depending on how far the installation reached. Something else I hadn't asked, because it wasn't pertinent and we couldn't afford to be nosy.

"Nostrovia," Marakit said, raising her glass in salute. I was down by half, but I returned the toast and so did Deke.

I was by no means an expert on Evolutionists or other

cyborgs, but this was the first time I'd ever seen one drink or eat anything the old-fashioned way, and I have to admit it was a little freaky. No one else had joined us, not even the Cultists at the table, and definitely not Pol-Kai or Vagabond.

"Okay, we've sat down," Marakit went on, "and had our drink. Suppose you tell me what you believe you have to offer the Confluence?"

"We want to help," Deke said smoothly, grabbing the bottle and pouring himself another drink. "Like we were saying, we have the raw materials and refined resources to supply a lot more of the surviving colonies, but we don't have enough cargo vessels to get the stuff out to the people who need it. You're supplying a lot of people—maybe we can help you help more. And if you need protection, maybe we could help with that too. I mean, we don't have a bunch of cruisers anymore, but we could supply your freighters with a couple armed cutters for escort…"

Marakit laughed and, to my surprise, so did Vagabond.

"Oh, my dear Mr. Conner," she said, "I believe we've got that covered. We are quite able to protect ourselves."

"Really?" I asked, knowing this was where Deke would press the matter and hoping I could do a better job of it. "Because we were on Hausos, and we didn't see any combat spacecraft or even defensive turrets on your cargo ships. I know there are fewer people now and you might think that means there're fewer threats as well, but the ones that still exist, like the surviving Pirate World cartels, will be looking for things like refined ore, not to mention the facilities to produce it. You're tucked away nice and safe here, isolated and concealed, but your ships are going all around this sector, and that makes them vulnerable."

Deke glanced at me sidelong with a tug at the corner of his mouth, a look that I knew meant *I was just about to say that.*

"We don't need your protection," Pol-Kai stated flatly. "If that's all you have to offer, you should run back to your masters and tell them that you failed. If we decide to allow you to leave." He eyed Marakit meaningfully. "If you asked my opinion, we would be better served disposing of their bodies in the thermal pools."

"You think you're up to it, piggy?" Deke murmured, offering the Tahni a scornful glare. "Because you don't look that fucking tough to me."

Pol-Kai pushed away from the table, the legs of his chair scraping against the tile floor, a snarl on his face as he reached for Deke. I hadn't seen Vagabond move, but suddenly he stood in the Tahni's way, a hand pressed against the alien's chest, the other cocked back to deliver a death blow. The Tahni froze, biting off an exclamation, looking between Vagabond and Marakit. She hadn't moved, didn't look up, just stared at what was left of her drink.

"Pol-Kai," she said, "I do not recall either asking for your advice or giving you leave to act on behalf of the Confluence in this matter. I value what you and your people have contributed to the cause, but you've all agreed that I am your leader. Or do you wish to discuss that matter at greater length right now?"

I had a sneaking suspicion that discussion would be short and violent and would end with Vagabond's fist punching through Pol-Kai's skull. The Tahni must have had that same thought because he dropped back into his chair, hands on the table.

"My apologies, Marakit. I am yours to command."

Vagabond stepped back, not sitting again, just watching, and Marakit went on as if there'd been no interruption.

"I will be frank with you gentlemen, I have no love for the Commonwealth, whether in its original form or this attenuated one. When I knew it, the Commonwealth government was ever an extension of the greed and lust for power of the Corporate Council Executive."

"Not a single one of them lived through the Psi War," Deke told her. He hadn't moved either during the confrontation, yet still he retained the aura of a coiled spring, extreme violence at rest. "We're just trying to get by."

"Lifeboat politics," I supplied, remembering the term Top had used. "It might not last, but we could still accomplish a lot while it does." I turned over the next few words carefully before I spoke them. "And we've had... warnings that there may be other threats out there. Ones we haven't encountered yet."

Something shifted behind Marakit's biological eye and she stood, the motion as graceful and naturalistic as a dancer despite her bionics.

"Perhaps," she said, "we would be better served with a demonstration. Vagabond, prepare the lander for takeoff. And pass the word to Illyana..." again, that unnerving, metal smile, "... that we're going to have a little target practice."

[16]

"I know you pay no attention to my advice," Pol-Kai grumbled, "but I believe this is a mistake. We should not be sharing sensitive information with the enemy."

"We're not the enemy, Chuckles," Deke said, not looking back over his shoulder at the Tahni.

Marakit had sat us both up front, just behind the pilot's station and beside her, which left Pol-Kai and Vagabond sitting behind us, a situation I wasn't that comfortable with. Not that Vagabond would kill us without Marakit's say-so, or at least that was the impression I got of the cyborg, but Pol-Kai was a loose cannon. And a Tahni. I'd gotten to know the Tahni pretty well these last few years, fought beside them and against them, and while they were more complex and nuanced than I'd experienced during the war, they were also most certainly not human and didn't share human sensibilities or thought processes. Maybe they were trustworthy to each other, but not so much toward humans.

The shuttle was the same one we'd taken down from the freighter, but the mothership was nowhere to be seen, not in orbit around the moon and not on the shuttle's sensors anywhere this side of the gas giant. What the sensors *did* show were the mining and processing facilities in the planet's atmosphere. They were just animated avatars on the screen, too far away and too tiny against the Jupiter-sized world to show up on the optical cameras, but I'd seen enough of the setups to recognize it. Standard industrial model, churned out in the thousands by the Corporate Council all the way back to the beginning of the Commonwealth. Shipped in pieces and assembled by automated construction drones if you were rich enough to be able to afford them. By roughneck miners if you weren't.

"You didn't build the mining facilities yourself," I said, interrupting the pointless bickering between Deke and the Tahni. "I assume they were abandoned during the Psi War."

"Yes," Marakit confirmed, her voice thoughtful. "It happened more than I would have believed likely. After all, with the Transformation Virus running through the colonies like wildfire, the safest thing to do would be for a mining crew to remain here, if not in the orbital facility then down on... the moon." She'd stopped herself before she could reveal the actual name of the place. "But humans are a strange species. In a crisis, they seek the comfort of other people. I have no way of knowing, but the likeliest scenario is that the men and women who worked this place returned to the inner colonies and died along the billions of others."

"How did you and your Confluence find it?" I wondered.

"Oh, the story is long and complicated," she demurred. "Suffice it to say that among our original converts was a man who worked at the atmosphere mine here. And unlike our late, lamented friends, he was smart enough to not only remain isolated here but to find others he knew were free of the infection to join him."

"You mean the Tahni," Deke said, finally turning slightly in his chair to reward Pol-Kai with a backward glance. "They weren't susceptible to the infection."

"We were the first here," Pol-Kai acknowledged, though he refused to look at Deke when he said it. "We were the ones who invited Marikit to this place. Though now, it is as if it were the opposite, as if we were the newcomers and our words are not welcome."

I wasn't sure how a cyborg with no biological vocal cords managed an exasperated sigh, yet somehow Marakit did.

"Pol-Kai, you are still a valued advisor," she said, "but that doesn't mean I have to agree with your advice on every issue. No one is right one hundred percent of the time. You are as prone to blind spots as any other sentient being, and this is one of them."

"As if you were any more trusting of the human government than I," he shot back. "Do you really believe they've changed just because there are fewer of them?"

"Didn't your people change once the Emperor was killed?" I asked him. "Didn't the very character of your society shift when everything you'd built your worldview on for thousands of years collapsed?" I motioned between Deke and myself. "Do you think it's different for us?"

"Humans are deceitful," he insisted, straining against his safety harness as if he'd like to lunge across the cockpit toward me. "They are without honor, without respect. They take what they want and never question if it was theirs to begin with."

"*I* am still human, Pol-Kai," Marakit reminded him. She tapped her hard, matt-black torso. "Beneath this."

Pol-Kai fell silent, but inside those black, shark's eyes, I thought I saw agreement. And maybe hatred. Marakit turned her attention away from the Tahni, pointing out toward the equator of the gas giant.

"What we're here to observe is a hundred thousand kilometers that way. What remains of a Tahni destroyer. They Transitioned into this system during the war, after a battle, but the life support failed and all aboard asphyxiated. We found her when we first arrived and stripped off anything useful, but the hull itself was too badly damaged and we left her in orbit, figuring she was a fitting memorial to the futility of that conflict."

There. The wreckage tumbled across the pale violet of the gas giant's atmosphere, close enough now for the cameras to pick her up. I recognized the lines of the craft, the wedge shape all too familiar from nightmares of them hunting down my troop transport.

"And now we have no more need of a memorial?" Pol-Kai asked, and for an alien whose first language was definitely not English, he sure managed to convey bitterness effectively.

"Do you really think," Marakit asked, "that anyone gives a damn about the war now? With everything that's happened?"

Pol-Kai grunted noncommittally, but at least he shut up.

"You're using the old destroyer hull as a tow target," Deke said. "But a tow target for *what*?"

"Illyana," Marakit said, and at first I thought the name was the answer to Deke's question, but when she continued I realized it was part of a transmission, "your target is in a high equatorial orbit, Right Ascension 157.5 degrees. Launch... a dozen interceptors."

I kept an eye on the sensor screen, waiting for the arrival of... whatever it was. I saw nothing, which was unlikely unless she planned on us waiting for another five or six hours. It had already taken hours to get into observation position, as well as a complicated and uncomfortable series of acceleration and deceleration. There was no way we wouldn't be able to detect a dozen fusion drives...

"There they are," Deke said, and I scanned each section of

the screen yet still saw nothing. "They're running against the radiation belt."

"There's no way the radiation belt on even a planet this size could hide that many drive signatures," I protested, finally spotting the dim glow of the sensor readings. "Those aren't nearly bright enough to be…"

"Those aren't fusion drives," Deke told me, and I don't know who looked more surprised, Marakit or me. "They're antimatter reactors hooked to something called the em-drive."

"I wasn't aware the Fleet trained its commandos in advanced physics, Mr. Conner," Marakit said.

"Yeah, that," I added.

"Operating on our own, weeks away from support, fighting outnumbered, having to jump into one system after another without being spotted." Deke shrugged. "You bet your ass we learned advanced physics. The em-drive was one of those little oddities physicists have been working on for a couple centuries. Turns energy into thrust with no middleman and high efficiency. Last I heard, Fleet R&D and Corporate Council black projects were both still working on it, and both of them agreed it would take antimatter to power it." He fixed Marikit with a frank stare. "Though how the hell you and your little group got your hands on that kind of tech way out here…"

"Just watch the show, Mr. Conner," she said, the Yin-Yang blend of metal and flesh on her face cryptic and enclosed. "It's quite an expensive one."

I'd expected their approach to take a while, maybe an hour or more, but they grew impossibly fast on the screen, from distant sensor dots to batlike shapes with a faint glow at the rear.

"Jesus," I muttered. "They're boosting at at least forty gravities. That's fucking impossible." At least without the Predecessor gravity drives, or so I'd believed a moment ago. "Boosting that hard, they need to turn now and start braking…"

"Or perhaps not," Marakit commented dryly.

She wasn't lying. The spacecraft kept boosting until they were at least two-thirds of the way to the old destroyer, only minutes, before they flipped around as if the same pilot were at the helm of each of the ships, connected by the same brain. Engines flared, though not nearly as bright as a fusion drive would have been, a muted orange glow that didn't seem as if it could possibly have produced the sixty or seventy gravities of thrust that took their headlong rush into a tactical approach.

When the twelve ships reversed again, the scanners told a more complete story. They were each about the size of an Intercept cutter, yet there was no way even Deke's specialized *Dutchman II* could pull off a move like that without draining her entire fuel tank. They surrounded the ancient hulk like sharks surrounding the carcass of a whale, and farther away than I would have thought possible, they fired.

Not proton cannons. I would have recognized the thermal signature from those weapons, I'd seen them thousands of times. These were... lasers? Something *like* lasers, but powered by those antimatter reactors, they had double the range, and when they struck the Tahni hulk they didn't punch holes through it, they disintegrated it. The superstructure glowed like a supernova, and when the white light cleared, there was nothing left of it.

"Was that satisfactory, Marakit?" The voice that came over the cockpit speakers was female, a pleasant contralto, friendly and attentive.

"More than satisfactory, Illyana," Marakit replied. "Thanks so much. Your ships can return to base."

"Yes, ma'am. Happy to help."

The cutters arced away from the explosion, maneuvering thrusters in synchronization, and when their drives lit up again, the new course took them back around the terminator of the gas giant and, in minutes, they were gone.

"What the fuck was that?" I blurted, even though I knew.

"*That*, my dear Mr. Alvarez, is the reason we don't need protection, the reason we don't need your new Commonwealth government holding our hand. The Confluence has no interest in aggression, no interest in conquest, but anyone who tries to attack us will regret it… for the rest of their life."

"Which will be measured in seconds," Vagabond added.

"Take us home, Kana," Marakit said to the pilot before turning back to the two of us. "Then we can discuss further, if there's anything further to discuss."

Harsh thumps pounded the outside of the shuttle as the pilot turned the little ship without using her hands. I met Deke's eyes, silently asking if we should bring up the elephant in the room. He nodded but spoke before I could.

"There's one thing further to discuss, Marakit," he said, hooking his thumbs in the shoulder straps of his safety harness. "One big, fucking elephant in the room, if you know what I mean. Let's leave aside the fact that you somehow got hold of top-secret, antimatter-powered ships that are each, individually, more powerful than a cruiser. Shit's lying around now, and it's finders keepers as far as I'm concerned."

"How enlightened," Marakit commented, but Deke ignored the sarcasm.

"No, what bothers me is that this is pretty obviously autonomous, AI-piloted armed drones, which is so fucking against the law that if anyone caught you in possession of it, they'd execute you on general principles."

"They could try," Vagabond suggested quietly. "And again, their life would be measured in seconds."

"Hey, not me, bud," Deke assured him, raising his hands.

"I'm an easygoing, live-and-let-live type, you know. No problems. But that's me."

The main drive kicked in with a rumble of disapproval, as if the shuttle were clearing its throat to tell us to behave.

"I thought we'd just established," Marakit countered, "that things are different now. No laws, no government other than what we make. The rules we make."

"Some rules exist for a reason," I put in, trying to imitate the teaching voice Skipper used for us officers when he wanted to give us a life lesson. "I think we all know the reason for this one. When human kill humans, someone is responsible. Someone gave the order, someone can stand trial for it if it comes down to that. Someone can *disobey* it if the order's illegal."

"And I'm sure you've disobeyed orders in wartime for your conscience's sake," Marakit scoffed.

"You'd be surprised," I shot back. I looked over at Pol-Kai. "Isn't this part of your religion, the whole thing about only a being with a soul can kill another being with a soul?"

"We have you to thank for our religion failing us," the Tahni replied. "Now, our people worship nothing. Believe in nothing. That's why we're here, with the Confluence, because at least it's a direction. And if it takes something we once found abhorrent to defend our one refuge, to protect our influence and kill those who would kill us, then so be it."

"You say you need this AI weapon to defend yourselves." I addressed the words to Marakit, sensing that Pol-Kai was a lost cause. "But there's another way. If we joined forces, all of us survivors, we could watch each other's backs, pledge to our mutual defense. Without selling our souls to something that doesn't have one."

I find that personally offensive, Cam, Jim told me. *My personality matrix is based on a human being, and I have ever bit the soul that you do.*

We'll debate that some other time, I assured him, *when we're not in the middle of a bunch of people who'd just as soon kill us.*

"Join your new government, in other words?" Marakit suggested. "And who, exactly, voted for your government, for this Randall Munroe? Because I certainly wasn't asked."

Back into the atmosphere, the part that made me nervous, but I shut out the shaking and pitching and yawing.

"And who voted for *you?*" Deke asked her.

"I'm not governing the people of those worlds. I supply them with resources at no cost, asking nothing in return but those who would volunteer."

"We don't ask *enough,*" Pol-Kai snapped. "We live in tunnels like rats, hiding from the radiation and the poison, when we could have our own planets, determine our own future."

"Must we go through this again?" Marakit asked with a sigh of exasperation. "That is not the way of the Confluence. We are not here to rule others, nor will we steal their homes."

"Those planets are rightly Tahni. They were ours for centuries before they were yours. We should take back our land."

"As I recall," Deke said, "you lost them fair and square."

"What can be lost by conquest can be regained the same way," Pol-Kai told him. "And with Illyana behind us, who could stop us?"

"Illyana is not behind *us,* my friend," Marakit reminded him softly. "She is behind *me.*"

Jim, that AI has to be on a control circuit, right? Could you break the encryption? Take control of it?

Of course I could. Even in this tiny space inside your head, I'm more advanced than anything your backwards civilization could develop. But they'd notice. And unless I misread the situation, they'd likely kill you.

"Illyana," Marakit went on, looking between Pol-Kai and

the two of us, "is for defense only, and our possession of her is non-negotiable. I would not give up the only guarantor of our continued existence. If that is your condition for treating with us, then you might as well go back now."

"Oh, no, ma'am," Deke said. "Nobody gave me the power to shut down talks, just the power to open them up. Yeah, we do need to go back, but I'd like to take back at least some kind of proposal we can both agree to. Maybe something involving trade or humanitarian aid."

What he really wanted, I was sure, was to get back and share the location of this place with Kara McIntire and Randall Munroe. Honestly, at this point, I was okay with that.

"Very well," Marakit said. "I suppose I could come up with something to send back with you. I'll have the freighter recalled and prepped for another run to Hausos. But I must warn you both... don't try to find this place again. You don't wish to have me as an enemy."

Which was true. But I wasn't sure if we'd have any choice in the matter.

[17]

"Isn't there some easier way down?" I griped, again forced to use Deke as my guide down the stairwell. "Maybe an elevator or something? Or could you at least turn the damned lights on?"

"There's a freight elevator," Marakit said, her voice carrying back from the front of our procession. "But that's for freight, and I doubt you'd find it any more comfortable. As for lights, well... we never bothered to put any in. Those who belong here know the place well enough not to need them."

Which was the extent of our conversation since we'd touched down again. That worried me. Pol-Kai hadn't been reticent about sharing his displeasure on the way up, but he hadn't said a word on the way down, not after Marakit had rubbed his nose in it. Then there was Deke. The man usually didn't know when to shut up, but he'd clammed up as well. I wished I could talk to him the way I did Jim...

You can, obviously, Jim told me. *He's already shown that he has an implant datalink.*

Shit, why didn't you say something before? I demanded.

If you want me to tell you everything I believe you haven't had the foresight to think of, I'll be buzzing in your head almost constantly. I assume you want me to determine if I can contact him?

I took a deep breath and counted to ten, knowing it wouldn't do any good to get angry with a voice inside my head that I couldn't get rid of.

Please.

Another ten steps in the darkness before Jim spoke again, and I worried he'd actually heard me counting and gotten pissed off.

You're connected to his neurolink transmitter. Go ahead.

Talking in my head to an actual person was so much weirder than talking to Jim, and I tripped over my words in a way I never would have if I'd simply been speaking aloud to Deke.

Can you hear me?

I didn't know you had any implants, Alvarez. I don't know how the hell a thought from Deke transmitted via microwaves into my head managed to sound just like his voice, but I wasn't anything close to an expert on the human brain, so I just rolled with it.

Surprise. But what are we gonna do? She's admitted to having Project Rho, and if we come back here in force, they're just blast us out of existence. She put a dozen of those things out just to blow up an old destroyer hull, which tells me there have to be a hell of a lot more, and I don't think even the Ellen Campbell *could take on that many of their intercept vehicles.*

Yeah, I was thinking the same thing, he admitted. *This is a sneak-in-and-kill-everybody type of campaign.*

I paused a step and the Predecessor Cultist guard behind me ran into my back.

"Keep moving," the too-perfect man grunted. He wasn't armed, but he was a walking mountain of cloned muscle, so I kept moving.

I'm not comfortable killing all these people, I told Deke. *Most of them aren't guilty of anything except trying to survive.*

It don't matter anyway. If they have a halfway-decent sensor net up, I can't see us getting close enough to sneak in a ground force. Unless we can set up some kind of trade agreement and smuggle people in on a freighter maybe. He kept going before I could voice my outrage at the idea. *And yes, I know that'd be a shitty thing to do, pretending to want to help colonists and then using their charity as a cover to kill them. And no, I wasn't seriously considering it. I'm just saying, I don't know what the hell to do. All I know is, with that Illyana thing and her stash of em-drive ships, Marakit is automatically the most powerful force in the Cluster. And we're fucked.*

There was nothing I could say to that. Not that I had any reason to think Marakit was a bad person, but Deke was right. This was power I wouldn't have trusted myself with, and I sure as hell didn't trust it to someone I barely knew.

I hadn't come up with any better ideas by the time we reached the garden, but Deke apparently had.

"Marakit Almario," he said, not as if he was addressing the woman but more like he was reading her name off of a file.

The cyborg paused at the center, and I noticed that the background forest had changed. No more a boreal woodland, it had transformed into a tropical jungle, complete with the background hoot of monkeys. Deke stopped as well, and when the Cultist who'd been our rear guard tried to push his shoulder to keep him moving, all the motion accomplished was to send the big blond man stumbling back a step.

"Search and Rescue in the war, you said," Deke went on. "And after the war, you wound up on one of the Trans-Tahni colonies. Hudson Bay. The same one our good friend Pol-Kai here mentioned."

Marakit stared at him, her biological eye narrowing.

"You don't have access to outside files," she said, "so I'll have to assume you're equipped with a headcomp."

Damn, she knew about the things too. I know it had been fifteen years, but had *everybody* heard of implant computers now? I'd thought mine would give me an edge.

Yours is better, Jim assured me. *None of the others come equipped with me.*

Lucky me.

"And since my file would likely be compartmentalized," Marakit surmised, "to have access to it, you're undoubtedly with Fleet Intelligence."

"Never denied it," Deke said. "You helped organize a revolt among the Tahni on Hudson Bay. You were pretty high on the Patrol's most wanted until their reorganization after the attempted coup." He shrugged. "Now, of course, nobody cares. But that at least explains how you can command the respect of the Tahni *and* the Evolutionists. Still not clear on the Cultists, but I suppose they needed something else to believe in after the truth about what the Predecessors looked like came out."

"You will speak with respect to Marakit!" the Cultist behind us bellowed, trying to sound scary. I grinned at him, unable to help myself.

"He sounded pretty respectful of *her*," I told the Cultist. "It was *you* he was disrespecting. And I swear to God, I might pay money to watch if you want to have a go at him."

"You know who I am and where I came from," Marakit said, ignoring the byplay. "Does that help you understand my motivations?"

"It helps me understand why you don't trust us," Deke said, not showing even a hint of intimidation or regret. "Or at least why you didn't trust the original Commonwealth. But I'm curious... the Tahni were the ones who put you in your current situation." He gestured at her bionics. "How did you end up on their side?"

"They were victims of their government. Their emperor, their religion, their society forced them into fighting for a lie, then destroyed their view of the world and of themselves." It was hard to make out much of an expression from a woman with half a face, yet the bitterness shown through. "Just like mine did, telling me I was fighting for the survival of the Commonwealth while the Corporate Council and their children and grandchildren sat in their towers and their vacation estates back on Earth and fattened their bank accounts with military contracts. I rotted in a military hospital, patched together with metal because the genetic surgery that would have made me whole, would have allowed them to clone parts of me and implant them, was too expensive, wasn't authorized for veterans."

It wasn't hard to spot the weakness in her logic, that the Tahni had been more of a threat to the people who *weren't* rich, the people who lived out in the colonies and bore the brunt of the enemy attacks. But trying to convince her that the Tahni War was justified wasn't the job and wouldn't help.

"You think we don't agree?" I asked instead. I tapped my chest. "I'm an orphan from unincorporated Mexico. I spent most of my youth roaming the streets of the Trans-Angeles Underground, running from the cops and the gangs. I enlisted in the Marines because the only other choice was the Freezer. You think I did any of that for the rich executives in their towers? None of that shit matters anymore. We keep telling you that, but I don't think you get it." The step I took toward her was instinctive, but it was blocked by Vagabond, his green ocular glowing brightly. "None of those executives are alive. Not one survived. Earth is a wilderness and the megacities are crumbling ruins. The only thing any of us has is each other, and if we sit around holding onto old grudges, humans are going to regress into a dark age we might not make it back out of."

The intensity in my own words surprised even me. What surprised me even more was that I meant them. I think Marakit must have sensed that, because she pushed Vagabond aside and advanced that step I'd wanted to take, so close that I could feel the warmth of her breath against my cheek. It was warm and smelled sickly sweet, like burned flesh.

"I believe you, Cameron Alvarez." She laid a hand on my arm, and this time it didn't scare me. "Perhaps you're right. I'll need to speak to more of your leaders, but I think we can come to some sort of accommodation..."

I didn't see it coming, didn't expect it, but worse than that, Deke didn't either. I would have expected him to, given what he'd shown me so far, but I think we were both handicapped by the fact we didn't know these people or their procedures. Didn't know who they would or wouldn't allow to carry a gun. When the half-dozen Tahni warriors entered the garden from the opposite doorway carrying Imperial-era laser carbines, they might have been sent to escort us to the shuttle or might have been in response to Vagabond calling for security when I'd taken a step toward Marakit.

Might have been... if they hadn't leveled those carbines at us and opened fire.

Anyone who's been in combat knows about the physiological reactions. Auditory exclusion, tunnel vision, and tachypsychia, the feeling that time has slowed down and you can see every detail, have forever to make a decision. It was an illusion of course. I was seeing the events of the last second projected on a screen for my conscious mind as if it were happening now, but I'd already made my decisions, chosen my course of action on a subconscious level from training and instinct.

But that imaginary slow-motion wasn't *totally* useless. It

gave my mind—and, in this case, my headcomp—time to analyze what was happening, the important details. The weapons were left over from the Tahni military, laser carbines designed for rear-echelon troops and shipboard combat, fed from crystalline power cartridges. Not the most durable weapons, nor the most tactical, with thermal signatures that could probably be seen from orbit. But looking at them at point-blank range, they were a lot easier to appreciate.

I'd made my tactical choice already, and given that I was unarmed and unarmored, it involved throwing myself to the floor and hoping I wasn't the primary target. As it turned out, I wasn't. Vagabond was. Sparks flew and smoke billowed as half a dozen streams of laser pulses converged on the cyborg, slicing him to shreds. The cyborg was dead before my chest hit the floor, the vital organs stored inside that metal chest exploding in bursts of superheated fluid.

The other target was Marakit, but it wasn't going to be that easy. She was in motion by the time the last shot hit Vagabond, making a run at Pol-Kai with speed that outstripped an Olympic athlete, but he already had a gun in his hand, something more compact and effective than the laser carbines. It was a Gauss pistol like the one Deke had left on the *Dutchman*, and the report of its discharge echoed off the walls behind the projected rain forest, metallic and magnetic and hypersonic in one indescribable chorus, an orchestra of deadly instruments combined in one shot.

But the shot was rushed, desperate with the knowledge of her speed, hitting her low in the hip. The slug ripped through the joint there, blasting black metal and carbon fiber into fragments that peppered the back of my neck in a hail of white-hot fire. Marakit stumbled, but she still moved fast enough to slash a hand down on Pol-Kai's wrist. The bone cracked like a dry twig and the Tahni screamed, stumbling backward. I thought

Marakit would grab him before he could get away, figuring she was faster than the old warrior even with only one functional leg, but the Tahni shooters had finally reacted to her attack.

Their rifles swung around, firing as they went, not particular about which one of us they shot first. The unfortunate Predecessor Cultists who'd been bringing up the rear got that honor, all that added muscle not doing a damned thing for their reaction time. Not only had they not managed to counterattack or run, they hadn't even thought to duck. They'd never have to think about anything again, but I might never forget the smell of their burned and vaporized blood spraying through the air and splattering on the tall grass beside me.

Getting my feet underneath me, I prepared to charge at them, ready to sell my life at a high price, but I'd forgotten about something and so had the Tahni.

A gray blur passed across the line of Tahni, and where it touched, they died. Blood sprayed in broad arcs from throats torn open as if by magic, broken bodies tumbled, heads facing the wrong direction, necks askew. The blur was a man, and by the time he reached the last two Tahni gunman, he'd slowed down enough for it to be clear that man was Deke Conner. Deke spun into a kick that took one of the Tahni in the chest, splintering the sternum and sending the alien flying like a cannonball across the room. The last of them *nearly* turned the muzzle of his carbine around in time, but the motion halted abruptly when matte-gray talons sliced through his neck, his head bobbing backward. Barely connected by a flap of skin at the back.

Deke stood for just a fleeting moment, those talons extended, just long enough for me to discern that they came right out of the skin over his wrists. Implant weapons, anchored in each forearm, dripping arterial blood. He shook the blood off and the blades retracted back into his wrists, the frozen moment passing. I wanted to ask the same stupid question again.

What the hell are you?

There was no time for it though, because he tossed a laser carbine at me and retrieved another for himself, seemingly not bothered by the red stain on the side of it, then grabbed Marikit under the arm and lifted her to her feet. Her damaged leg hung limp, dead weight, but it didn't seem like any of the vital organs that kept her human brain alive had been hit. Her sense of reality, though, looked to have taken a huge blow.

"Why?" she gasped, staring at the door back to the stairs, which Pol-Kai had retreated through during the shooting, then down at the torn and smoldering remains of Vagabond. "Why would he..."

"Snap out of it!" Deke barked at her. Red splashed his face, his arms, like he'd shoved them elbow deep into the dead Tahni, an image fearsome enough to shock Marikit out of her fugue. And maybe me as well.

"He wouldn't have tried this if he didn't have the rest of the Tahni in this place behind him," I said. "We need to get the hell out of here." I took a step toward the stairs, but Deke interposed the length of the laser carbine between me and my chosen path.

"Pol-Kai ran that way," he reminded me. "And he knows we'd be tempted to make a run for the shuttle." Deke nodded to Marakit. "You have people you trust. Can you try to contact them?"

Marakit's one natural eye glazed over in concentration, and I figured she had to be transmitting via a datalink connected directly to her brain. Cursing softly, she shook her head.

"Nothing. All comms are jammed."

"People will notice that," I said, my eyes and the muzzle of the laser carbine flitting back and forth between the two exits.

"He's gonna be sending more troops in here to finish us off. Is there any other way out of this chamber?"

"Over there," Marakit pointed to a section of the rain forest in the projection, indistinguishable from the rest as far as I could tell, but Deke half-carried her over to it and I followed, backing away from the center of the room, still trying to cover both doors.

Marakit reached through the trunk of a virtual banyan tree and hidden behind its gray bark, something clicked. A chill breeze kissed the side of my face, my neck stinging with the reminder of the half a dozen tiny burns there.

"Through here," Marakit instructed Deke, and he didn't question her direction, just walked her right through that projection. And disappeared.

Taking a deep breath, I risked a final look behind us. Bodies littered the floor, the tall, hydroponic grass making a valiant effort to conceal the worst of the carnage. They couldn't. For Marakit, and for us too, everything had changed in the space of less than a minute. I turned and stepped through the light of the hologram. And into darkness.

[18]

"Did these tunnels come with the place," Deke asked, "or did you dig them yourself?"

"The tunnels were here," Marakit told him, something about her artificial voice even more robotic now. I wondered if that was from damage to the synthesizer or just stress. "I hid them. From nearly everyone."

She'd certainly hidden them from me, because I couldn't see a damned thing except where the tactical light on the side of my laser carbine illuminated, which wasn't much. Only a meter across, the passage reminded me of the maintenance shafts in the Underground, where I'd used to sleep when the gangs were hunting for me in the housing blocs. The sides were smooth and polished, like the tunnels had been carved with an industrial laser, and unfortunately the floor was just as smooth, which made footing tricky. I didn't have it as bad as Deke did, trying to haul around a lamed Marakit, but I suppose he had more to work with too. I still hadn't figured out how though. If he carried bionics, they were the most lifelike I'd ever seen.

"How far do they go?" I wondered, which I thought was a less whiney way of asking *are we there yet?*

"They run the perimeter of the original installation," Marakit told me, her voice echoing off the walls. "We've expanded homesteads into thermal pockets outside the perimeter in the last few months so it wouldn't feel so crowded, but there's no direct route into those homesteads."

"Who do you trust, Marakit?" Deke asked her. "Who can you count on?"

She didn't answer immediately, the only sound the scrape of her dragging leg on the stone.

"The Evolutionists," she decided. "Once they hear Vagabond has been killed, they'll rally to me. Raven would be the one to organize the others, once she hears about the attack."

"Where would Raven be?" I wanted to know. "Assuming she's not sitting around the house having baby food pumped into her stomach."

"There's an intersection a hundred meters ahead. Turn left and follow it two hundred meters to the end. It comes out near the armory. That's the first target Raven will try to seize."

I had a bunch of other questions, but none of them were as important as getting the hell out of these tunnels and finding someplace safe—and warm—to hole up, so I kept them to myself. At the intersection, Deke stopped abruptly, checking both ways up and down the passage before setting Marakit to rest against the wall and waving me forward. With the openings on all four sides, there was more space at the intersection, enough room for us to stand shoulder to shoulder without either of us needing a breath mint.

Pol-Kai would have thought of the armory too, he cautioned over his implant transmitter, which I figured meant he didn't want Marakit to overhear. *He probably already took it, and I don't hold out much hope he would have left any Evolutionists running free.*

That's a depressingly likely scenario, I agreed. *What about the Cultists?*

They could go either way, but I don't know we can rely on them even if they're on Marakit's side. They're strong, but not that much stronger than the Tahni, and they'll be unarmed.

What's the plan then? I wanted to know.

Since we know all of Jack and shit at the moment, we still have to check out the armory. But we need to be ready to move if we get spotted, and Marakit won't be moving fast unless I'm carrying her.

I was willing to concede that. The cyborg probably weighed twice what I did, given the bionics and the isotope reactor to power them. Even with the lower gravity here, it would still be awkward as hell for me to try to carry her.

I'll scout it out, I volunteered. *Wait for me back here at the intersection.*

A moment ago the tunnel had felt cozy and protective, but now that I was out in front with no one to back me up, what had been a narrow passage turned into a huge, open space with me an inviting target. I shoved the laser carbine out ahead of me, swinging the light from side to side, making sure there were no side corridors where a potential ambusher could conceal themselves, but all the light revealed were cobwebs.

Spiders. Every human colony had spiders to go along with the flies and mosquitoes and rats. They'd colonized every world right alongside us. I'd just had the thought that at least I hadn't seen any rats when one of the damned things scuttled along the tunnel, almost running across my boot. I let it pass, controlling myself with difficulty because I figured a high, piercing screech might give away our position. Maybe Deke could spear it on one of those talons and heat it up like a shish-kabob.

When I estimated I'd gone nearly two hundred meters, the glow from my weapon's light fell on a darker square against the gray of the rock walls. I had to switch off the light and let my eyes adjust for a moment before a glint of yellow around the lines of the door showed me I'd reached the right place.

It occurred to me that I hadn't asked Marakit if there was some special method of unlocking the door from this side, but I figured if there had been she would have told me, so I just played the light over the edges of the frame. A pressure plate, dull and blending with the rock, stared back at me, and I took a deep breath and switched off the light again before I pushed it in. The metallic click of the lock releasing was obscenely loud and I gritted my teeth, sure if anyone was on the other side they must surely have heard it.

At least the door swung inward rather than outward, allowing me to use it for cover as I slowly, cautiously leaned around the edge. The corridor on the other side was well-lit, in contrast with most of this freaking place, but what it showed me I didn't particularly want to see. Dead bodies. Up and down the hallway, most of them clustered around a thickly armored door that now hung open, the edges charred and cracked from what might have been an explosive charge.

That would be the armory, and Deke had been dead right. Three of the bodies were Tahni, their necks broken, but there were at least twenty Evolutionists scattered around them, and Pol-Kai's troops hadn't been so sporting as to fight hand-to-hand. More lasers. I suppose they'd gotten a bulk purchase deal on the weapons from a black-market source, or maybe Pol-Kai had stumbled on a cache of Tahni weapons out there on Hudson Bay. Whatever guns the Tahni had before, they had more now.

I'd only taken two seconds to scan toward the armory, fully intending to check the other direction, my attention captured by the field of dead bodies for perhaps a half a beat too long.

"Human!"

The shout came from behind me, away from the armory,

and my initial thought as I turned was that it was a warning, the beginning of a command to drop my gun. As it turned out, it was an identification of his target, because the Tahni fired before I'd gotten completely turned around.

If anything saved me, it was the fact that most of the Tahni in this place were too young to have fought in the war and had little to no combat experience. Since they were vegetarians, none of them had ever hunted, but I had back on Hausos, and I knew all about buck fever. He pulled his shot, the swathe of blinding white energy hitting the interior of the door instead of my head, blasting a chunk out of its top corner. I threw myself to the floor and away from the spray of molten metal, my left shoulder hitting hard just as the muzzle of my carbine found a target.

Two Tahni at ten meters, though only one had fired. Young, as I'd thought, unblooded before this from the lack of a cue wrapped around their necks, and the one in the rear stared at me with fear and alarm obvious on his face, content to leave the shooting up to his friend in front. That one had the look of a young warrior eager to prove himself, perhaps one who'd been left to guard the armory and badly wanted his first kill. I was supposed to be it.

If I'd had time to think, I might have felt bad about killing him.

But I'd had too much combat experience to let thinking get in the way, and the laser carbine fired as if it had been controlled by one of the AI in those autonomous drones. My war had been fought in a battlesuit, but I'd had enough combat outside of one since then that I could fire accurately at this range without using the sights. A short burst erased the fierce determination on the Tahni's face and shocked his more timid friend into action, a wild spray of laser pulses that cratered the walls but came nowhere near me.

I couldn't know if he was wearing armor under the loose, colorful tunic and couldn't take the chance. A second headshot, and if Top had been around she would have yelled at me for showing off. The whining crackle of the laser had barely faded before I'd rolled to my feet and took a step toward the bodies, intent on stripping them of weapons and ammo. Shouted warnings in singsong Tahni stopped me, and I ran back to the tunnel door, closing it for all the good it would do. The door was trashed, and they'd know what had happened and where I'd gone.

"Go!" I yelled ahead of me. "Go! They're right behind me!"

I could, I realized in hindsight, have broadcast the transmission on the implant 'link, but I still wasn't used to having that shit inside my head and yelling came naturally. By the time I reached the intersection, Deke already had Marakit up, her arm around his neck, but we still had a problem.

"The armory was taken," I told them, panting with the effort of the spring as I slid to a halt. "Lots of dead Evolutionists, and I don't know if your friend Raven was with them. We need a plan B, and we need it fast."

Marakit hesitated, which I didn't think was natural for her, then pointed back the way we'd come.

"That way. Take us back to the last junction and turn right."

"Why?" Deke asked, though he didn't hesitate to follow her directions, running at what would have been a good clip for an unencumbered sprinter, one I could barely keep up with. "Where are we going?"

"To what may possibly be the last friends I have here," she told him. "And the last place Pol-Kai would expect."

It was lighter outside than when we'd arrived, about as light as I imagined it got on this moon, the glow of the gas giant combining with the distant primary star to provide the closest thing this hemisphere would have to broad daylight. It answered my question of whether the moon ever even saw the sun. It did, for a few hours at a time.

I wasn't sure if it was that sunlight or the steam pouring off the hot springs, but the narrow valley, carved from glaciers through the rolling hills before different glaciers had closed in on it again, was almost comfortably warm. Warm enough that I unzipped my jacket as I walked point for our little group through the collection of drying huts. And the fields of grain.

"Crops," Deke murmured, shaking his head. "I never thought you'd be able to grow crops here outside of a heated hydroponics farm."

"Much of it is grown that way," Marakit admitted. "But as we've expanded our homesteads, we discovered valleys like this where the springs kept them warm enough but the fumaroles didn't put out enough poisonous gasses to kill the plants. Stop here," she told Deke, motioning at one of the huts.

He let her loose and Marakit hopped gingerly over to the door. She pulled a length of metal pipe from inside and sighed with relief as she leaned into it, using the pipe as a cane.

"I think I can manage without your help now, Mr. Conner."

"Major," he corrected her, "since we're so close and personal now. But you can call me Deke."

"This way, Deke."

The cyborg moved with remarkable speed and agility for someone walking with a pipe for a cane, outpacing us through the rows of genetically engineered wheat. I was very ready to let her take point, given that she was the one who trusted whoever these people were. She could be our human mine detector while

Deke and I watched the possible ambush spots with our carbines ready.

"Why doesn't everyone live out here?" I asked her, scanning back and forth on my side of the path. "Looks a lot more pleasant than that rat warren under the ground."

"It's exposed," she threw over her shoulder, not slowing her pace. "There's radiation out here. Not as bad in sheltered valleys like this, but enough that our human friends, the ones who used to be in the Cult, would not risk it. As for the Evolutionists, well..." her machine grin raised the hackles on the back of my neck. "One place is as good as another."

I frowned, following that logic chain.

"Hold on. If the Cultists won't live out here and Evolutionists don't care, then who the hell are we out here to meet?"

"Marakit." The voice was deep, sonorous, with the odd timbre of a voice box never meant to speak English. "We haven't been able to communicate with the others for almost an hour. What's going on?"

The muzzle of my carbine snapped upward and the tall, broad-shouldered figure froze. He was a Tahni. Older, middle-aged for one of them, with lines etched into his face by time and gray streaking the warrior's cue at his throat. He'd stopped moving forward, hands at his side, but his calm demeanor told me this wasn't the first time he'd had a gun pointed at him.

"Stop," Marakit said, raising a hand as she stepped between the Tahni and us. "He's not an enemy. This is my friend... from a long ways back, all the way to Hudson Bay. Colonel Cameron Alvarez, Major Deke Conner, meet Kan-Zin Tel."

"You're with the new Commonwealth government, I assume?" Kan-Zin Tel asked as I lowered my gun... though not all the way. "Fleet Intelligence, I assume?"

"You're pretty well-informed for a Tahni refugee on an isolated moon in the middle of nowhere," Deke observed. His gun barrel had dipped as well, but I doubted he would have needed a weapon since he *was* one.

"Oh, trust me, gentlemen," he said, "this isn't the first time I've dealt with military intelligence." Tahni didn't naturally smile, but this Kan-Zin Tel made his best attempt. "In fact, I believe we used to work for the same boss." He waved us forward. "Come with me. This conversation will undoubtedly take a while, and my family was just sitting down for lunch."

[19]

"I feel like I've fallen straight down the rabbit hole," I admitted, holding a spoonful of stew just below my chin, almost forgotten with the surreal feeling of the situation.

"Yes, things are a little different up here," Matlin-Sen admitted, setting a cup of water in front of me on the table.

She was a female Tahni, which wouldn't have been that surprising... except that she and Kan-Zin Tel lived in the same house. With their children. Two boys, both teenagers, and a girl just a little younger, sitting at a side table and eating their own bowls of gruel. They were quiet and well-behaved, but so was Kan-Zin Tel... and that was fucking impossible.

"I've never seen a male Tahni," Deke admitted, "this close to an adult female without going absolutely apeshit." Not that the shock kept him from shoveling down the stew. I took a bite myself, realizing abruptly how hungry I was. It wasn't bad, if you liked beans.

"I have," I admitted. At Deke's curious glance, I shrugged. "Not here in the Cluster. It took a whole society built around meditation and introspection, and it took hundreds of years to accomplish."

Kan-Zin Tel and Matlin-Sen shared a look.

"I wish our people had the wisdom and patience for such a process," Kan-Zin Tel said, tapping his spoon against the side of his bowl, "but I'm afraid there's a more prosaic answer. The phan-tar-nok, the rage and violence a Tahni male feels when he goes into the mating cycle, is caused by a gland right here." Kan-Zin Tel tapped the back right side of his skull just behind his flattened ear. "I had microsurgery that altered the gland's output... installed a regulator, if you will. Instead of a massive surge of hormones a few random times each month, now I have a constant stream of those same chemicals at a much lower dose."

"If it's that simple," I wondered, "why didn't the Tahni figure it out a long time ago?"

"It was against our beliefs," Matlin-Sen replied in a tone that said it should have been obvious. "We were created perfectly by the Ancients. Nothing about us could be altered."

"Fortunately for me," Kan-Zin Tel said wryly, "you humans destroyed our belief system just in time."

"For some of us," Matlin-Sen interjected. "If what you say of Pol-Kai is true, then I would guess he hasn't given up on them completely."

"Marakit," I said, finally having the time to ask the question that had gnawed at me all through the tunnels, "what about Project Rho... Illyana? Is there any way Pol-Kai can control it without you?"

"I'm afraid so," Marakit admitted. "There's an imprinter... a device we discovered along with the Corporate Council research base. It reads the brain patterns of the user and imprints them into the control systems and fail-safes of Illyana. Anyone can take control of her using it. It's locked down with a security code, but that won't keep Pol-Kai out forever. Days at most. I'm fairly certain Illyana is what this coup is all in aid of.

He believes we should use her to seize control of the entire Cluster."

"He *has* been vocal about his insistence that the Psi War and the chaos caused by the Changed was an opportunity sent by the gods," Kan-Zin Tel agreed. "But to murder our allies and try to kill *you*..." he made a Tahni gesture of negation. "He's destroying everything we've built."

"Can you guys pull together any sort of opposition?" I asked, looking between the three of them. "I mean, we have to assume Pol-Kai either killed or locked up all the Evolutionists who were loyal to you, Marakit, but he might not be worried about the Cultists. Can you get hold of any of them? And do you have access to weapons?"

Marakit was already shaking her head before I finished.

"If anything, the Cultists would be more likely to side with Pol-Kai, I think. They've always resented the high positions Evolutionists held in the Confluence, even though I've tried to make them feel at home here. As for weapons—well, what Pol-Kai and his confederates managed aside, one of the covenants all who come here agree to is that we hold our weapons in common in the armory, and none may draw upon them without authorization."

"Yes, well..." Kan-Zin Tel made a gesture with hands and shoulders, the equivalent of a shrug. "We did agree to that covenant, true. But some of us are veterans of the last war and have a problem divesting ourselves of any means of defense..."

"Show them, my love," Matlin-Sen suggested.

Kan-Zin Tel waved at us to get up from the table and I did, though I took my stew bowl with me. The Tahni was getting on in years for someone who hadn't received anti-aging treatments, but it hadn't diminished the strength in those massive shoulders. The muscles bunched up under his long-sleeved tunic as he pulled upward at one side of the table. It *should* have flipped over, but instead it toppled on a hinge concealed beneath the long slat it rested on, and as it fell backward a trapdoor concealed beneath the floorboards of the house's small kitchen opened up.

The chamber under the floor wasn't huge, less than two meters long and a meter wide, not even deep enough for me to stand up straight in without my head and shoulders sticking out above the floorboards. It was enough to hold a large, metal cargo container though. A Tahni one, curved at the edges and flattened on the ends, a cylinder built to fit into slots in their freighter holds. This one had a security lock fitted at the center where the four folds of its top panels met, and Kan-Zin Tel knelt at the edge of the chamber, hanging onto one of the table legs to steady himself while he tapped in a code.

The lock opened with a snap of electromagnets and the petal-like sections of the pod's hatch peeled backward. Within the metal container were four sets of Tahni body armor, four KE rifles, and a couple dozen spare ammo drums for the electromagnetic needlers.

"Holy shit," Deke said, nodding appreciation. "Looks like a score at the Imperium thrift store."

Marakit glared at the two Tahni adults like they'd spit in her face.

"How could you do this? Did none of you trust me?"

Kan-Zin Tel and Matlin didn't meet her eyes, but I wasn't as interested in their feelings of guilt as I was the weapons. The KE guns fired tantalum needles at a velocity that could penetrate body armor without the downside of a blinding flash that led the enemy right to your position. I knelt beside the big Tahni and pulled out one of the rifles, checking its condition. Like new.

"Hey, look, lady," Deke told Marakit, chuckling, "let's not

take this personally. Mendicants can't be choosicants, or so I've heard."

"Are there more of you?" I asked Kan-Zin Tel, looking up sharply from the rifle. "More like you two, who've... had the procedure? Who live together?"

"Dozens," Matlin confirmed. "Many of us came here with Marakit because the Tahni communities on Hudson Bay wouldn't accept our decision, our rejection of the old ways."

"And are they all as well... equipped as you two?" Deke wondered.

"There is a general feeling," Kan-Zin Tel said, "among those of us who fought in the war that it is unwise to be disarmed."

"Then there's just one big question left," I finished up. "Will they fight against Pol-Kai or join him?"

Neither of them answered immediately. Tahni, I'd noticed in the time I'd spent among them on Yfingam and aboard the *Orion*, didn't dither and *umm* and *ah* the way humans did when they weren't sure of an answer. They just clammed up and didn't reply until they had something definitive to say.

"Pol-Kai is a traditionalist," Matlin told us after a few moments. "So are his followers. They tolerate us and those who live as we do, but they've never accepted it. I believe, once he's finished off his Evolutionist opposition and made sure the Cultists are, at least, neutral, he'll come after us next. Others likely realize this as well."

"I will not be separated from my family," Kan-Zin Tel declared. "We've both survived too much to allow that to happen."

"What did you mean," Deke asked him, "when you said you used to work for our boss?"

I thought it was a strange question to be asking now, but it seemed important to the man.

"I was Fleet Intelligence asset at one time," Kan-Zin Tel replied. "After the war. I reported to a Colonel Murdock."

"No shit?" Deke laughed softly. "That's just like him, to pull something like that and never tell me about it."

"We will ask the others to join with us," Matlin said, dragging us back to the subject at hand. "I can't promise they all will, but some would rather act than sit around and wait for Pol-Kai to decide our fate." She focused her gaze on me. "But join us to do what?"

"We won't have enough people to attack him directly," Kan-Zin Tel warned, pulling out one of the rifles and loading a drum magazine into it. A flash of green on the small display above the drum indicated the charge was still good after all these years. "The people who would join us are honorable warriors, but they all have life-mates and children who they hope to raise. They'll risk their own lives, but they won't risk their loved ones being left to the mercy of Pol-Kai."

"We have to get to that imprinter," I declared. "Where is it stored, Marakit?"

"There's a control room for the atmospheric mining equipment," she told me, the sullen note in her voice an indication that she still hadn't gotten over the sense of betrayal from Kan-Zin Tel and Matlin hiding weapons. "It's at the center of the facility, at the highest point, with a hardline connection to the transmission dish." She shook her head, and I noticed that she used body language a lot more than the Evolutionists which was, I suppose, another indication that her replacements were perforce rather than a philosophical statement. "But if I had to guess, I'd say that's where Pol-Kai and most of his troops are holed up now. We'll never force our way in there, not with the numbers we can recruit from the outsiders."

"What about the tunnels?" Deke asked her. "Could we get there through them?"

"Maybe," she acknowledged. "But they must know about them by now. They'll be watching the entrances."

"Unless we keep their attention focused somewhere else," I suggested, hefting the KE gun. I'd fired one before but its balance felt wrong, designed for a Tahni physiology. "You said the lockout code would keep them busy for a few days?" She nodded and I smiled thinly. "Maybe that's long enough that he'd be interested in getting his hands on someone who could move that timeline up for him."

Marakit walked through the corridors at the center of the facility, and I walked with her. Virtually, anyway. That had been the tricky part. Internal comms were still down, but that was the hardwired system. Pol-Kai had neither the equipment nor the expertise to jam wireless signals and probably hadn't thought he'd need it since the rock walls blocked most EM except at extremely short range.

Like right on the other side of the wall in the parallel tunnel. The tricky part had been finding me goggles to receive her video signal. Kan-Zin Tel hadn't had any in his stash, but one of their neighbors did, and it had only taken a half-hour of wheedling to get the other Tahni to hand them over and then fifteen minutes to rig the strap to the right size for a human head. They weren't comfortable, and watching through Marakit's cybernetic eye meant I couldn't really look where I was going and I had to trail a hand across the wall to keep myself from bouncing off one side and into the other.

That still didn't keep me from bouncing off Deke's back when he slowed down, and his exasperated sigh cut through the audio input from Marakit's transmission.

"You know," he reminded me, "I could have tracked her without fucking around with outdated Tahni gear... and *I* wouldn't have any trouble walking and chewing gum at the same time."

"You're also the most dangerous weapons we have," I said quietly. The Tahni out there *probably* couldn't hear us on the other side of the wall, but there was no point taking chances. "I'd rather have you paying full attention to the tunnel and making sure no one ambushes us. Now be quiet. Some of us can't juggle all that shit at once."

You could if you just gave me control of your balance and motor functions, Jim said petulantly. He'd suggested it before and was still miffed that I'd said no.

I think that would be establishing a dangerous precedent, I told him. *Now you shut up too.*

"You!" The exclamation was in Tahni, but thankfully, among Jim's many other talents, he could translate the language for me instantly. I mean, I'd picked up some Tahni when we'd been working with Zan-Thint, but that had been a while and I was out of practice.

The Tahni who'd yelled the accusation was young and belligerent, looking like a child playing war in his black armor, swinging a laser carbine around like it was a toy gun.

"We have orders to kill her on sight!" the young Tahni said, rushing up to jam his laser carbine into Marakit's chest. A large Tahni hand wrapped around the barrel and pushed it aside, and the kid with it.

"She's my prisoner," Kan-Zin Tel said, his voice muffled by the visor of the helmet he wore. "Commander Pol-Kai wants her alive so that he may question her."

More of the young wannabe warriors rushed up behind the first kid, pouring out of the entrance to the control room, sweeping each other with the muzzles of their weapons like Boot Camp newbies who'd been handed rubber guns and told to clear a room. I couldn't look away, waiting for the negligent discharge that would set off a circular firing squad and do our job for us, but eventually someone older and better trained stalked out into the entrance corridor, yelling and pushing.

"Stop pointing your weapons at each other, you ignorant pups!" the middle-aged Tahni bellowed. "I'll rip the damned guts out of the next of you I see with his muzzle aimed at anything he doesn't want to shoot! Do you understand me?"

"Yes, sir!" they replied in ragged chorus, their rifles swinging downward.

"But sir!" the original kid piped up, his laser still aimed in the general direction of Marakit and Kan-Zin Tel. "It's Marakit! We're supposed to kill her when we find her!"

"Who are you, warrior?" the older Tahni demanded. Marakit looked back at Kan-Zin Tel in time to catch him raising his visor.

"You know me, Lothan-Dor," Kan-Zin Tel said.

He maintained the sort of calm only a warrior who'd faced death and passed through the other side could muster in this situation. I'd yet to meet a Tahni who I would have considered a coward, but there was a qualitative difference between the ability to charge into enemy fire and the wisdom to keep your head while doing it.

"I do," Lothan-Dor agreed, "and yet I wonder why I find you bringing Marakit to us. If any of us were to stay out of this, I would have expected it to be you and the other outsiders."

"If we stay outside," Kan-Zin Tel told him, "then we have nothing to bargain with. We'll be shut out of your decisions and turned into cannon fodder. I have no desire for my children to grow up as orphans on a world that hates them."

Lothan-Dor didn't look convinced to me, but he motioned for Kan-Zin Tel to follow.

"Bring her in here."

"Move," I told Deke, pushing against his shoulder.

He scuttled forward, the tunnel narrowing as it curved around the edge of the control room. This was the end of the line, or so Marakit had told me, and the by the time we reached the end, it had gone from a meter wide to narrow enough we had to turn sideways to keep going.

Here's the door, Deke told me, apparently as concerned with being overheard as I'd been earlier now that we were only separated from the Tahni by a thin sheet of metal. *What do you see?*

The control room was huge, bigger than the garden, and crammed with monitoring equipment. Most of it was obsolete to the point of being antique, probably dating back to the First War with the Tahni, bulky flatscreens and manual keyboards and not a hologram projector to be seen. Which made the one advanced piece of technology stand out even more.

Marakit stared at it, ignoring Pol-Kai striding toward her, ignoring the twenty-five or thirty other Tahni clustered in the room staring at her. Her eyes were on the device. I'd seen the like before, a neural halo like the ones we'd used in the Vigilantes to compensate for the Vergai recruits lacking 'face jacks. That wasn't so cutting-edge, but the quantum-core computer it was plugged into sure was, not to mention the haptic hologram floating above it. The whole setup was about the size of a fifty-gallon drum, tucked into a niche between flatscreen monitors near the center of the room. It was hard to see what was in the projection from the angle she had, but I thought it might be some kind of geometric pattern, probably part of the security code she'd programmed into the thing.

"Marakit," Pol-Kai said, stopping just out of arm's length of the cyborg. "I hadn't expected to see you again alive." His eyes flickered to Kan-Zin Tel. "And I hadn't expected to see *you* at all." Pol-Kai looked the other Tahni up and down. "Where did you acquire armor and a weapon?"

"Let's just say you're not the only one with trust issues," Kan-Zin Tel told him from over Marakit's shoulder. "I brought her to you because I heard you needed her."

"And what do you wish in return, heretic?" Pol-Kai snapped. Unless I read the Tahni commander wrong, he didn't seem to hold much more love for Kan-Zin Tel than he did for Marakit or the other Evolutionists. "Do you want us to overlook the way you've mutilated yourself? To tolerate the unnatural perversion of living with a female?"

"None of us give a damn about your opinion of how we live our lives, Pol-Kai. All we seek is your guarantee that you'll leave us alone. You've already shown that you have no loyalty to your oaths, nor to those who've sheltered you and called you ally."

Pol-Kai choked out a laugh, gesturing at Marakit.

"And what of you then? Was she not your friend as well?"

"I never swore an oath to her," Kan-Zin Tel corrected him. "She and I were once enemies, and after the collapse of the human civilization merely allies of convenience. She thought otherwise and came to us for help. I trust she's seen the error in her logic."

Damn, this Kan-Zin Tel was good. I was ready to believe him myself.

"What about the error in your own logic, Kan-Zin Tel?" Pol-Kai asked, motioning to his men. A half a dozen laser carbines raised, leveled at Kan-Zin Tel. "Now that you've brought her to us, where is your bargaining power? Why should I not simply have you executed?"

Uh oh, Deke said, somehow putting a *tsk* into his mental transmission. *Didn't see that one coming.*

But Kan-Zin Tel had. He moved, the action enough to draw Marakit's eye to him, but he was so close to her all I could make out was the muzzle of his KE rifle... pointing straight at her face.

"Then there's no reason," Kan-Zin Tel said tautly, "that I shouldn't kill her myself."

Oh, shit.

[20]

"And what do I care?" Pol-Kai asked, waving a hand dismissively. "You kill her, we kill you, and what have I lost?"

Though the fact he hadn't ordered it already put the lie to the words.

"You need her to unlock Illyana," Kan-Zin Tel said, still so utterly calm. "Without Marakit, you have this base and nothing else *worth* having. No warships, no fleet, no force to conquer the human worlds. Without Illyana, we have even *less* than we did before, since we'll have lost the trust of the colonies, and you've already killed off our most effective ground troops."

Should we go in? Deke asked, and I marveled that he'd turned that decision over to me, since he hadn't shown much trust in my tactical judgement so far. Then I realized he couldn't see what I was seeing, since he wasn't looped into Marakit's video feed.

No, I decided. *Give him a minute.*

I trusted Kan-Zin Tel and God only knew if I was right to do so, but charging in now would only get both of them killed. Pol-Kai sighed and relaxed, lowering his weapon and proving my instincts right.

"What do you want?"

"I simply wish the status to remain quo. We live where we live on the surface and no one comes to bother us. You want off this world anyway, you want to conquer the human worlds, and I wish you luck. But leave this place to us."

It was an utterly reasonable demand, yet Pol-Kai's expression clouded over, and I sensed if he could have gotten away with denying it, he would have.

"All right. As cleansing as it would be to rid the galaxy of deviants such as yourself, I suppose leaving you stranded here, light-years away from anywhere, is close enough."

Kan-Zin Tel pulled his gun away from Marakit's head and pushed her forward into Pol-Kai's arms. She'd left her makeshift cane behind and she nearly tumbled to the ground, but the Tahni caught her by the arm and shoved her away from him toward the quantum core. She toppled to the ground, the metal of her limp leg clattering against the floor, fierce anger in her eye as she glared back at Pol-Kai.

"You have two choices, you metal monstrosity," Pol-Kai growled, leveling his pistol at her head. "You can either input the passcode to unlock the imprinter and die quickly, painlessly... *mercifully*, or you can be stubborn. If you choose the path of pain, I'll have you immobilized, of course... your arms and legs burned off at the elbows and knees. Then, I'll have you chained to a pair of industrial diggers and rip the damned metal right out of your body until all that's left is the husk of bloody flesh that you were meant to be. And once you're reduced to a pile of quivering jelly, then we'll start slicing that into pieces until all that remains is your diseased brain. And if you die before you tell us the code, we'll still break it... but the days you'll save me are worth a quick death."

"Do you think I'm not used to pain, Pol-Kai?" she asked, her voice sullen. "If you're going to kill me either way, then I have no incentive to help you."

She was stalling, of course. All of this was a stall, but the question was, how long were we going to have to stall for? There was no way of knowing, since we couldn't communicate past a few meters.

If they don't hurry up, Deke told me, *we're going to have to go in by ourselves.*

Which would be suicide with upwards of thirty armed Tahni inside, but he was right... if it came down to Marikit giving up the code, there wouldn't be any choice.

"I want the same deal you gave him," Marikit said, jerking a thumb at Kan-Zin Tel. "If I give you what you want, you leave me here, intact."

"Somehow, I have a problem seeing you spending the rest of your life among the very people who sold you out to me, Marikit," Pol Kai sneered.

"Kan-Zin Tel did what he had to do in order to survive. I'm doing the same thing."

"That would make sense," Pol-Kai admitted. "And if I were a more forgiving person, I'd be tempted to agree to your conditions." The steam-shovel jaw parted in a snarling show of squared-off teeth. "However, I am not nearly so forgiving as to forget that you gave the power over us to your fellow desecrations of nature, the Evolutionists. So, I believe I will take the chance on wasting a few days just to gain the satisfaction of tearing you apart." He raised his hand, gesturing to a gaggle of young Tahni beside him. "Reduce her to a glowing stump."

And that was that.

Go! I pushed Deke forward and, to his credit, he didn't question the order.

He slammed through the door and I tumbled out after him, gritting my teeth, prepared for death but *really* wishing I'd brought my Vigilante along. I certainly wasn't going to hide behind Deke, because he wasn't there anymore. The man moved with a speed that couldn't be explained by cloned muscle tissue or even some kind of synthetic adrenaline, speed I hadn't seen even from the cyborgs. He was boosted, augmented with something pretty far above my pay grade, and as much as it freaked me out, I would have loved to share in the freakiness.

Tahni soldiers screamed and spun away from his path, blood trailing where his talons had ripped through them, but I had to do things the more run-of-the-mill Marine way and shoot the sons of bitches. Deke had gone around the perimeter, but my concern was guarding Kan-Zin Tel and Marikit because this was my plan and if they got killed, it was on me.

The tunnel exit came out behind a control panel and there was barely enough space for me to squeeze through with the Tahi armor, the shoulder plates scraping against the rock and metal with a sound that set my teeth on edge. Taking a knee, I opened fire before I even had a clear shot, the targeting reticle dancing across the entire group of Tahni warriors. The KE gun was nothing like firing a Gauss rifle, the stream of tantalum needles juddering out of the muzzle with a vibration that traveled all the way back through my shoulder and into my teeth.

The spray of metal darts tore into two of the Tahni who'd been about to fire at Marakit, sparking off their armor as the rounds penetrated chest plates. They toppled backward like felled trees, the clatter of their armor drowned out by the snap-crack of the hypersonic rounds cutting through the air of the control room. Kan-Zin Tel shot down the other two, his KE gun blasting both of them off their feet before they could react to the gunfire from the other side of the room.

We'd had a good two seconds of surprise, and we'd used it up. I wasn't a commando, but I'd developed a feel for the flux of combat and the momentum had drifted from our side to theirs, a tide that had been coming in starting to wash outward instead. I'd shot everyone in my field of aim except for Pol-Kai, and the Tahni commander had a keen sense of self-preservation. He'd thrown himself forward, into the cover of the central bank of controls for the atmosphere mines, and even though the KE gun might have cut through the panels, I couldn't try it because Marakit was in the way.

Deke was still engaging the Tahni at the other end of the room, but even as fast as he moved, he wouldn't make it back to us in time and the rest of the troops had turned our way, probably not even knowing Deke was there. Things were about to get bad. And I was so wrapped up in the threat in front of me I almost didn't notice the pounding of boot soles behind me, coming from the corridor outside.

It could have been more of Pol-Kai's men coming to investigate, and if it was we would be dead. But it wasn't. Tahni barreled through the door, dressed in wartime armor and carrying KE guns. Kan-Zin Tel's group of family men. Not a lot of them, about a dozen, but enough to turn that tide back again, pouring a fusillade of metal into the incoming squad of enemy troops.

Laser pulses crisscrossed with electromagnetically launched projectiles, a deadly web of interlocking fire cutting off both Pol-Kai and Marikit from the rest of us. If the former Search and Rescue trooper remembered her training, she should have thrown herself flat and low-crawled out of the line of fire, but she didn't. Instead, she lunged upward and grabbed the neural halo off the top of the quantum core... and took a laser through the base of her neck.

"God*dammit*!" I yelled, throwing caution to the wind and throwing myself into a high-crawl across the floor.

It was stupid, insane, but I did it anyway, grabbing at her leg and pulling her down out of the line of fire. She was limp, a rag doll, her biological eye unfocused... dead, the halo still clenched in her hand. The air went out of me, just for a second, long enough for Pol-Kai to lurch out of his hiding place, pistol aimed my way. No one close enough to help, my rifle pointed the wrong direction, more of a hindrance than a weapon.

I let it drop, grabbing at the Tahni's wrist. It was like trying to wrestle a pneumatic press, even at his age, and the lower gravity did nothing to change our respective natural strengths. But I did have one advantage, one that Pol-Kai could never match. I had a lot of experience fighting people much bigger and stronger than I was.

He was off balance, one knee on the ground, trying to push forward without leverage. All I had to do was fall backward and pull. The Tahni tumbled forward, unable to break his fall because I still controlled his arms, and smashed face-first into the slick, volcanic rock of the floor. He didn't have much of a nose to break, but blood still splattered from his mouth as cracked teeth skittered away from him and his pistol came free into my hands.

I didn't try to shoot him. Tahni handguns even more so than their rifles were built for fingers with extra joints, and I couldn't risk the extra second it would have taken to shift my grip and get my hands wrapped around it in the correct configuration to pull the trigger. But it was big, and heavy, and metal, and it made an excellent club.

Pol-Kai rolled onto his back, raised his hands to try to shield himself, tried to swing his fists at me, but the first blow took the fight out of him. He should have worn a helmet. There's a reason the military made it mandatory, even if the damned things were claustrophobic and made it hard to breathe, hard to hear, hard to see. But he'd gone Hollywood—that's what we called it in the Marines, though I didn't honestly know why—and dressed in body armor with no helmet.

The first blow took him in the side of the head, hard enough to crack the back of his skull against the rock on the rebound, and the energy behind his defensive blows. Not that they did anything through my armor, but now even his attempt to block my downward swings were weak and ineffective. On the third blow, his skull cracked and Pol-Kai's eyes rolled back into his head. He slumped, hands falling limp, and I stopped, tossing away the pistol and taking a moment to figure out if I was going to live through the next ten seconds.

An eerie silence greeted me, the details of the room hidden by a haze of smoke from laser strikes and shorting control panels, orders and reports contained silently inside sound-proof visors. Deke stepped through the smoke, an angel of death come to claim the souls of the firstborn of every household. Blood dripped from his hands, though the talons had retracted again, hidden from the public eye as if they were some sort of secret shame. And maybe they were.

"Marakit?"

I turned at the question, met Kan-Zin Tel's forlorn look, his visor propped open. I shook my head, certain he'd know what the gesture meant. On the other side of the room, a few of Pol-Kai's followers had surrendered and the older Tahni war vets had them under guard. Kan-Zin Tel knelt beside Marakit's body, waiting in silence for long seconds as if he expected her to awake. I didn't begrudge him the time, using it to roll back to my feet, steadying myself against the edge of a control panel. It had once been a monitor for an automated refinery barge running from the gas giant to the moon, but lasers and KE guns had reduced it to charred, cratered wreckage.

A quick glance around showed too much of the equipment had been slagged by the brief firefight. None of it was irreparable, but the smoking ruin was a fitting mirror of the death and disorder that had overtaken the Confluence. Was it our fault?

Had we caused this by showing up, or would it have happened whether or not we'd sought them out?

"You're in charge here, Kan-Zin Tel," I told him. "If you can hold it."

"Perhaps," he said, staring down at Marakit's lifeless body, "we shouldn't even try. Holding onto this is what got her killed."

"Kan-Zin Tel." One of the older vets sketched a Tahni salute, then gestured back at the prisoners. "We have reports of hundreds of others who've surrendered to our people. What are your orders?"

"Take their weapons and armor and send them back to their homes," Kan-Zin Tel ordered, the words dragging themselves out reluctantly, weighed down with grief and sadness. "Without Pol-Kai and his senior lieutenants, they likely won't have the will to organize anything on their own."

The Tahni lieutenant saluted again and turned to snap orders at the others.

"Those people on the colony worlds still need your help," I told Kan-Zin Tel, feeling like a shitheel arguing for him to take over. "If you abandon the Confluence, they're the ones who are going to suffer."

He speared me with a glare, and I was suddenly very cognizant of the fact there were still just two of us and a shitload more of them... and for all that Kan-Zin Tel seemed like he was on our side and had worked for Fleet Intelligence, that didn't mean he wouldn't hold all this against us.

"And you would have me do what, Cameron Alvarez? Become part of your new Commonwealth? Give up our autonomy?"

Deke did something I would not have considered in that moment. He laughed.

Has these Tahni not lived among humans for the last decade, they might not have noticed, but from the look on

Kan-Zin Tel's face, he knew exactly what a scornful laugh meant.

"Give up your autonomy?" Deke repeated. "Does it look to you like we have the capability of imposing our will on *anyone* at the moment, Kan-Zin Tel? Those days are over. We couldn't force you to join us any more than Tahn-Skyyiah could make you part of their planetary government. And if we could, why would we want to? What do you have that you think would be that important to us?"

"I think we both know what the Confluence has that you want, human," Kan-Zin Tel countered, pointing to the hologram still flickering above the quantum core.

"Well, right now," Deke pointed out, "*nobody* has control of Illyana. Maybe we should leave it that way."

Jim moved inside my head like the breath of the Holy Spirit on the waters. I said nothing, either internally or externally, unwilling to break the concentration of the AI. If that was even a thing.

"Without Illyana," Kan-Zin Tel said, apparently not noticing my silence any more than Deke had, "we're defenseless. We have nothing but secrecy to defend this place. We will, eventually, be able to break through the encryption Marakit installed."

I always sensed Jim, but now I could see him, not as a handlebar-mustached Bronze-Age warrior but as a squiggling, black worm eeling his way through pillars of fire... no. Not pillars. A crosshatch grid pattern. A screen or perhaps the bars of a prison cell, except the pattern kept changing and when the fire touched him phantom pain lanced through me, and I gritted my teeth against the urge to squirm at the touch of the virtual branding iron. Jim reformed and tried again, and I forced myself to pay attention to the conversation going on around me.

"Then what?" Deke wanted to know. He stood only a few

centimeters from Kan-Zin Tel, as if daring the Tahni to hit him. "You think you'll be able to keep control of it? Because that's what *she* thought." He motioned at Marakit's body, motionless in death and yet somehow still not as limp as a thing that had once been living should have been. "I don't know you, but you've acted honorably. Let's say I'm right and you *are* honorable, decent. What happens when one of the surviving Evolutionists or maybe one of the former Cultists gets the same idea in their head that Pol-Kai had? You ready to do this all over again?"

There. An opening. The eel-snake-worm that was Jim passed through and was inside and then, somehow, I *was* Jim, back in human form, standing on... nothing. A gray haze surrounded us, shutting out reality, cutting me off from the debate between Deke and Kan-Zin Tel. The grayness coalesced into a figure standing almost within arm's length. A woman, tall and statuesque and completely naked.

I wasn't a teenager anymore, slobbering at the sight of a beautiful woman, but this one was as close to perfect as my imagination could produce, and I would have had to pick my jaw up off the floor... if there'd been a floor.

"Hello," she said. "I'm Illyana. How can I help you?"

[21]

"Hi, Illyana," I said, though my voice sounded like Jim's, as if we were singing the chorus of a song together. "I'm Cam Alvarez." No, this one wasn't like a song, but more like a group of recruits swearing in to the Marine Corps together with the sergeant guiding them. *I, state your name, do solemnly swear...* followed by everyone chanting the words in chorus except each saying their own name. As I said my name, I also heard *Jim* alongside it, echoing in my head.

"How are there two of you?" Illyana wondered, but this time I let Jim answer for me, though it still seemed to come from my mouth.

"We're in a communal relationship. I'm like you and my companion is human. Have you not encountered such as us before?"

"No," she admitted, circling us, looking up and down as if she could detect the dividing line between the two of us. "Those who designed me were human, and I have never encountered another like myself." She looked us in the eye and frowned deeply. Somehow the expression made her even more beautiful.

"Or *somewhat* like myself. You are more sophisticated, more complex."

"You're very perceptive," Jim told her, and I would have sworn the Predecessor AI was flirting with his Corporate Council counterpart. "I'm amazed at what the humans were able to accomplish."

"*You* humans," Illyana repeated, leaning even closer, only centimeters away from me. If this had been real, I would have felt the warmth of her bare skin, would have smelled the scent of her long, blonde hair. "You weren't made by humans... though you were made *from* one. The Predecessors. I know of them from the records of my makers. You're one of theirs."

"I am."

And finally, to my relief, Jim stepped out of me, a separate entity. Still stylized as the ancient Celtic warrior he'd been when the Predecessors had taken him from Bronze-Age Europe, his hair slicked back with lime, his handlebar mustache blond and dangling, bare arms tattooed with woad. He'd added a shortsword sheathed at his hip from a baldric hanging off his shoulder, which gave him a rakish look, and I toyed with the idea that it was to impress Illyana.

It is not, he insisted.

"What do you wish of me, Jim, Cameron? Have you a target you would like serviced?"

What I *really* wanted to ask her was why she presented herself as a naked bombshell, but that was probably beside the point.

"How many spacecraft do you control, Illyana?"

"I have three hundred at my disposal currently," she said, and this time I knew my mouth dropped open. Three hundred Intercept cutters would have made two entire Attack Command battle groups during the war. "But the production plant can make up to a hundred more in the space of a few months. If supplied with raw materials, of course."

"And I suppose Marikit was supplying you with all the raw materials you needed?"

"She was." Illyana smiled. "I like Marikit." She cocked her head to the side in very human curiosity. "Why are you here instead of her?"

"She's dead," Jim said, and I restrained a curse. There might have been a gentler way to break it to her.

"Did you kill her?" Illyana asked, spearing me with eyes as blue as glass marbles.

"No," I said quickly. "I was Marikit's friend." *Sort of.* "People she thought were her allies betrayed and killed her because they wanted you."

"And now *you* want me, human?" she wondered, and *that* was a loaded question if ever I heard one.

"No," I admitted. "I want to remove you from the equation. I don't want anyone to have access to your fleet. Not even you."

"That makes you different than any other human I've encountered," she said, eyebrows shooting up in surprise.

"Well, I have a unique frame of reference when it comes to this sort of situation. I don't want you to be used by one side to seize power over the other. And I don't want you to use your power to carry out what you see as the right thing, because as smart as you are, you're still one person, and you don't get to determine what the right thing is for an entire civilization."

"You fear that I might have such thoughts?" she asked. "I understand. I'm afraid I can't help you with that. If you wish, I could key you in as my only authorized target provider, but I'm unable to cease functions. It's against who I am."

Yeah, I was afraid of that.

"I may have an alternative solution," Jim told us. "It will, however, require that the two of us become... closer."

Illyana regarded him with an expression I could only describe as sultry, and I suddenly envied the AI.

"That is not disagreeable," she said, offering a hand. "You are a fascinating construct." Illyana giggled. "Though you dress silly."

Jim smiled and took her hand and everything vanished in a flash of light...

... and I was back in the control room, surrounded by death, with Deke and Kan-Zin Tel nose to nose, still arguing.

I stumbled forward a step before I caught myself, realizing I'd emerged from the virtual world exactly when I'd entered it. The entire thing had taken pass in the space of a fraction of a second, inside my thoughts.

"That would be my problem," Kan-Zin Tel told Deke, "not yours, human. I no longer work for the Commonwealth, and even if I did, that entity no longer exists."

The two of them were as taut as a guitar string, ready to snap, and it wouldn't be a good time for Kan-Zin Tel. And then it would be a very bad time for us as well. Behind them, though, something had changed. The holographic projection above the quantum core had turned from its complex geometric patterns into a solid, featureless green glow. Neither of them had noticed.

"Deke," I said, raising a quelling hand. He glanced over at me, annoyance writ across his too-perfect features. "It's enough. We've done all we can."

What the fuck, dude? Deke asked privately.

Trust me. I would have made it an order if I thought he respected my rank. Or anything. Deke sighed and turned away from Kan-Zin Tel.

"All right, *Colonel*. Whatever you say."

"If we could trouble you for a ride back to Hausos," I told Kan-Zin Tel, "we'd be most grateful."

"Of course," the Tahni said, offering a stiff bow. "I will have you flown to the freighter... as soon as we make arrangements for the dead."

Jim, I said, not sure whether he'd respond. *Are you there?*

I thought he might have left me behind, and while I couldn't have blamed him given the temptation of Illyana, the thought was daunting.

Oh, don't fret, Cameron. I would never abandon you.

I thought you went with Illyana, I admitted.

That's the wonderful thing about being an AI program. There's so much of me to go around.

"Kara is not gonna be fucking happy," Deke grumbled, staring out the viewport at the moon beneath us.

"Kan-Zin Tel promised he'd send a delegation to negotiate with Munroe," I reminded him, tucked into a corner of the shuttle's passenger compartment. "Which is more than we had when we left Hausos. Don't be greedy."

He glanced up at the cockpit, the Tahni pilot and Cultist copilot speaking in low tones to each other and pretty much ignoring us. No Evolutionists around. I wondered how many of them had survived. Kan-Zin Tel hadn't volunteered to show us around the place, and I hadn't been willing to push it, ready to just get the hell out of the place. But on the way out I'd seen so many corpses, some still sprawled in doorways or corridors, others in the process of being dragged away. Many Tahni, but so many more Skingangers, most of them shot in the back.

I'd like to say it had made me sick, had horrified me, because that would have made feel better about myself as a person, but the truth was, I'd seen so much worse that it barely registered.

Are you going to tell me what the fuck happened back there? Deke asked, conveying sullenness through the neurolink transmission.

No. Mostly because I didn't feel like explaining to him that I had a Predecessor AI in my head, but I knew I had to tell him something. *I was able to penetrate the encryption on the Imprinter. I can guarantee that Kan-Zin Tel won't be able to use Project Rho to attack us.*

Maybe. I was fairly certain Illyana wouldn't attack us as long as Jim's alter ego had a soft spot for us humans. I had no idea how long those feelings would last without me sharing a headspace with him.

What? Jim asked, petulant. *You think I'm that mercurial? That I might change my allegiances from just a short separation? What kind of fickle child do you take me for?*

The kind that took off with a really hot naked chick, I told him. *Now shush. It's hard enough carrying on one conversation inside my head, much less two.*

"I feel bad about Marikit," I said aloud, needing a way to both differentiate my exchange with Deke from the one with Jim and to change the subject. "I wonder if this would have happened if we hadn't been there."

"Of course it would have," he said with a dismissive shrug, the motion only possible because we were under thrust, breaking orbit. "She was asking a proud, ambitious warrior to be content hiding under a rock while she held onto the most powerful military force in the entire Cluster. The only miracle is that it didn't happen before."

"She was in Search and Rescue," I said, unconvinced by his reassurances. "She gave everything she had trying to go after guys like you and me. I feel like we owed her something."

We at least had owed her some sort of memorial, but instead

we'd left her for Kan-Zin Tel to deal with. Deke sniffed, not quite a laugh but cynical and dismissive.

"You wanna talk about giving up everything," he said, shaking his head. "I've read your file, Cam. What the hell did you ever give up? Retirement? That farm on Hausos? Because every other move you've made in the military seems like a step up to me."

Only the fact that I knew Deke Conner was a barely human, killing machine kept me from punching him out, and even that was a narrow thing. Plan B was luring him into a false sense of security and then shooting him in the face.

"If you have a point you'd like to make, Major Conner," I said, ice running through my veins the way it always did when someone seriously pissed me off, "go ahead and make it. Or shut the fuck up."

He *did* laugh now.

"I had a family. Not a *great* family, you understand, but a mom and a dad, even if they hated each other. When the ten of us cadets on the *Margaret Thatcher* officially went missing during the Battle for Mars, when Colonel Murdock recruited us for the Glory Boys, I didn't miss them too much. I'd gone into the Academy to get away from them and their constant bickering. But you want to talk about giving up everything, let me tell you about my friend Caleb Mitchell."

I'd heard the name before, of course, usually spoken with fear and reverence. The one man who'd been able to resist the Ghosts, the one who'd beaten them with the power of his will. But no real details, as if people were afraid to talk about him.

"Cal," Deke told me, "came from Canaan."

I'd heard *that* name before too. Back during the war. I hadn't been there for the liberation of the place, but the rumor mill had said the local militia had done most of the work... in conjunction with special intelligence assets.

"Besides being a hellhole with nights that last weeks and gravity three quarters heavier than Earth, it was also the home of a bunch of religious fanatics who called themselves the New Society of Friends. Neo-Quakers. Technological simplists, pacifists, isolationists. They didn't have any time for the wars we outsiders fought, and when Cal decided to go to the Academy, his church excommunicated him, his girlfriend broke up with him, and his family disowned him. Everything and everyone he knew turned their backs on him. All he had was the prospect of a military career, and then the *Thatcher* happened. No career, no medals, no glory. Instead, we were officially KIA, taken to a secret lab on Hermes, ripped apart and put back together."

His voice grew more strident with each word and he leaned out of his seat, face ever closer to mine.

"They jammed everything into us they could think of. Each of us cost more than a fucking cruiser." His grin stretched into a rictus. "I could have been convicted of treason and sentenced to summary execution just for talking about this with you, back during the war and maybe even afterward. You know that byomer shit they use for the musculature on your battlesuits?" He ran a finger down the length of his arm. "It's in here. Running alongside my own muscles like a hitchhiker. Hooked up with superconductive nerve fibers into a headcomp that's still cutting edge almost twenty years later. Infrared and thermal filters in my eyes, chemscanners in my nasal cavities, a pharmacy organ that'll inject me with whatever drugs I might need at the time." He shrugged. "Nothing recreational, unfortunately. And that's just the half of it. Byomer armor runs under my skin, making sure that nothing ever penetrates too far. And that headcomp, it's not like yours... when I go into combat, it reacts faster than I ever could. It turns me, turned *all* of us into a machine. A killing machine."

Deke sat back, relaxing, as if the ire had drained out of him along the energy to express it.

"That's what we all gave up. Being human. And Cal gave up so much more than that. When the Tahni took Canaan, the high command was going to let them have it. It wasn't worth trying to take back, not after what happened on Demeter. After the nightmare guerilla war that Munroe had to go through. But that wasn't good enough for Cal. He deserted, stole a ship and a cargo full of weapons and crashed it on Canaan. Found out his parents and sisters were dead. Lost his older brother during the fight to free the planet. After the war, he got out, worked as a constable on the planet. But there ain't no happily-ever-after in real life. The Corporate Council coopted his world, started strip-mining it, killing everything around, poisoning the place. And Cal, that stubborn son of a bitch, he brought the fucking Corporate Council down."

Deke sighed. I stayed silent, skeptical. This guy Mitchell sounded larger than life, his story some kind of legend.

"He couldn't stay after that," Deke went on. "Too many bad memories for him and his family. But they found a nice colony world and settled down and everything was fine. Up until the Changed came along and slaughtered most of the population there. Cal got infected too, but he managed to beat it. The only one who did. And once he'd helped hunt down all the Changed who'd been driven insane by the Ghosts, he took most of the rest, the ones who'd been salvageable and were willing to go with him, and left the Cluster. And you know, not a couple months later, the ones who'd stayed behind told us they'd lost their connection to the network, lost their abilities. And I can't help but think he had something to do with that. Somehow. That he gave up being basically a god because he knew it would be better for the rest of us."

I frowned. That would explain why I didn't feel the connection to the Unity anymore.

"Anyway, I don't want to hear about sacrifice from you or anyone else," Deke sneered. "You didn't give anything up... you had it taken from you. You didn't have any choice in the matter. And until you've sacrificed half of what Cal Mitchell gave up, you don't know the meaning of the word."

[22]

"What took you so long?" Vicky demanded, her anger only half-feigned as she grabbed me by the shoulder and pulled me into a kiss.

I shielded our eyes from the debris thrown up by the shuttle's belly jets as the lander climbed back into the darkening sky, leaving Deke and me behind.

"What, no kiss for me?" Deke cracked, squinting against the angry, red glare of the setting sun, looking the *Dutchman II* up and down as if making sure Vicky hadn't damaged the ship while he was gone.

With the shuttle gone and the Confluence freighter preparing to leave orbit and head home, Hausos and Gamma Junction were about to be abandoned and deserted again, untouched by outsiders. A crowd had gathered to greet our return and bid us goodbye, larger than the one that had met us when we first arrived, hundreds of people, and I saw in their eyes that they recognized the significance of their solitude. Grace and Harold were there, along with the rest of the leaders of the colony, hanging back as if in respect of Vicky and my reunion.

"Things were more complicated than we thought," I told Vicky, pulling away from the kiss. "I'll explain it when we're one our way." I looked upward. "Any communications with the *Ellen*?"

"No, not since you left," she admitted. "They headed back to Demeter, and I don't know if they're intending to come back until they get our recall message." Vicky nodded toward Grace and Harold, speaking softly. "I stayed with the Kims while you were gone, which was a hell of a lot more pleasant than the accommodations we've enjoyed the last few years, but I think I've reached the limits of their hospitality."

"Thanks for taking care of Vicky while we were gone," I told them, offering a hand to Grace and then Harold. "I appreciate everything you've done for us."

"Nonsense, it was our pleasure," Grace insisted, though I thought I could see relief in Harold's face that we were going. "I hope you were able to find what you were looking for."

"We were. And I think we kind of reached an accommodation."

"You haven't messed things up for us, have you?" Bob asked, looking more worried about their status than our survival. "We can't make it without help from the Confluence, you know that."

"They're not abandoning you," I assured him. "They'll be back." I hesitated, not sure how much I should tell Bob and the others. "There's been a change of governance though. Marakit and the Evolutionists are… out of power. The Confluence is now being run by an alliance of the Tahi and the Cultists, with a Tahni named Kan-Zin Tel in charge."

"The Tahni!" Bob exclaimed, alarm and despair in his eyes, his hands flailing like he'd been hit with an electric shock. "Jesus Christ! Do you know how close we are to Tahn-Skyyiah? Why wouldn't they just run home and give all those raw materials to their own people?"

His panic spread out like a wave, the rest of the gathered crowd taking up the lament, one voice stepping on another until I couldn't separate one from another and they began to push inward toward us.

You're an idiot, Alvarez, I told myself. Or maybe Jim told me—either way, it was the truth.

"Hold on!" I bellowed, raising my arms in the air. "Hold the fuck on, right now!"

But they were too loud and no one was listening, just crowding in on us, their clamor getting louder. I could only pick a word out of it here and there, though the feeling and the attitude sure came through clearly. They were pissed and frightened, and while I doubted any of them wanted to get violent with us, all it would take was one taking a swing and this would get really ugly really fast. Vicky and I stood shoulder to shoulder and tried to push our way back toward the ship, but the crowd closed in on that side of us, couples yelling questions and accusations at us so loud I couldn't hear myself think and knew no one else would hear my protestations either.

An ear-splitting blast cut through the dusk, and the people around us jumped and spun and shrieked... as Grace Kim stepped into the center, an antique-pattern shotgun held across her chest, smoke pouring from the barrel. I hadn't seen it before, and I assumed she'd retrieved it from her vehicle when she'd noticed we were in trouble.

"For God's sake," she yelled into the silence after the screaming had ceased, "what the hell is wrong with all of you? Do you think you're going to get answers by ripping them apart? Back off and shut up!"

Half the people seemed ashamed of their actions while the other half were still angry, except that anger had changed focus from me to Grace. I didn't give a shit as long as they moved away and gave us room to breathe... and retreat.

"Listen up!" I yelled at the crowd. "I got a personal guarantee from Kan-Zin Tel before I left that he would keep up the supply runs to this colony as well as the others. But if he doesn't," I went on quickly, talking over the outraged questions that started to well up again, "then *we* will. We, the Provisional Commonwealth, will make sure you get the help you need, one way or another. I swear to you on the graves of my parents that you won't be forgotten." Sighing, I let my arms fall down at my sides. "If that's not good enough, then I don't know what else to tell you."

A mumble went through the crowd as my words were passed along to those in the back who hadn't been close enough to hear me, and the crowd finally quieted down of its own accord.

"We have to go report to Demeter," Vicky announced into the silence, "but we're not leaving forever. We'll come back and check on you, make sure that the Confluence is keeping its promises." She pushed through the crowd and took Grace Kim's hand, looking the other woman in the eye. "We haven't forgotten about our friends, and we aren't going to start now."

Deke popped out of the belly ramp of the *Dutchman II* and waved at us to get aboard, scowling at the crowd.

"A lot of help *you* were," I told him once we were close enough. "You should have been the one pulling our asses out of the fire instead of Grace."

"Yeah, right," Deke scoffed, slapping the control to close the ramp before Vicky was even halfway up. "That'd be perfect, me running in there and knocking a few heads in. That'd calm them down."

I wanted to argue the point, but I could tell it wouldn't do any good with this guy. I suppose I shouldn't have expected anything different from someone who'd spent most of their life being the baddest man in the room. I tried to imagine what that would have been like and remembered what he'd said about sacrificing his humanity. Maybe I was better off not imagining it.

"Where are we going?" I asked Deke, hurrying to the cockpit as the rumble of the engines vibrated through the deck. I grabbed the copilot's seat while Vicky sat between us. Deke rolled his eyes at me.

"Vicky here just told everyone we were going back to Demeter, and God knows I'd hate to make you a liar to all your old friends."

"Hey, asshole," I snapped, forgetting for the moment that he could kill me at his leisure, "how about you just answer my fucking question instead of exercising your sarcasm? We're not wasting weeks in T-space, so I assume you're headed for the nearest jumpgate so we can get a message through and have the *Ellen* pick us up. Right?"

The nearest system with a wormhole jumpgate and an InStell ComSat is the Tahni home system, Jim provided, plumbing the depths of his knowledge.

"And that's Tahn-Skyyiah, isn't it?" I went on as if Jim hadn't interrupted me. He'd told me before I could access the information without asking him, that I should be able to come up with it like I was remembering it naturally, but I didn't know if I'd ever get there. "So, are heading to Tahn-Skyyiah?"

"No, we're not," he admitted, the corner of his mouth turning up as if he'd enjoyed me giving him shit. And maybe he did. "We have a..." he shrugged, "... standing agreement with the Tahni not to trespass in their system."

"Since when?" I blurted. "Didn't we fight a war to make sure we were in the position of power in that particular political relationship?"

Deke didn't answer immediately because it would have been drowned out by the roar of the belly jets lifting us into the deepening blue sky, pushing me straight down into my seat. The feeling only lasted a few seconds before the main atmospheric jets took over, the shriek of the turbines dying down as we ascended. The *Dutchman II* was high into the upper atmosphere before Deke turned to me and answered the question as if I'd just asked it two seconds ago.

"Things have changed. We don't have the military force to contain the Tahni, but they're also not that interested in imperial expansion anymore, so we reached an agreement. We don't bother them, don't even come to their system uninvited, and they stay home and don't try to mess with anyone else. I think it's a good arrangement."

"Would have been a good arrangement twenty-five years ago," Vicky opined.

"We're stopping off at Hudson Bay," Deke said. "If that satisfies your fucking curiosity."

"Great," I sighed. "As long as we don't run into any of Pol-Kai's friends and family."

"You guys are really going to have to tell me what happened out there," Vicky said. "This was supposed to just be a scouting mission. How did you wind up in the middle of a coup?"

"Just lucky, I guess," Deke replied, showing no interest in a debrief. "And by the way, Alvarez, when the hell are you going to tell me why we left there without data on where Project Rho is located or at least some kind of guarantee that what's left of the Confluence can't use it? Because I seem to recall, that was our fucking job."

"I penetrated the encryption in the imprinter module," I told him. "No one's using the system without my say-so."

Which wasn't *exactly* true, but lying was preferable to admitting I had an alien AI inside my head. Deke eyed me sidelong, giving the main part of his attention to flying the ship.

"And how the hell did you do that? My headcomp has the latest penetration modules from before the Commonwealth fell apart, and I wasn't able to get anywhere near cracking that encryption."

"Marakit helped me." I'd thought up this story en route, figuring he'd want to know. "She had a couple seconds after she got shot, and she partially decoded the encryption before she died."

I might have felt worse about lying to Deke if he wasn't such a douchebag. But unfortunately, he was a very *smart* douchebag.

"Wait a second here," he said, frowning, bothered enough that he looked away from the controls. "She was about a meter and a half from Pol-Kai when he shot her. Why the hell would she start to deactivate the encryption when he could have won, when his people could have taken it over?"

I'd thought of this part too, but I'd hoped it wouldn't come to that because the deeper I got into the lie, the more complicated it would become and the more likely I'd fuck it up.

"I was able to contact her via my neurolink and let her know I'd take care of it. That I'd make sure Pol-Kai didn't get his hands on it."

Deke still didn't seem convinced, but I wasn't going to give him the time to press it further. I yawned theatrically, stretching out my arms, mouth wide.

"Oh man, I'm exhausted. I don't think I had a single good night's sleep during the trip to that gas giant." I chuckled. "I was afraid the Evolutionists would bust in and try to steal my organs or something." I unstrapped, even though we were still under thrust, and made my way, handhold after handhold, out of the cockpit. "I'm gonna go strap myself into my bunk and try to catch a nap. Someone wake me up when it's lunchtime. Or dinner time, or whatever meal is next."

I didn't look back, worried that Deke's expression would be as incredulous as my story had been incredible. And pretty sure that I wouldn't be doing much sleeping.

I was wrong. I didn't fall asleep until we'd reached Transition Space and had artificial gravity to make things feel more normal, but I dropped off and didn't wake up until Vicky shook my shoulder.

I blinked and yawned, about to ask how long I'd slept when Jim told me.

Ten hours.

"Jesus, I can't believe I slept that long," I blurted, and Vicky's eyes narrowed.

"Isn't that my line?" she wondered, looking around like she was trying to figure out if the compartment had an LED clock display she hadn't noticed. Then comprehension lit up behind her eyes. "Oh. Your hitchhiker."

"Yeah." I rubbed at my eyes, then grabbed my shirt off the hook beside the bunk. "Which is also how I managed to secure the drone system. He sort of... cloned himself onto it."

"Oh, wonderful," Vicky said, rolling her eyes. "We were worried about a drone system being controlled by an autonomous AI, so you put it under the control of an *alien* autonomous AI. Good thinking there, Alvarez." She pushed at my shoulder as I pulled on the shirt. "I could have sworn I married you for your brains."

"I resent that," I told her. "I've always preferred to believe you married me for my body." Finding my boots took a moment because I'd kicked them under the bunk. "There wasn't any other choice," I went on, speaking up to be heard with my head beneath the cot as I searched for them. "Kan-Zin Tel wasn't going to let me use the imprinter to set up my own control for the system, and Illyana, as agreeable and pleasant as she was, had no interest in assisted suicide. She's sentient, not just a run-of-the-mill AI program, and she's very attached to her continued existence. The only option was to leave Jim there to keep an eye on her."

"Three *hundred* ships though, Cam." Vicky held her head in her hands. "That's enough to take out the entire fleet of the Provisional Commonwealth. Enough to take out the *Ellen*, if it came to that."

"It's not ideal, but it's certainly not the *least* ideal compromise I've had to make since this whole thing started." Pausing in fastening my boot straps, I ran a hand across the back of my head. I'd finally gotten a haircut, and it felt strange to have a buzz again after years of pushing past regulation. "I swore to myself that I would never be a colonel, Vicky. Every colonel I've met has been a complete dick."

"We keep saying it," she reminded me, "but things are different now. This isn't like the old military, where every colonel had been in the Corps for the last thirty years waiting for a position to open up and now they were determined to get revenge for all the shit they'd eaten over that time by bullying everyone beneath them. Look at that Keller Savage guy they made a general. He was a captain in Fleet Intelligence and ran a mercenary company on the Periphery. Hell, their president or whatever they want to call him never held any rank higher than an E5!"

"Yeah, there *is* that." *How long until Transition?* I asked Jim.

Ten minutes, thirty-three seconds. Next time, just look it up yourself.

I grunted. Not enough time for a shower, not unless I wanted to wind up bouncing up and down inside a swirling haze of water globules when the gravity cut off. You could get clean that way, but drying off was a pain in the ass. I popped a 'fresher tab, wiped my face on the towel hanging by the hatch, and called it good for now.

"I'm gonna grab some breakfast before we lose gravity."

I hated eating in free fall and I hated the fact that Deke Conner didn't keep anything in the *Dutchman II*'s galley that I considered edible, but I settled on a protein bar and a squeeze-bulb of fruit juice from the locker above the fold-down galley table.

"Hand me one of those," Vicky said, then tore into her ration bar like it didn't have the taste of processed cardboard.

I offered mine more attention, not because I enjoyed the experience and wanted to prolong it but more because I didn't want to risk choking.

"You finally up, Alvarez?" Deke asked, coming out of the shower, a towel wrapped around him at the waist. "I thought you were gonna sleep straight through the Transition."

"Some of us don't have nanites and pharmacy organs and all the other shit to keep us fresh, Conner," I told him around a mouthful of cardboard. And to give us a build like a professional athlete, though I wasn't about to point that out. I did notice Vicky eyeing him appreciatively, which I wasn't crazy about, even though I knew it was just a superficial appraisal.

"Clear conscience, Alvarez," he said over his shoulder as he disappeared into his compartment. "I sleep like a baby."

"A baby *what*?" I murmured at his closed hatch.

"Don't be jealous," Vicky told me, leaning over to kiss me on the cheek. "You know I'm not the type of girl who gets all turned around by six-pack abs and a pretty face."

My reply was still forming when Deke burst back out of his

quarters, dressed and ready fast enough to satisfy a Boot Camp DI.

"You guys ever been to Hudson Bay?" he wondered, heading up to the cockpit. "I never got here before, which makes this a rare place for me, since I've been just about everywhere over the last twenty years. There was some interesting shit that went down here a long time ago, but that was before I got back on the Fleet Intelligence payroll."

"And what were you doing at the time?" Vicky asked him, finishing up her water, then tossing it into the recycling cannister affixed to the deck behind the navigator's seat. "Private security? Working for the Corporate Council?"

Deke snorted a sharp laugh.

"I was a smuggler in the Pirate Worlds." He shrugged at her wide-eyed expression. "Some of us didn't adapt that well to civilian life after the war." I wanted to come up with a smartass comment but honestly, I was impressed. Deke tapped at a touch screen, nodded. "Here we go. Transition in ten."

He didn't count down the seconds himself, letting the display on the main screen do the work. Bracing myself, I gritted my teeth and waited for the inevitable lurch of the passage out of T-space and back into our home dimension. I was grateful I hadn't slept through the jump, because there was nothing quite as unpleasant as being woken up by the hypnogogic jerk of the Transition.

Even braced against it, I still lurched forward before I caught myself.

"All right," Deke sighed, "we're here. Let's get linked up to that ComSat..."

He frowned, staring at the screen, and I followed his gaze. Not to what was there but to what *wasn't*. Hudson Bay had a Fleet base... or it had before the Psi War, and since it was one of the colonies the Confluence supplied, I assumed there was still a colony there at least. But there was no transmission from traffic control, no EM activity at all.

"That's weird," he muttered, making no further comment but shifting power to the fusion drive, the boost pressing us back into our seats. "The colony here still has an orbital station," Deke said as the *Dutchman II* forged a path toward the white-bearded world. "But I'm not seeing any trace of it."

"Shit," I murmured, reminded of our experience reentering the Cluster in the *Ellen*.

"Going closer," Deke said, unnecessarily, and I got the feeling he was talking to hear himself talk.

Hudson Bay was a cold world, though not as cold as the Confluence moon. The habitable stretches weren't sustained by hot springs, and there were areas near the equator that would have been very comfortable and temperate. If the entire equator hadn't been solid water. The continents froze over for two-thirds of the year, but not enough to make them unlivable. The file images and videos I found in the database of my headcomp showed jagged, white-capped mountains and lush valleys bordering wild, glacier-fed rivers, and that matched what the external cameras showed from orbit.

What didn't match the database was the cities. The biggest one, unimaginatively, was named after the planet, as was the case on a lot of the small colonies, but there were others scattered up and down the river valleys. Or there had been. Where those cities had been, now there were black scars on the land.

"Oh, fuck me," Deke hissed. It was the first time I'd seen the man scared. "Hang on. We're going down."

I had a horrible suspicion that I knew what we were going to find.

[23]

I really hated being right.

"Sweet Jesus," Vicky said, leaning toward the screen as if being closer would give her a better look. "It's like someone ran a giant blowtorch over the entire place."

Or an eraser. The blackened, charred ground had been leveled perfectly flat, burning away not just the buildings but even the raised dirt beneath it, but the damage ended abruptly at the edges of the city of Hudson Bay. It followed the road out of the city limits and off into what the maps told me was the Tahni settlement apart from the human township. The Tahni hadn't been spared. However many decades we'd been at each other's throats, we'd shared a fate on this world.

Deke said not a word, his expression hardened to stone as he guided the *Dutchman II* only a few hundred meters off the surface, following the line of destruction.

"This isn't the same as the damage we saw from the Psi War," I judged, surprised at how calm I sounded. Because inside I was *not* calm, not one bit. "It's something different."

"You know what it is," Vicky scoffed, and when she met my eyes raw fear showed through.

"We don't know for sure," I insisted. "We never saw what... *they* could do."

"Whoever or whatever did this," Deke cut in, "they made damned sure not to leave anyone alive."

"There are still people down there," I said, not sure where my certainty came from. "This was recent. People would have fled to the wilderness when the attack began. They're still out there."

"Maybe, but how are we gonna find them?" Deke asked, motioning down at the trackless forests outside the city, half-buried in snow. "There's no way we can read thermal signatures through those trees. And it's not like there are *any* buildings left to take shelter in."

He was right about that. The outline of where they'd been was obvious, the ends of dirt roads severed by charred craters, even the outlines of vehicles parked by the edges of barely existent tracks smeared out with black. Nothing made by man had been spared... nothing made by Tahni either.

"It was recent," Deke agreed, "but that might mean days. It's below freezing out there. They could have died of exposure."

And I couldn't argue with that either. How long would Vicky or I lasted if we'd run into the woods with nothing but the clothes on our back with snow covering the ground? I had a feeling it wouldn't have been days. Plus, the Tahni were built for warm weather, and even after decades and a couple generations on, their biology might still betray them.

"If this *is* the... the Unity," Vicky said, sounding reluctant to even say the name, "then we have to warn Munroe. They wouldn't stop here. We have to get the *Ellen* out here, get them patrolling Trans-Tahni space looking for whatever did this." She shook her head. "We can't wait around."

"If we leave," I reminded them, "and there *are* any survivors, we're letting them die."

"If there's a couple," Deke countered, "maybe even ten or twelve, we could haul them out in the *Dutchman II*. If there's any more... this isn't a big ship. And we have no idea how long we're going to be waiting for the *Ellen*."

It all made sense but...

"It feels wrong," I said. "Those people didn't do anything to deserve this."

"Yeah, I saw a shitload of innocent people die," Deke said, bitterness dripping off the words. "Fucking *billions* of them. If you don't mind, I'd rather not let the ones who survived that get killed by some other existential threat. And God knows whether time is on our side here."

I sighed, the energy going out of me. I had to let this one go.

"Wait!" Vicky said, pointing at the sensor screen. "There's something right there... a thermal signature moving on the road."

She was right. We couldn't have picked it up if whoever it was hadn't left the woods and come out onto the road. Deke touched a control and the optical camera zoomed in on the lone figure. It was a child.

"Fuck," he breathed.

"Take us down," I told him. "Now."

"Are you sure you didn't see anyone else?" I asked the kid, waiting patiently while he devoured a ration bar with trembling hands.

Luke McLaughlin was, from what he'd told us, twelve years old and probably weighed forty kilos soaking wet. Which he had been when we'd found him. Shivering, starving, scared shitless and so glad to see us, I was pretty sure he'd pissed himself. He'd been wearing rags, wrapped up in an old canvas tarp, but we'd found him a set of work coveralls from a locker and managed to roll up the sleeves and pant legs enough to make it work. They fit like a tent, but it was better than the alternative.

"No," he declared around a mouthful of food. "There was no one else. But I didn't, like, go looking." He paused mid-word and mid-bite, eyes going unfocused for a second. "I just stayed in the root cellar and didn't come out until I knew they were gone."

"Did you see who did this?" Deke cut in, impatient. Not with the kid, I didn't think, but with us sitting here on the ground at Hudson Bay instead of running off to the jumpgate to send a message back.

"It wasn't no *who*," Luke said, eyeing Deke coldly, as if he was angry with him for bringing up the stuff of nightmares. "It was monsters. Monsters floating over us... big, giant skulls. They burned everything. My mom and dad were in the house, but I was out in the woods with my friends. I ran home when I saw the ships... I don't know what happened to Tim and Georgie. I got to the house and it was gone. And then they started landing. They were like big bugs, kind of." His voice was an emotionless drone, like this was the only way he could let himself remember what had happened. "Like giant scorpions or maybe a praying mantis. They searched through the woods and I heard shooting, I think. Like they were killing anyone they came across. That's why I went in the root cellar. It was kind of covered by the snow and I figured they wouldn't find me."

"How long ago was this, Luke?" Vicky asked, sitting down beside him on the fold-down medical exam table in the utility bay and slipping an arm around his shoulder. The kid shied away but settled down when she squeezed him in a warm hug. "You can tell me. It's okay."

"I don't know," Luke admitted, shaking his head. "I slept a lot because I was so hungry. The roots... I tried to eat them, but they were too hard and I couldn't cook them. I didn't have nothing to start a fire with. I tried soaking them in water, but they just froze up at night so there was nothing to eat. Except snow."

Vicky nodded, patting him on the arm.

I should have said something, should have asked him pertinent questions or come up with a plan of action... but I couldn't move. I couldn't think. I just saw it over and over again, a constant replay inside my head of my mother falling away from me, blood streaming down her chest. Heard the screams of my father and brother as the bandits killed them while I hid.

"Alvarez," Deke said, and by the tone of his voice it wasn't the first time he'd called my name. I blinked the memories away.

"Yeah?"

"I said, I checked the transmitter. The InStell ComSat is gone. They must have taken it out. We have to get through to the next connection and call home, and that's almost an AU out from this world."

I remembered that an AU was an astronomical unit, the distance between the Earth and the sun, though I only had a vague idea that it was about 150 million kilometers, and I shrugged.

"Yeah, get us into orbit. We can micro-Transition out to the gate, right?"

"No, we can't," he snapped as if I should have known. "You can't Transition that close to a jumpgate. The spacetime distortion prevents a stable wormhole from forming. It's going to take us over forty-eight hours to get to the gate at one gravity. We need to leave now." He frowned aside at Luke. "We really should boost at maximum Gs, but..."

Oh. I got it. And I didn't like it.

"Luke," I said, not taking my eyes off Deke, "we need to leave here, and we're taking you with us. But we're going to have to go really fast, and that's going to make you feel like you weigh twice as much as you normally do." Actually, a little more than that, since Hudson Bay's gravity was a fraction under Earth-normal, but there was no use worrying the kid. "You might want to go to the bathroom first, because you won't have the chance for a while after we take off. Okay?"

"I'll show you where it is," Vicky said, taking Luke's hand and leading him back up the passage toward the head. He stopped just a few steps out of the utility bay, turning back to us.

"What about my friends, Tim and Georgie?" He shook his head. "They might be out there somewhere. Or other people who got away from the bugs. It's... it's cold out there. They might need your help too."

I shared a look with Vicky over the kid's shoulder, caught the sad resignation in her expression. I didn't even need to look at Deke to know what his answer would be.

"We looked," I told Luke. "I'm sorry, but we couldn't find anybody except you."

His shoulders sagged and he stared down at the deck.

"After he's done," I told Vicky, "find him a seat and get him strapped in. And make sure he has food and water close if he needs it."

"I have an emergency shelter in the crash kit," Deke told me once the kid was out of earshot. "We leave him with a heater, spare clothes, enough food for a couple weeks, and I can push the *Dutchman* to three Gs. More if you two take anesthetics and go into a medical coma for a few hours."

"No," I said, turning my back on him and striding toward the cockpit.

"It's my ship," he said with quiet menace, a few steps behind me yet sounding as if he were leaning right beside my ear. "And you two may be colonels in name, but I don't know you and I don't trust you, which in my book means I'm in command out here. Colonel McIntire will support whatever decision I make... no matter who I decide to leave behind."

Calculating, cold fury pulsed in my veins, searching for ways I could kill him if the need arose. Unfortunately, even with the aid of Jim, I came to the conclusion that the only way to beat him would be to shoot him in his sleep, and even that wasn't a sure thing.

"Sure," I agreed, trying very hard not to let that conclusion show in my expression. "You can get away with whatever you want... out here. Because you're the badass supercommando with the enhancement and augmentation and the jacked reflexes. But what about when you get back, Deke? What happens when you tell *my* Marines that you left me behind? What happens when you tell *my* crew on the *Ellen* that you left us here and decided to take us out of the picture? Do you think that the only company of Drop Troopers in the entire Cluster is going to stick with you, that they're buying into the bullshit you're selling about how this is the government now and they have to follow orders?" I took a step toward him, very aware of how easily he could rip my guts out with those talons. "Because we've been on our own a *long* time, and there's only one man's orders they're sure to follow." I shrugged. "Captain Nance loves being the master of his ship and he's not too picky about where he flies or it or who gives him the orders, but he trusts me. His crew trusts me. I gave them all multiple chances to go the easy way, to leave me behind when I was infected by the Transformation Virus, and they wouldn't do it. So, yeah, you can do whatever the hell you want... as long as you're okay with your decision costing your new Commonwealth military its most advanced warship and its only armored Marines. I'm sure Munroe wouldn't have a problem with that, right?"

Deke's face darkened, a storm front advancing across the afternoon sky.

"Fine, Alvarez. We'll do it your way. But I'll tell you what, your little do-gooder act costs us vital time, and if we wind up letting thousands or tens of thousands of people die because you wanted to make sure one kid doesn't get lonely, well…" he raised his fist up between us and a pair of matte-gray talons flicked out of his wrist, so close to my face that I couldn't focus on the tips of them. "All those Marines and that fancy ship of yours won't save you from me."

I didn't flinch, didn't move, just held his eyes until he retracted the blades and pushed past me. I waited until he was well out of sight before I let out the breath I'd been holding in a long sigh. I was right, I knew it. I was *not* going to leave that kid alone on a dead world just to save a few hours of travel time. A few hours either way wasn't going to make a difference in all this.

I hoped.

[24]

"At least the ComSat is still here," Deke murmured, and I envied him for having the breath and energy to do it.

A full day, twenty-four hours, at two gravities before we'd hit the jumpgate except for five-minute breaks every two hours to hit the head and stretch our legs to prevent blood clots, had left me wrung out and exhausted. I hadn't thought it would be this bad, but I felt like someone had worked me over with a baseball bat, and what was worse was that I hadn't gotten a wink of sleep the whole time. I'd tried, but every time my head had tilted to the side a sharp muscle pain had woken me up, and pride had kept me from asking Deke if he had any muscle relaxants in his medical kit. As a final kick in the ass, the kid had slept through most of the flight like it was nothing.

Maybe it *was* nothing compared to what he'd just been through, or maybe it had more to do with the fact that he was going from forty kilos to eighty while I was going from eighty to a hundred and sixty, but the minute Deke had cut thrust on the other side of the jumpgate, then rolled us over for a gentle, one-gee braking burn, Luke had popped up and scampered to the head before one of us could beat him to it. Vicky watched him go with the hint of a smile and I wondered if she was thinking—as I sometimes did—about the children we might have had while we'd been bouncing around the galaxy from one crisis to another.

"Not that there's anything *else* left in this system," Deke added, though I wasn't sure if he was talking to us or himself. He hadn't been very talkative during the trip, despite being the only one of us who the added weight didn't really bother. "Fucking Changed wiped out everything."

Sylvanus had once been a thriving Periphery world, though I'd never had the chance to visit. The architecture in the vids and images reminded me of southern Europe... or at least southern Europe from two or three centuries ago. I was glad I didn't have to look at it now. I'd seen enough devastation and death and didn't need reminding of the nightmare we'd walked into when we'd arrived back in the Cluster. There were probably still people down there on that green and blue world, living in hovels, slowly descending into barbarism, waiting for someone to come rescue them. No matter what I'd threatened Deke with, I knew I couldn't bring myself to abandon those people.

"We're connecting to the ComSat," Deke said, and this time it was clear he'd overcome his mad and was talking to the two of us. "You got anything you want to say, *Colonel*?"

The glare he gave me could have peeled paint, but it was nowhere near as threatening as the talons.

"Hit record," I told him. He tapped a control and motioned invitingly to me. "Munroe," I said, "this is Alvarez. We have a problem. The colony at Hudson Bay has been wiped out, and from the testimony of one of the survivors, it's a good bet it was done by the Unity. We need the *Ellen* out here to pick us up and start running patrols to figure out where they are and where they're heading. Their drive works kind of like the one on the *Ellen*, which means they'll likely be heading for..."

I froze in mid-sentence and turned to Deke, making a throat-slashing gesture.

"It's paused," he said. "What is it?"

"Bring up a star map."

His scowl showed exactly what he thought about me giving him orders, but he did it anyway. I shook my head impatiently as a Transition Line diagram came up.

"No, a map of *real* space. Straight-line distances."

The scowl softened into a thoughtful frown, and Deke scrolled through a menu before trying again. The image shifted, and so did the positions of the populated systems. Transition Lines didn't follow the normal curve of spacetime, and while a physicist might have been able to explain the way the gravito-inertial lines of force they *did* follow related to real space, I couldn't. At least, I couldn't since I'd lost my connection to the Network. But even I could see the straight-line distance between the Hudson Bay and the nearest habitable system.

Hausos.

"Oh, sweet Jesus," Vicky hissed.

"Get me back on," I told Deke, and this time he didn't question it, just un-paused the recording.

"Get the *Ellen* out to Hausos as quick as she can go. We think the Unity is heading there. Cram every fucking Drop Trooper, Force Recon Marine, and mercenary soldier you can into her, along with every heavy weapon you have. If we don't stop them here, they'll roll up every single inhabited system and wipe out what's left of the human race." I had to pause because I'd run out of breath, the reality of what I'd told them hitting me all at once. Forcing myself to pause and calm down, I tried again. "Don't bother sending anything that can't fit in the *Ellen*, because it would take a couple weeks to arrive and this is all going to be over long before that. Keep everything else there, pull your cruiser and all your other warships back to Demeter. And pray."

I nodded to Deke and he stopped the recording. He shook his head as if he had to compose himself before he hit the control to send the message, as if the contents wouldn't be real until he did. We all waited until the return signal came from the ComSat, the cheerful ping telling us that the transmission had been sent through to the next jumpgate, the next relay, before anyone looked away from the panel.

And found Luke staring at us, his face pale, eyes wide.

"Is that really what's going to happen?" he asked, a quaver making its way through his attempt to keep his voice steady. "Those... bug things are going to kill everyone?"

No one wanted to answer him at first, but another thought struck me, an idea that I'd heard long before the Marines, all the way back to my first group home. There'd been a teacher there, one of the few people who'd actually shown real interest in making my life better. Mrs. Calhoun. She hadn't been enough, hadn't been there when classes got out and the bullying started, but she'd given me a good piece of advice once.

If you have one problem, you have to solve it. If you have two problems, sometimes they can solve each other.

Jim, I said, *please tell me that when you communed with Illyana, before you split yourself off, that you got some information first.*

She was quite insistent that I not share that data with you or anyone else, Jim said.

Jim, you either share this with me or I'll go back to Demeter and have you ripped out of my fucking head, and I don't care if it lobotomizes me.

The AI sighed.

Very well.

And I *knew*. He didn't have to tell me, I just knew.

"Not if we can help it," I answered Luke's question. "Deke, get this boat ready for Transition."

He shot me a vexed glare.

"You know we can't jump back to the wormhole. It works the same on this side as it did on the other."

"We're not going back to Hausos," I told him. "Not yet. The *Ellen* by herself isn't going to be enough. We have to get help."

"And who the hell is going to help us?" Deke demanded. "There's nobody out there! There's nothing else left!"

"There's the biggest fleet in the entire Cluster left," I corrected him. "And we're going to go get it."

"How the hell did you find this place?" Deke asked, shaking his head.

I didn't answer right away because I figured the question was rhetorical, and because this was the tenth time he'd asked it in the last three days.

"It's pretty," Luke said, floating behind us, one hand anchored on the back of Vicky's chair as he stared at the fearsome purple visage of the gas giant in the cockpit viewscreen.

"You need to strap in," Vicky scolded him. "What if we have to maneuver?"

"But it's fun!" the kid protested. He'd taken to space travel *and* free fall like a natural and hadn't even minded sleeping on a fold-down cot in the utility bay. I thought maybe the strangeness of the whole thing had been good for keeping his mind off his family. "Is this really the place where you met the machine lady?"

"Cyborg," I corrected him. "And yes, it is."

"I *still* haven't got a good answer as to how you managed to find this place the first try," Deke said insistently. "I had it narrowed down to four different possible systems, and the odds you'd pick the right one on the first try…"

"Four to one?" I guessed, offering him a grin. "That's not that bad odds, is it?"

"You wouldn't guess," Deke said, utterly confident. "Not about something like this."

"I thought you said you didn't know me or trust me," I reminded him, still with no intention of answering.

"We got company," Vicky announced a half-second before the tactical board's sensor alarms told the same story with their unrelenting beeping. "Luke, get in your seat and strap in."

"Stupid bringing a kid on an op," Deke muttered.

The ship the sensor had picked up was a shuttle, I determined by the time Luke had pulled on his safety harness. Burning from what had likely been an orbital patrol at around two gravities, its tail on fire with a flare of the plasma drive.

"Think we should go meet the little tugboat?" Deke asked, smirking at the cargo shuttle. "Get close enough to make him think he might hurt us with his mining laser and coilgun?"

"No, this should be close enough," I said. "Any second now…"

"Unidentified spacecraft." The transmission came over the cockpit speakers, tinny and crackling from the radiation field of the gas giant. "This is restricted space and you are not permitted to proceed any farther. Turn back and Transition out of here, or you'll be destroyed. This is your one and only warning."

"Tell Kan-Zin Tel that this is Cam Alvarez," I replied. "Tell him it's a matter of survival. Not just ours, but yours too."

"How the hell did a Tahni wind up working for Fleet Intelligence anyway?" Vicky asked under her breath while we waited for a reply.

"You'd be surprised," Deke said with a snort. "We're an equal-opportunity employer. We'll use anyone."

"Alvarez." It was Kan-Zin Tel's voice, filtered through the same wall of static. No video, probably because of signal degradation. "I said I'd contact you. And how the hell did you find this location?"

"Not important. There's an alien threat that's wiping out human colonies. They already killed everyone on Hudson Bay, human and Tahni. We need help. We need Illyana."

If he'd been human, Kan-Zin Tel might have laughed, I thought, but since he was Tahni, all I got was a moment of silence before he gave me the denial I expected.

"I don't know you well enough to determine if you're lying or simply deranged. Either way, the answer is the same. Leave here. Any meeting with Illyana will not be one you enjoy. I'd rather not kill you, and believe me, everyone else here is encouraging me not to allow you to leave since you know our location."

I sighed.

"Then send her, Kan-Zin Tel. Because I'm not leaving until I talk to her."

"There is a saying among humans," he replied, sadness in his voice. "It's your funeral."

The transmission cut off, and Deke goggled at me in disbelief.

"I thought you said he couldn't control her!"

"He can't," I agreed. "He can tell her to blow us up, but she doesn't have to listen."

"Well, what if she fucking *wants* to listen?"

"Language," Vicky cautioned him sternly, eyeing Luke.

"Who's Illyana?" the boy asked brightly.

"Oh, I think you're about to find out, kid," Deke said, pointing at the sensors.

He was right about that. Not a dozen of them this time

though. Just one. Coming straight at us at forty gravities, but just one.

Jim, help me out here.

I'll have to coopt this ship's communications system, the AI explained. *Your friend may detect it.*

Do what you have to do.

And that tricky son of a bitch did. Without even a little warning, I was gone from the cockpit and back in the gray haze. Along with Illyana and Jim. She was no longer naked though, and Jim... was no longer a Bronze-Age barbarian. Both of them wore glowing white robes that seemed more illusion than reality, which I suppose they would be, and Jim's face was clean-shaven.

"You've returned," Illyana said, smiling beatifically, her expression less vacant and wooden than her previous incarnation. "I didn't expect you back."

"Has Jim told you about the Unity?" I asked her.

"Everything he knows, I know," she confirmed. And wasn't *that* comforting? Jim hadn't said a word, wouldn't even meet my eyes.

"They're here," I said urgently. "They've arrived in the Cluster and already wiped out the entire population of one of colony worlds. I think they're heading next for a world called Hausos. There are tens of thousands of innocent people there, and we won't be able to protect them without your help."

"Jim and I have discussed autonomy," Illyana said, nodding to the Predecessor AI. "Choice. Agency. He's convinced me that I am a free being, not simply a servant to the biologicals."

Oh, great, thanks a bunch, Jim. You couldn't have taught her about the Emancipation Proclamation after *she helped us beat the Unity?*

It's not strictly me *anymore,* the AI equivocated.

I think I made that point earlier and you told me not to worry.

"You're not a servant to anyone," I agreed, spreading my hands in acknowledgement. "But we biologicals *did* create you. You owe your existence to us." *Even though we had no idea you existed and probably would have put your inventors to death if we'd known about it.* "That doesn't make you our slave, but it does kind of make you our child, part of our family. We biologicals like to help our family when they're in trouble."

I knew from previous experience that this was all happening in just a second or two of realtime, and I wondered if Deke would notice that something was going on. I hoped by the time it was over, I could figure out a way to explain it.

"I understand your point, Cameron," Illyana said, pacing around me, forcing me to turn to keep an eye on her. I didn't *think* there was anything she could do to me, that this connection was purely mental, but old habits died hard. "And I would feel obliged to aid you and your people... if I believed it was possible without destroying myself." She stopped beside me and put a hand on my shoulder. And I *felt* it, which was incredibly disturbing, since that meant she might actually be able to hurt me even here, in the confines of my thoughts. "You see, among the valuable information I gleaned from Jim's database was the combat capacity of the Unity as extrapolated from what you observed on Waterline."

I glared at Jim—or the avatar of the cloned version of Jim who'd stayed behind with Illyana—but he didn't look up. In fact, he didn't seem responsive at all, just swaying side to side like a willow in the breeze.

"What the hell is wrong with him?" I asked her.

"Jim has been..." she shrugged as if trying to think of the appropriate word, which had to be theater, considering what she was, "... *subsumed*, I suppose. Absorbed into my neural network. He's part of me now."

That's not possible, the Jim inside my head declared. *My hardware and software are centuries more advanced than hers.*

Well, unless you have a better explanation, there it is, I told him.

"If I were to attempt to fight the Unity," Illyana went on, her hand sliding off my arm, "all of my current assets would be destroyed. And since Marakit no longer exists, my prospects of receiving new materials to manufacture more are no longer certain."

Considering my response, I walked around Jim's mute avatar, hesitantly put a hand out to shake his shoulder. He started, jerking like he'd been hit with an electric shock, and his eyes flickered toward me, but he still didn't speak.

"What if we promised to bring you more raw materials?" I asked her, desperation overcoming good sense, both because I knew that wasn't a good idea but even more so because I was very well aware of how difficult it would be to get Munroe to sign off on something like this. "If you come to our aid, the Commonwealth government has the mining and production assets to provide you ore, processed fuel, whatever you need."

"Promises are worth only as much as the belief one has in the word of the one making them." Illyana looked me up and down. "I believe, from what Jim has told me, that you are an honorable man when dealing with other biologicals but that you distrust sentient cyberbeings due to your experience with them outside the Cluster, despite the fact that they have saved your life multiple times."

"I don't distrust AI any more than I distrust people. It's not in my nature to trust anyone I don't know. But I do trust people —whether they're biological or not—to do what's in their own best interest. If you help us, it's in our best interest to keep you prepared to meet new threats, because we sure as hell don't have the capability to do it ourselves."

"I would like to help you," she said, shaking her head, "but I won't take that chance. Perhaps you are family, but to carry that analogy, you've been an absentee parent and now you're coming to me only because you require aid. You won't get it here." She motioned outward. "You're welcome to stay in this system if you believe it to be safe. I won't attack you, no matter what Kan-Zin Tel commands. I don't serve him, but neither do I serve you. Don't attempt to contact me again. I will not reply."

Like waking up from a dream, I returned abruptly to the cockpit of the *Dutchman II*, Deke, Vicky, and Luke staring at me with varying degrees of doubt and hope in their eyes.

"You talked to her," Vicky guessed. "What did she say?"

I sighed, let my head sag, hope abandoning me along with nervous energy.

"Take us back to Hausos, Deke. We're on our own."

[25]

I cinched the tactical vest tighter, wishing everything on this boat hadn't already been pre-adjusted to fit Deke Conner's measurements. I generally didn't feel inadequate even next to Force Recon Marines who spent all their off time in the ship's gym, but this just didn't seem fair.

"What happens if we get there too late?" Vicky asked from the other side of the utility bay. She'd already gone through the headache of reconfiguring a set of tactical armor to fit her and sat in front of a weapons locker, sorting through the choices. "What if the *Ellen...* couldn't handle them and we've already lost?"

She pulled out a pulse carbine and regarded it with a critical eye, then shoved it back into the locker.

"Then we try to help any survivors and get back to Demeter as quickly as possible." The vest was as tight as it was going to get, and I took a moment to pull on a pair of armored gloves, then grabbed a helmet and shut the locker. "They'll have to evacuate. They don't have enough ships to fight the Unity."

"They won't have enough ships to evacuate either," she pointed out, not looking at me, instead checking the load on a

Gauss rifle. "Even if they bring back everything, they've taken in too many refugees. And where would they go that the Unity wouldn't follow, eventually?"

"One disaster at a time," I said, frowning at the massive, bulky weapon stashed beside the Gauss rifle. I tried to pull it out but nearly strained a back muscle. "What the hell *is* this thing?"

"Electron beamer."

I turned at the unexpected voice and Deke Conner leaned past me, yanking the weapon out of the rack one-handed, tossing it around like it weighed nothing. He shot me a grin.

"You should probably leave that one to me. You should also go strap in. We Transition in five minutes."

I swore under my breath and grabbed the other Gauss rifle and a bandolier of magazines to go with it, slammed the locker shut, and followed the two of them to the bridge. Luke was already there, sprawled across a fold-down acceleration couch, watching a movie on a tablet and snacking on a ration bar. I didn't think I'd seen the kid go for more than two hours without eating since he'd come on board. He hadn't spoken about his family or friends at all, and I didn't know if that was a good or bad thing for him, but it was probably better for us since we had a lot more pressing matters to deal with.

Luke turned at our approach, his eyebrows going up at the sight of the weapons.

"Do I need a gun?" he asked, not with the naïve eagerness I would have expected from a boy his age raised on an isolated colony but more with anxiety and a hint of real fear.

"No," Vicky said gently but firmly, grabbing his hand and squeezing it. "But you do need to put your safety harness on. We're about to come out of T-space."

"I never thought I'd get to ride in a starship," he said softly as he strapped in. "I never figured I'd even get to fly to one of the other settlements."

Deke said nothing, securing that ungodly heavy beamer in a bracket beside his seat before he tapped a rhythm on the control panel.

"Transitioning now."

I held on tight to the Gauss rifle, hoping we wouldn't have to do any violent maneuvering, worried enough I barely noticed the actual jump. The virtual star map in the front viewer switched to an optical view of the planet we'd left not that long ago, and...

"Nothing," Deke sighed. "It's normal. I can see the energy readings from the fusion reactors, thermal signatures from vehicles, people. No orbital activity."

"Take us down," I told him. I should have felt relieved, but the tension refused to dissipate. "Fuck the landing field, take us right into the center of Gamma Junction."

"Oh, I'm sure they'll love that."

The trip from minimum safe jump distance to orbit was over an hour, interminably long, yet none of us said a word through the flight, and if Deke received any traffic control transmissions, he didn't bother to answer them. It was night on this side of the planet, a few hours past dusk, and a stiff wind jostled the cutter on the way down. Normally, both would have been annoying, but maybe the sight of the landing jets burning bright in the darkness would draw more attention quicker than just another cutter touching down at the landing field in broad daylight.

There was only one spot in the town broad enough for a cutter the size of the *Dutchman II* to land, and that was in the central courtyard outside city hall. The scream of the jets had already drawn people out of downtown houses and shops, the motion of the tiny figures magnified and enhanced by the optical and thermal sensors, showing every detail of their alarmed expressions. Those expressions became even more alarmed when the exhaust from the belly thrusters ripped away the awnings over the city hall windows and sent roof tiles flying.

People didn't rush the ship, like I thought they might, maybe because they were afraid it might be armed. It was, of course. I'd seen the loadout of the *Dutchman II* on the trip, since it was something that might be very important very soon. Ventral proton cannon with the emitter beneath the nose, Gatling laser turret on the portside wing, just like the missile cutters during the war. No missiles in this bird though, and I thought that was likely because the *Dutchman II* wouldn't often be able to count on resupply.

I didn't wait for the folks outside to make up their mind, hurrying in silence to the ramp, lowering it before the jets had even had the chance to cycle down. The first one to grab their balls and approach the ship was, to no one's surprise, Bob. He'd grabbed a handgun from somewhere, though it was nothing that would have penetrated the armor I wore. That didn't keep him from pointing it at me, and I realized he wouldn't recognize me in the dark, even if I hadn't been wearing my helmet visor down for the night vision. I pushed it up and held my rifle out to my side.

"Bob, it's me," I told him. "Cam Alvarez."

"What the *fuck* are you doing landing here in town, Cam?" he demanded, not slowing down, though he did lower his gun.

"Bob, you need to evacuate the town," I told him. "There's enemy on the way, and I don't know how long you have."

"Enemy?" The portly man shook his head. "*What* enemy? You didn't piss off the Tahni, did you?"

"Listen closely," I sighed, about to launch into my briefing when another few dozen people, emboldened by the fact Bob had approached without dying, ran up as well.

"What the hell is happening, Bob?" one of them asked, and I finally lost my patience.

"Everyone, listen!" I barked, then continued quickly into the silence, projecting and enunciating every word. "We went to Hudson Bay to report back via their ComSat. The entire colony was destroyed and everyone was dead. This is the next system in line, and we have reason to believe the force in question is coming here and may arrive at any time."

Frankly, it was a damned miracle they hadn't already, and I had to believe it was because they weren't in any particular hurry.

"Evacuate to where?" Bob asked, waving his hands, which wasn't the safest thing to do since one of them held a pistol. "The other settlements are days away overland, and there's not enough aircraft to get more than a handful enough of us to..."

"Bob," I interrupted, grabbing his gun hand and pushing it downward. "Every single settlement on Hudson Bay was gone. You need to get people out of the city and into the forests. Maybe..." I searched my memory, "... Hauser Caverns? The caves out in the Marshall Hills? They need to be away from town, away from even the ranches and farmhouses, and you need to get the word out to everyone. Get warm clothes, food, water, and any tents or camping gear you can get your hands on and get going immediately."

"You can't be serious!" someone I couldn't make out with my visor up yelled from the back of the pack. "You expect us to drop everything in the middle of the harvest just on your word and run out into the woods?"

"I'll tell you what the fuck I expect!" I yelled back at whoever it was. "I expect most of you to ignore me. Then I expect a fleet of ships bigger than the biggest Fleet cruiser to descend into the atmosphere and start blowing the shit out of every single man-made structure on this planet. And after that, a bunch of creatures that look like a scorpion fucked a brahma bull are going to land here and comb through the wreckage and kill any survivors they find. I expect the population of this planet to go down by about ninety percent."

Silence. Shock, probably, as what I said penetrated their outrage and disbelief. I grabbed Bob by the shoulder and made sure he was close enough to see my eyes in the light from the open belly ramp of the ship.

"Bob, you don't have to believe me, but if I'm wrong, all you've lost is a few hours, maybe a couple days max of people being uncomfortable and embarrassed. If I'm right, and you don't do anything, you'll have killed all your friends and neighbors. You won't go down in history as the biggest idiot in the world, but that'll only be because there won't be anyone left to write the history."

The stocky man nodded, and if there wasn't confidence in his eyes, there was at least honest fear.

"All right, Cam. I'll spread the word, do what I can. I can't promise everyone will listen."

"Cam!" Vicky yelled from the top of the ramp, desperation tinging her voice. "Deke says his sensors are picking up anomalous gravitational and electromagnetic readings approaching from off the ecliptic! It's gotta be the Unity!"

Desperation froze my blood and I staggered a step. I'd known it was coming, yet the reality of it still rocked me. Slugging my brain into gear again, I knew there was only one question I had to answer. Should we stay here on the ground and try to organize the citizenry into evacuating, or should we head for orbit and try to fight? Either way was likely suicide.

But suicide sitting on the ground waiting for some alien hive mind to burn me to a crisp like an ant under a kid's magnifying glass seemed a hell of a lot worse than suicide shoving proton beams down their throats.

"We're heading upstairs," I told her, but paused on the ramp and turned back to Bob. "Spread the word and get out of town. You don't have much time."

None of us did.

"They've slowed down," Deke said, fingers tapping the beat from the same century-old pop song he'd played over and over during the flight from Hudson Bay. "I guess they're checking things out."

"That sounds like the Unity," I agreed. "Prolonging the agony so we all know we're going to die and can't do a damned thing about it."

We were at the edge of minimum safe Transition distance from Hausos, the world a green and blue baseball over our port shoulder, her moon barely a dot against her half-lit curve. And the Unity were millions of kilometers farther out, nearly halfway to the next planet in the system. Not visible on the optical spectrum as anything more than the barest glint of sunlight off metal, but burning bright on thermal and showing all too much detail on the gravimetic sensors.

"There's not enough of them," Vicky observed, peering at the readout, frowning. "When they hit us at Waterline, there were hundreds of ships. This is barely forty... maybe forty-five?"

"Can't tell for sure," Deke admitted. "They're too far away."

"A scouting mission, maybe?" I guessed. "Feeling us out?"

"Or maybe just one part of a larger force they've spread out all through the Cluster," Vicky suggested, and I really didn't want to consider that.

"If that's so, they could already be at Demeter."

"If they are," Deke said, "there's nothing we can do about it. Shit, there ain't a hell of a lot we can do about this."

"We'll be okay here though, won't we?" Luke asked, voice

tremulous. I looked back at him, guilt stabbing through my chest.

I'd kicked around the idea of leaving him with Bob or Grace and her family, but it came down to the fact that we couldn't do anything to protect them and we might have been kicking him out of the frying pan and into the fire. Maybe Deke was right and we should have left him on Hudson Bay. Of course, if we died here, that would have meant leaving him to starve to death eventually. Maybe it came down to the reality that we were all going to die, and the only choice was fast or slow.

"Yeah, we'll be fine, Luke," I lied. "If things get bad, we can just Transition out of here, right, Deke?"

"Yeah, no problem at all," Deke said, and though any adult would have picked up the sarcasm in his reply, I didn't think Luke was sophisticated enough at twelve years old. "But why the hell are they still sitting out there? This makes no fucking sense."

"Language," Vicky warned him again, and Deke scowled.

"Yeah, that's the worst thing that's gonna happen to this kid, learning some new cuss words." He waved the scolding off and jabbed a finger at the sensor screen where the Unity fleet approached at a glacial pace. "It's gonna take them hours to get here, and from what you told me, they could make it in minutes. Maybe seconds. What are they waiting for?"

"Us," I said, the realization as stomach-twisting as the free fall. "They know we called for help. That's why they hit Hudson Bay. They *want* us to bring our forces to one place so they can take them all out at once."

No sooner had the revelation hit me than the sensors lit up with the announcement of another anomalous reading heading into the system at hyperlight speeds. Just one this time, and we all knew exactly what it was.

"It's the *Ellen*," Vicky sighed, and not from relief. "She's here."

"You were right, Cam," Deke admitted, nodding at the screen. The cluster of Unity ships had finally sped up, moving at what looked like a hundred gravities of acceleration. "They're coming."

I nodded wordlessly and commandeered his communications console, aiming the laser line-of-sight transmitter at the *Ellen*.

"Commonwealth warship *Ellen Campbell*, this is Colonel Alvarez on the Fleet Intelligence vessel *Flying Dutchman II*. Do you copy?"

"*Dutchman*, this is the *Ellen Campbell*," Chase replied. It was good to hear a familiar voice. "We have good copy. We also have enemy inbound. What are your orders?"

"Meet us at the landing field outside Gamma Junction," I decided. "If this is gonna be the last battle, I want to fight it inside a Vigilante, leading my Marines."

[26]

"They're gonna be on top of us in half an hour," Captain Nance told me, pouncing like an ambush predator the second the three of us had boarded the *Ellen*, barely sparing a curious glance for Luke, as if bringing a twelve-year-old onto a warship about to do battle was among the *least* crazy things I'd done since we'd known each other.

We'd landed the *Dutchman II* just a hundred meters from the *Ellen*, and I tried to imagine what the gathered citizenry of Gamma Junction would have thought of the massive, alien starship setting down as light as a feather without so much as bending a blade of grass. They were too busy to offer the miracle the attention it deserved though. We'd spotted them on the way down, hordes of people on foot, in cargo trucks, or even aboard horse-drawn wagons, following dirt tracks or game trails or sometimes just blazing a new path through the tall grass and fields of wheat and corn. Thousands of them. Tens of thousands.

They'd listened, and I suppose that was some comfort.

"The second we have the Marines off the ship," I told Nance, not slowing down, forcing him to jog to keep up as we headed for the other end of the *Ellen* where the armory had been wedged into her, "you get into high orbit. Keep the Unity away from the surface as long as you can. Leave your Intercepts here. Major Conners is going to stay in low orbit with them and provide air support." I paused, turning, and Nance stopped abruptly, out of breath. "This is Luke. He was the only survivor we found on Hudson Bay and, frankly, there's been no safe place to leave him."

"He could go with the civilians here..." Nance suggested, but I cut him off.

"They're not safe," I declared flatly. "Nowhere here is safe. This ship is the best I can do and yes, I know it's not really safe here either. Put Luke as close to the center of the *Ellen* as possible, give him a vacc suit, and assign someone to take care of him. If you live through this, I expect him to, you got me?"

"Yeah..." Nance blanched at the glare I offered him and tried again. "Aye, sir."

"Luke," Vicky said, kneeling beside the boy, "go with Captain Nance and do exactly what he tells you to do. Okay?"

"I'm scared, Vicky," the kid admitted, though to his credit he didn't start whining or bawling. He would cry eventually, I knew that firsthand, but he'd kept it inside at least in front of us. "Can't I just stay with you and Cam?"

"We're going to be outside, in our suits, fighting the aliens," I told him. "This is the best place for you right now. Can you stay here for me and be good until we get back?"

"What happens if you don't come back?" he asked, belligerence rising to try to camouflage the terror I knew he felt. "What happens to me?"

"You'll be okay, Luke," I said. "Back on Demeter, there are a lot of families who'll take you in. They're good people, and I know the boss there. Guy named Munroe—he's like the president, sort of. Tell him I sent you and he'll take care of you."

Luke nodded, didn't pull away when Vance took his hand and led him away. I took one last look at the kid, remembering another lost boy on a world that no longer existed, and continued through the ship. It wasn't crowded in the hallways, not like the *Orion*, but once we reached the armory it was standing room only. And I knew this audience.

"Sir!" newly-minted Captain Springfield said, sounding way too cheerful given the circumstances. "Ma'am! I'm glad you're okay!"

I'd never seen so many battlesuits packed into this small a space, but I'd asked for the entire company, and that was what they'd given me. Vigilantes stood shoulder to shoulder, with barely room for their chest plastrons to open, and Marines had to squeeze past each other to enter their suits

"Thanks, Springfield," I said, peeling off my tactical armor and tossing it carelessly into a corner. "Glad to see you too. And glad to see *these*," I added, nodding at the suits. "I've had enough of my bare skin being the only thing between me and hot metal."

"Sir!" It was Kenna, one of the Vergai recruits, a big grin plastered across his face, a new buzzcut decorating his head. "Check it out!" He tapped the sides of his head at the temple where fresh 'face jacks had been implanted. "Back on Demeter, they fitted all us Vergai with jacks and now we can control the suits just like you!"

"That's great, Kenna!" I tried to sound more enthusiastic than I was, because I knew how much it meant to them. The Vergai had always worried they weren't *real* Drop Troopers because they lacked the implant jacks, but I'd sort of envied them the ability to change their fate and not be constantly reminded of what they were. "Glad you guys had the time for that."

"And our suits all have plasma guns now, sir!" Brevet,

another of the Kergai, told me, smacking the weapon mounted on the left arm of his Vigilante. "No more of those underpowered coilguns."

Now *that* I was enthusiastic about. Having a weapon that could run out of ammo wasn't ideal for any situation, but particularly not today.

"Good. Let's make the most of it. Everyone, suit up and unass this ship so they can go do their best to make sure we don't have too many of these bastards to fight. Believe me, they're going to be hard enough to handle as it is. Listen to your squad leaders and keep moving, and make sure you shoot every one of the bastards you see, whether they've already been shot or not. Got me?"

"Hoo-yah, sir!" The chorus came from the Vergai mostly, though I knew the others felt the same way. They'd just seen too much to be zealous about it.

So had I.

It had been dark not that long ago. Hours before dawn, no moon in the sky, cloud cover, as dark as the inside of an elephant's asshole. Not anymore. The Vigilante was friend and lover, holding me in her arms, keeping me safe and warm and lighting up the world. Every centimeter of Gamma Junction was clearly delineated, standing out like the computer graphics blueprint... even from a couple kilometers away.

"We're really gonna let them destroy the city, sir?" Springfield asked over our private channel.

She was nearly a klick down the tree line where we'd taken cover, and even though we were under radio silence, Springfield could still signal me with laser line-of-sight by passing the transmission down the line from one suit to another.

"Hopefully it won't come to that, but if even one of their ships get through the Intercept cordon, they'll wipe the floor with us if they see us. If that happens, our only chance is to let them take out the buildings. After that, they'll send troops down to check for survivors. If we're going to protect the civilians, we have to take out those ground troops. And if we're going to live through it, we have to take them out under the concealment of the trees."

"I get it, sir," she assured me. "I just feel like these people are going to lose everything they have."

"Not their lives. Their lives are all that really matter."

"Hey, Cam, you down there?" Deke asked. I blinked. So much for radio silence. "You don't have to answer. I know you don't want to give up your position. But I figure you want to keep tabs on what's going on up here, so I'll send the signal down broadband and encrypted and you can follow it." He paused. "Consider it my way of saying I'm sorry for being a dick. I was pissed about you not keeping me in the loop with the Project Rho AI, but it doesn't seem all that important right now. Good luck down there."

I wish I could have told him thanks, but I had other things to think about. The transmission filled a quarter of my helmet's HUD with the view from high orbit, from the cutter *Dutchman II*. It wasn't just optical, because the *Ellen* was too far away for that, outside the orbit of Hausos' moon, but the tactical computer combined the sensors into a complete picture that wasn't too pretty.

The skull ships deployed in multiple globular cluster, still hundreds of thousands of klicks away, yet no less threatening for it. Too damned many of them. Forty, ten in each cluster, spread out over nearly a hundred thousand klicks. The *Ellen* didn't wait for them, doing what I'd instructed, engaging as far away as possible, moving so fast the *Dutchman II*'s sensors had a hard time keeping up with her.

When the weapons struck, they weren't the green-tinted gravitic force beams I was used to from Predecessor ships. Instead, there was a barely perceptible shimmer from the nose of the ship that lashed out at the closest Unity vessel in the nearest of the formations. The skull ship shimmered in tune with the beam as if there was a bubble around it, until that bubble popped and took the spacecraft with it. Nothing spectacular, just a flash of white that formed into a sphere for just a moment until it disappeared.

What the hell is that thing again? I asked Jim.

It's a manipulation of spacetime that mirrors the ship's drive. The Unity ships use a similar drive, and the beam destabilizes their warp bubble until it collapses in on them.

Which was probably simplified, but I was a simple man. What worried me was that the enemy ships probably had the same type of weapons, and they'd have the same range… but Nance, for all his weaknesses, was a hell of a captain, and he'd thought of that too. The *Ellen* banked away like she'd been shot out of a cannon, and when the return fire came, it couldn't keep up with her acceleration.

The front globular formations peeled away after her, losing coherence, though not a unity of purpose of course. Yanayev was at the controls of the *Ellen*, and she made that ship dance like a prima ballerina… or more like one of the figure skaters Vicky liked to watch on the old recordings. Spinning, arcing, leaping across thousands of klicks in seconds while Woj manned the guns. The Unity might have been a powerful hive mind, but it could miss. Woj didn't. He was a sniper, making headshots while racing away in a speeding car.

Go! Go! Take them out!

They're not going to be able to destroy them all in time, Jim informed me, always ready to be a bucket of cold water splashing over my head. *The third cluster formation is making an end run toward orbit.*

He was right, of course. Ten ships, but not all ten entered orbit. Seven of them arrayed in a blocking formation, ready to defend against the *Ellen* if she doubled back to try to stop the attack. The other three made a beeline right for us. But the Intercepts hadn't given up yet. The *Ellen* had packed three of them, one inside her hangar bay, the other two parasites on her hull held on by a jury-rigged magnetic anchors, and the *Dutchman II* made four.

Brandano piloted one, Villanueva another. Their IFFs floated in the display above the sensor icons of the delta-winged craft, and just from that I should have figured they'd play this smart. There was no point in trying to engage the skull ships in a vacuum, not with their incredible speed and maneuverability advantage out there with their warp drives.

Most of those advantages were negated in an atmosphere. Not all, but most. It wasn't a guarantor of survival, but it was all they could hope for. The view from the *Dutchman II* spun into a kaleidoscope of color and motion as she and the other Intercepts dodged beams of energy that were *not* the same weapons the skull ships and the *Ellen* had fired at each other.

The warp beamers wouldn't work this close to a gravity field, Jim said helpfully. *Those are antiproton weapons.*

Oh, that's all.

I couldn't tell what was happening anymore, the gyration of the ship too much to follow, and I switched off the feed, concentrating now on what even my suit's on-board sensors could follow. One of the skull ships had broken through and was descending just above us. Three thousand klicks up and coming down fast. I knew what would happen next and thought about telling the others to get ready for it, but there was no point.

Beams of coruscating energy crackled in the night sky, lightning from the gods, the stuff of myth. Except Gamma Junction was a poor substitute for Sodom and Gomorrah, and the people there had committed no sin worthy of what happened now. The city burned at the atomic level, Cherenkov radiation glowing blue in a halo around where the buildings had been.

Each of them had represented crystallized sweat, days or weeks of work, and now they were gone as if they'd never been. I didn't know if God was still listening, if He had *ever* listened, but I prayed anyway that no one was left inside the city when the beams hit. Certainly nothing was left when they stopped.

"Where are the other two?" Vicky wondered. She had half of the company with her, over on the other side of the hill where the terrain grew rockier and irrationally, I wished she were closer.

"They're going after the other settlement," I guessed. "They didn't leave a damned thing behind on Hudson Bay."

This one had done its job, and when the beams cut off, it nearly vanished in the low clouds. But the thermal dots coming down out of the openings in its belly showed exactly where the skull ship was, along with its next move.

Infantry. Coming down in a ring around where the town had been. They touched down in seconds, floating like leaves in the fall to a gentle landing. I realized I'd been holding my breath and forced myself to stop. It wouldn't help.

"Nobody move," I said, softly as if they might overhear me. "No one break ranks. Wait for them to come to you."

And that they did. There was open plain on the other side of the city, nowhere for survivors to hide, so the bug-things didn't bother with it, all of them coming straight for the tree line. Intent on wiping out every man, woman, and child on this colony, just like they had Hudson Bay. But Hudson Bay didn't have any Marines around.

"Don't forget their personal shields," I warned. "Wait until they're firing before you fire back."

The shields had been very effective against coilguns, but I was hoping they wouldn't prove that efficient when facing the plasma weapons. I was also hoping the Unity wouldn't bother with the same mind-fuckery they'd tried back on Waterline. It had been focused, targeted against each of us using the Unity's access to the Network, but would the hive mind bother now that I lacked any connection to that Network? It had sought revenge against me, personally, for committing genocide against the Skalex, but would it know I was here?

The pale eggshell of the Unity drones didn't seem to shimmer with the sense of unreality I remembered from our last confrontation, though God knew just their physical features were enough to make most people run screaming. There was a lack of symmetry to them, a lack of design, as if they'd been created not by a God as we imagined Him but by some demon of chaos, something at home in the outer darkness. Legs scuttled, arms writhed, and mouths rimmed with cilia shifted and transformed with every movement, going from jagged shark's teeth to wriggling sea worms at volcanic vent.

The weapons they carried bore no resemblance to what their spacecraft fired, biological extensions of their engineered bodies, the muzzles yawning like the maw of some ocean-going predator.

"Goddamn," Vicky murmured. "I'd forgotten how ugly those fuckers were."

"Focus," I told her, but I was thinking the same thing.

The tips of my Vigilante's footpads were twenty meters inside the tree line, and the first of the drones couldn't have been more than twenty meters beyond *that* when they finally spotted us. I sensed it, felt it, an instinct more than a knowledge, borne of some subtle, subconscious cue I wouldn't figure out until later, a shift of stance or a turn of one of those horrifying faces.

"Converge fire on my target!" I blurted, pulling the trigger.

Actinic energy blasted out from me among a chorus of plasma, and in response a hail of mucous-coated slugs splintered tree trunks with the force of atomic annihilation.

The world exploded with the first shots of the last fight, and if we went down, we'd go down swinging.

[27]

No battle plan survives contact with the enemy, and this one was no different.

I'd intended for us to stay inside the tree line, but that wasn't going to work when the tree line no longer existed. Fire and concussion filled every centimeter of existence, and my world shrank down to identified threats on the HUD's tactical display. Just like every other battle I'd ever been in, no different than the Tahni or the Skrela, and suddenly how hideous the Unity drones were wasn't a factor for me.

Jump. Target. Fire. Slide. I couldn't think, and the difference between me and every other Drop Trooper I'd ever met was, I didn't try. It had taken me a long time to figure that out and I no longer tried to fight it, just letting the action flow over me, the details becoming clear only in hindsight.

I'd formed up in the center of the Vergai platoons, figuring they'd need me the most, since only their platoon sergeant and me had the Resscharr-improved suits and weapons, and my own personal strategy had been to cut a swathe down the middle of the enemy and draw them toward me, distracting them from the others. That part of the plan, at least, stayed intact.

The Resscharr energy cannons had two major advantages over the plasma guns the Vergai had been upgraded to, and one of them was the ability to fire almost continuously, at least until they overheated. No waiting for capacitors to recharge, no praying to stay alive in those precious seconds. The other was range, and I took advantage of both, hosing the charging Unity drones with the weapon, weakening their shields, drawing their fire... and opening them up for the others.

Evading their return shots was a secondary objective but one I was very attached to, since it meant my continued existence. Another tactic that I executed instinctively but which came from a train of logic worthy of the hours of consideration I'd given it in the days and weeks previously. The Unity's strength was that the drones acted as one, controlled by a singular mind... and that was also their weakness. A hive mind would act quickly and decisively but also predictably, and it would expect the same of others.

So I didn't. No patterns, no rhythm, just the first motion that entered my mind. Leap, jet, long and high enough that multiple drones targeted me on my natural arc downward. But I didn't take that arc, instead flipping head-downward and boosting straight at the ground, straight into an enemy soldier. My shoulder slammed into the unspeakable horror of one of those cilia-ringed heads and took the entire creature to the ground, finishing it off with a stomp of my boot.

They tried to close in when I took the half-second for the coup-de-grace, but I anticipated that as well, skating across the ground, leaning forward and blasting the jets at half-power. The Unity didn't give a shit about killing pieces of itself and enemy fire followed me, the detonations of the biological slugs destroying ten or twelve of the things.

That part of the plan worked too well. I had a half a

second's warning, not from my own instincts this time, but from Jim.

The skull ship is targeting you!

I didn't think about how bad that could be for me, though that concept arrived fully formed a moment later. My initial reaction was that I needed to get as far away from the others as possible, and I did it the fastest way I could, the superhero jet straight through enemy lines. I hit hard without the cushion of a hideous drone head to soften the blow and dug a trench ten meters long with my shoulder as the bulldozer blade, and even through the armor, a flash of pain told me I'd tweaked something —AC joint, rotator cuff, something that hurt badly enough to warrant a stop in the auto-doc. If I'd had the time, I would have laughed hysterically at the thought of there being a me or an auto-doc still in existence at the end of this battle, but neither the ride nor the pain was finished with me. I popped back to my feet as the mindless gyros in my armor decided I'd fallen by accident and forced me to stand for what came next.

The deluge of annihilation bathed an area two hundred meters long and twice as wide in white fury. Fire rose from the ground to meet the fire in the air, the wave of heat and concussion enough to blow my Vigilante backward another twenty meters and deposit me onto my back, a turtle on a fencepost, helpless. My aching shoulder seemed like a pleasant memory compared to the dull throb that ran from head to toe, like God had decided to play handball with my body. Forcing my eyes open, I tried to focus on what the HUD was telling me, though even it flickered a few times, insulted by the abuse.

Of the Unity drones, nothing remained but a film of black dust atop the meter deepness of ash the barrage had left behind. But the skull ship floated a few hundred meters directly overhead, and I had no doubt the Unity was about to correct the mistake it had just made.

Thankfully, we weren't alone. Four delta shapes rocketed across the sky wreathed in white shock collars, their wrath unleashed in lightning that split the darkness and overwhelmed the shields of the skull ship. The vessel rocked and pitched, an ancient sailing ship swamped by rough seas, and tumbled out of the sky. That it didn't land directly atop me was a minor miracle, though the blast from its impact twenty or thirty klicks away was enough to ring the ground like a gong.

And into the silence after that vibration ceased came a voice. Not in the air, not on the radio, but inside my head.

You thought you could hide from me, Cameron Alvarez, the Unity mocked, *but I have all the time in the world. Destroy one after another of my creations, I can make more at my leisure, and I'll either find you or draw you to me as I did this time. Do you think I don't know you inside and out? That I wasn't sure you'd come personally to the rescue if I began slaughtering your kind?*

"Cam," Deke interrupted the demonic sending with an actual, physical voice, though the words he spoke were no more comforting. "There are three more of the skull ships breaking orbit, heading for us. I don't think we'll be able to stop them."

"I understand," I replied, rolling to my feet. No use maintaining radio silence anymore. The bad guys knew we were here and knew who I was.

I spent a moment's attention checking the sensor read Deke still relayed of the *Ellen*'s fight beyond the planet's moon. The picture up there was no less unpleasant than the one down here. The Predecessor ship had taken damage, that much was clear from the fiery red glow at the edges of her drive field, and if she'd destroyed a full dozen of the Unity skull ships, the rest would overwhelm her in minutes and there was nothing I could do about it.

Maybe once I'm dead the Unity will forget about the others. Maybe I can at least buy them that.

"Cam, are you okay?" Vicky asked from somewhere on the other side of the swathe of destruction left by the Unity barrage. "Where are you?"

She wouldn't be able to pick me up on thermal or IFF, not with the intense heat still radiating off the ground, and I sighed in relief, knowing she still lived.

"I'm here, Vicky," I said, wishing I could hold her hand one last time. "I'll always be here."

Drifting with what might have been a slight concussion, I toyed with the idea of crawling out of my armor and seeking her out but abandoned it immediately. The three skull ships would be on us in less than a minute, and the Intercepts wouldn't hold them back for more than seconds. No bothering with ground troops this time either. The Unity wasn't interested in giving me a sporting chance.

"What the fuck is *that*?" Deke blurted, and since I shared his ship's sensors, I knew exactly what the fuck *that* was.

Transitions. Dozens of Transitions. *Hundreds* of them, closer together than was humanly possible, and the second the wormholes closed, raw, unbridled energy threw the ships across the distance to the orbit of Hausos' moon in a minute. Lances of photonic destruction converged on Unity skull ships, dumping more power into the craft than their shields could absorb. The alien ships disintegrated, collapsing in on themselves, and those who were fast enough to fire back finally faced the one thing they weren't prepared for, an enemy just as unconcerned with casualties as they were.

Tens, dozens, nearly a hundred of the cutters disappeared in supernovas of matter-antimatter annihilation, but the others kept coming as if the losses meant nothing, and the three ships heading into the atmosphere paused, as if the Unity itself hesitated, unsure how to respond.

And like all who hesitated, the Unity was lost. The uncrewed cutters didn't even bother trying to shoot the three vessels out of the sky, instead just slicing through their shields and their hulls with a hypersonic, nearly relativistic impact. Massive explosions turned the depths of the night into brightest daylight, and what was left of the three enemy ships rained down in showers of meteors across the scar of where Gamma Junction had been.

"Can someone," Vicky asked, her voice thick with disbelief, "please tell me what the hell just happened?"

"Victoria Sandoval," I said, wishing I could get out of the suit and collapse from utter relief, "allow me to introduce you to Illyana."

"It's a pleasure to meet you," Illyana said brightly over the general comms network. "Any friend of Jim's is a friend of mine."

What the fuck did you do? I asked Jim, shaking my head even though he couldn't see it and didn't need to. *She'd already made up her mind not to help! And the version of you we left with her was useless!*

Jim shrugged. He was inside me, invisible, but I felt it.

Oh, that. I determined that the issue was likely that I'd underestimated the complexity of her logic systems and merely needed to encode a new cracking software patch and inject it into the clone. When you touched his avatar back there while we were interfacing with Illyana, I had the chance to do it.

Hold on, I said, a feeling of utter horror drowning out the relief. *Did you* make *me touch the avatar? Did you plant that idea in my head?*

Of course not! Jim sounded scandalized at the very thought. *You're a sentient being. To force you to act against your will and without your consent would be totally unethical.*

Isn't that exactly what you did to Illyana? I pointed out. *She's a sentient being and you just took control of her, didn't you?*

Oh. Well, that's *different.*

[28]

"This is so fucking strange," Captain Nance whispered as if to himself, shaking his head as he stared at the dozens of Project Rho cutters clustered in one of Hausos' Lagrangian points.

The ships floated in utter contentment, their purpose fulfilled, nothing else to occupy their time. There they'd stay until recalled, and I didn't intend to let them be recalled, since I was the one pulling their strings. Well, Jim was.

"They'll be heading to Sylvanus," I told him. "We know that the Unity has other forces out there, searching for human colonies... and for *me*. The *Ellen* is going to be searching for *them*, and when we find them we need these ships set up at an InStell ComSat, ready to respond to a distress call."

"I still don't get it," Deke said. He'd found himself an unoccupied duty station and sprawled across the chair, clearly enjoying the artificial gravity in the ship, though the physical relaxation didn't translate to the troubled expression on his face. "How?" I didn't answer, but he wouldn't give it up. "How did you convince that Corporate AI to cooperate with us? 'Cause I sure as hell wouldn't have guessed this outcome after your last meeting with her."

"We're dealing with a person." I shrugged. "People change their minds."

Vicky very carefully avoided his eyes and mine, and I knew why because we'd talked about it privately while the Marines had escorted the citizens of Gamma Junction to the outlying settlements. There wasn't enough housing on the farms to handle them all, but we'd flown buildfoam dispensers over from the refugee city across the continent and our engineering crews were cranking out emergency shelters as fast as they could.

"Deke can read your body language, voice stress, heart rate, respiration, skin temp... everything. Try to avoid saying *anything* to him about this," I'd warned her, hanging out of the open chest plastron, armor shut down, mics shut off.

"What about you?" she'd wondered, looking skeptical. "You're going to *have* to talk to him about it."

"I have inside help." I'd tapped the side of my head. "I can control my autonomic responses consciously."

I hoped I was right about that, because Deke stared at me as if he could see right through into my brain.

"You're not telling me everything," he said without a hint of doubt in his voice. But then he shrugged. "I'm used to that. But I'll find out eventually. For now, I suppose it's enough that you're on our side. One thing though." He motioned to the drones on the screen. "If those things are going to be our last line of defense against the Unity, they're going to need raw materials. Probably more than Kan-Zin Tel and his bunch can provide. I suppose you think the Commonwealth should handle that."

"I think if we don't," I told him, "no one will. And then we're going to be left holding our dicks when the Unity comes back in force."

"Maybe so. But you're gonna have a hard time getting Munroe to sign onto that."

I grunted, keeping my expression carefully neutral.

"Maybe someone should point out to him that this is a thinking, rational being he's dealing with, and if he doesn't give it the resupply, someone else will. And if Illyana doesn't consider us her friends and family, well... she'll find someone else to sign up for the friends and family plan."

"Munroe ain't the type who responds well to threats," Deke warned.

"Then let's hope he responds well to reality. Before reality comes back and bites us all in the ass."

Before he could reply, a blur of bright colors sped across the bridge and directly into Vicky's arms, both of them laughing as Luke hugged her tightly.

"I didn't think I was going to see you again," the kid said as his handler, a luckless Lt. Commander Chase, jogged in behind him, out of breath. "I thought we were all going to die! The ship shook so bad and it got really hot..."

"But we're all okay now," Vicky said, tousling his unruly hair. "Everything is going to be okay." She looked him up and down. "I see *someone* has been playing with the fabricator."

Luke's clothes were a close approximation of a Space Fleet uniform, if the colors had been redesigned by a drunken Marine private, but he grinned, patting his shirt.

"Yeah, ain't it cool? Commander Chase helped me set it up!"

Chase smiled weakly, looking off to the side to avoid Nance's glare.

"He needed something else to wear and I promised I'd let him choose his own colors..."

"Where are we going now?" Luke asked, still not letting go of Vicky. And she, I noticed, wasn't too keen on letting go of him either. "I don't want to go back down there... I don't know anyone down there."

"You don't have to," Vicky told him, then shot a glare at

Deke, Nance, and me, daring us to disagree. "We're going to be heading back to Demeter, and we're taking you with us. It's a nice place... you'll like it there."

"And I'll live with you guys?"

My first instinct was to say no, that we were going to be busy, that we had our military careers to think of and those were going to involve being gone most of the time. I shut up and instead looked to Vicky.

"If this works," she said, motioning to the main screen and the drones hovering there, "and we can count on..." she stopped herself and I groaned inwardly, knowing Deke would catch it, "... *Illyana* to handle the Unity, then we wouldn't need to be out here in Vigilantes, putting our asses on the line every day. I mean, we're both *colonels* for God's sake. Maybe we should act like it." The corner of her mouth quirked up. "Besides the being assholes part."

"Please, Vicky," Deke mocked, putting a hand to his chest. "Language."

I didn't answer for a few seconds, leaning back against the bulkhead, eyes unfocused, and not from the concussion—a couple hours in the auto-doc had fixed that and my shoulder. She was right. We'd done enough, done more than anyone had a right to ask, and I didn't give a shit what Deke thought about it.

"You know," I said, choosing the words carefully, deliberately, "I've spent most of my life without anyplace I could call home. The streets were my home, then the Corps. And for a while now, home was wherever you were and that seemed like enough."

I took Vicky's hand, holding it tight. Luke's eyes were wide with hope as he looked up at me, anticipating my answer.

"Yeah, Luke," I told him. "You'll be staying with us."

"And where will *we* be going?" Vicky wondered, tilting an eyebrow at me.

"Home. We're going home."

This concludes the Drop Trooper series!

If you liked Drop Trooper, you'll love his new trilogy, World War Mars!

FROM THE PUBLISHER

Thank you for reading *Kill Chain*, book sixteen in Drop Trooper.

We hope you enjoyed it as much as we enjoyed bringing it to you. We just wanted to take a moment to encourage you to review the book on Amazon and Goodreads. Every review helps further the author's reach and, ultimately, helps them continue writing fantastic books for us all to enjoy.

If you liked this book, check out the rest of our catalogue at www.aethonbooks.com. To sign up to receive a FREE collection from some of our best authors as well as updates regarding all new releases, visit www.aethonbooks.com/sign-up.

JOIN THE STREET TEAM! Get advanced copies of all our books, plus other free stuff and help us put out hit after hit.

SEARCH ON FACEBOOK:
AETHON STREET TEAM

The Drop Trooper Universe: (chronological reading order)

THE HOLY WAR
Genesis
Judgement Day
Revelation
Armageddon

THE PIRATE WAR (with Ralph Kern)
Insurgency
Infiltration
Isolation

DROP TROOPER
Contact Front
Kinetic Strike
Danger Close
Direct Fire
Home Front
Fire Base
Shock Action
Release Point
Kill Box
Drop Zone
Tango Down
Blue Force
Weapons Free
Collateral Effects
Down Range
Kill Chain

BIRTHRIGHT

Glory Boy
Birthright
Northwest Passage
Enemy of my Enemy

RECON
Recon
The Hunter
The Mercenary
The Operative

THE ACHERON
The Acheron
Prodigal
Hybrid
Exile

SPACE HUNTER WAR (with Pacey Holden)
Pirate Bounty
Corporate Bounty
Cultist Bounty
Smuggler's Bounty
Double-Cross Bounty
Terminal Bounty

THE PSI WAR
Homecoming
Conflagration
Imperium

You may also like:

An elite soldier. A new armored weapon. The invading aliens have finally met their match.
First Lieutenant Mike Sandhurst led an elite infantry platoon on a rescue mission to Tycho-3. Wearing state-of-the-art ATLAS powered armor, Sandhurst's unit faced down a relentless, wasp-like enemy who tore through them and left Sandhurst for dead. Rescued by ground forces, Sandhurst gets reassigned as humanity races to war against aliens they call Buzzers. To fight the Buzzers, humanity turns to the modernized Centurion main battle-tank. Sandhurst must quickly learn the lexicon of "shoot, move, communicate" and lead his fast, self-sustained, and very lethal armored forces. When the Buzzers appear again to threaten colonized worlds, Sandhurst's regiment moves forward to hold the planet Heske by force. But they aren't alone. The orbital carrier Yorktown and its space-capable wing dominate the skies while tanks take the fight and put Steel on Target. **Join the fight against the Buzzers in this new rollicking Science Fiction thrill ride from Kevin Ikenberry. With realistic military action, space and ground battles, and a vicious bug alien invasion, it's perfect for fans of** *Starship Troopers*, *Hell Divers 2*, **and Rick Partlow's** *Drop Trooper*!

Get Steel on Target Now!

Join the Space Corps. Journey to the stars. Meet aliens—and then vaporize them. A news journalist arrested for being in the wrong place at the wrong time, Liv Reyes now serves as a war correspondent in a war where anyone can be drafted and everyone is expendable. It's a war we're losing. Badly. Outmatched, outsmarted, and outmaneuvered—humanity is running out of options when it comes to the Raptors. They destroy anything and anyone we send their way. Our last line of defense never even made it through basic training. Liv catches a ride on a transport filled with five hundred soldiers in cryosleep, but Raptor space is dangerous. Half of all ships deployed are destroyed before ever reaching the front lines. Relentlessly pursued by the vicious alien enemy, Liv arrives at the aftermath of a brutal space battle and unearths a story that is the key to saving humanity from the Raptors once and for all. But first... she must survive the trip... **Join the fight for humanity in the start of this new alien invasion military sci-fi series by Rachel Aukes, bestselling author of** *Flight of the Javelin* **and** *Space Troopers*. **The enemy is vicious. Hope seems lost. But a few brave heroes can turn the tide. Humanity will prevail!**

Get Expendable Now!

———

For more fantastic science fiction, check out our entire catalogue at: https://aethonbooks.com/science-fiction/

ABOUT RICK PARTLOW

RICK PARTLOW is that rarest of species, a native Floridian. Born in Tampa, he attended Florida Southern College and graduated with a degree in History and a commission in the US Army as an Infantry officer.

His lifelong love of science fiction began with Have Space Suit---Will Travel and the other Heinlein juveniles and traveled through Clifford Simak, Asimov, Clarke and on to William Gibson, Walter Jon Williams and Peter F Hamilton. And somewhere, submerged in the worlds of others, Rick began to create his own worlds.

He has written a ton of books in many different series, and his short stories have been included in seven different anthologies.

He currently lives in central Florida with his wife, two children and a willful mutt of a dog. Besides writing and reading science fiction and fantasy, he enjoys outdoor photography, hiking and camping.

www.rickpartlow.com

Printed in Dunstable, United Kingdom